*Oblivion* is a deeply intellige
ly drives a writer to write, ;
success in one's lifetime is,
struggling or successful, to
*Never Told Me: A Memoir.*

:-
'y
<now,
'r

MW00436316

Robin Hemley has written a whole new kind of ghost story with *Oblivion*, both hilarious and profound: an ode to humility and pride, to ambition and failure, to Kafka and to the Yiddish theater, and above all to artistic vanity, to which he gives a good thrashing. A delightful romp of a read all the way through. **Helen Benedict,** author of *Wolf Season* and *The Good Deed.*

*Oblivion* is a compulsively readable meditation on the life, death and afterlife of writers and their work. Hemley's narrative brilliantly describes the sine wave between narcissism and despair that fuels the creative act, capturing all its absurdity and irresistibility, and managing in the process to hit notes both of high comedy and plangent melancholy. The book subjects the notion of posterity to a thorough examination, then skewers it mercilessly. It's a glorious achievement. **James Scudamore,** author of *Heliopolis* and *English Monsters.*

The whole time I was reading *Oblivion,* I lived in the fantastic world Hemley created; it entered my dreams, inspired my mental debates, and, in the manner of the very best literature, infused my life with mystery and meaning. **Stephen O'Connor,** author of *Thomas Jefferson Dreams of Sally Hemings.*

A man travels a lot and as often returns home, though not without feeling a bit of a dybbuk, reinhabiting and repossessing his old body and self. In his travels, meanwhile, through time as well as space, he also finds himself inhabiting his great-grandmother when she was a winsome, wannabe actress in Prague, at the same time, as it happens, that a young Kafka was just beginning to inhabit himself, but not without a boost from a devoted dybbuk you might mistake for Robin Hemley. And so rescued from oblivion this fine novel, aglow with warmth, wisdom, and speculation. **David Hamilton,** author of *Deep River* and *A Certain Arc.*

Robin Hemley's best book to date – and a highly original and thoroughly absorbing one to boot. **Geoff Dyer,** author of *Out of Sheer Rage*

Robin Hemley's novel, Oblivion: An After Autobiography, is positively the best travel guide for anyone contemplating death...This brilliant existential speculation on artistic ambition and obsession examines why anyone writes when few are called to the greatness of a Kafka. Philosophical, engrossing and very, very funny, this book deserves its own shelf in libraries from here through eternity. In particular for authors, minor or otherwise, this book is you. **Xu Xi,** author of *That Man in Our Lives*

Hemley's masterful prose, and his willingness to completely inhabit this dream/ world space, makes Oblivion a stunning and truly original book that not only succeeds on its own, but blazes a trail for other writers to follow. If they dare." **Sue William Silverman,** author of *How to Survive Death and Other Inconveniences*

Irony and humility in this cafe of broken and unbroken dreams. Get me a table, a schnapps! I want to drink and read. **David Lazar,** author of *Celeste Holm Syndrome,* co-editor, *21st Century Essays.*

Now that time is starting up again (after more than a dozen months of sequestration's superseding sleepy gear-slipping déjà vu-ing) Master Horologist, Robin Hemley's time machine of a book, Oblivion, materializes out of the occluded tick-tocked atmosphere, initiating portals and wormholes of asymmetrical chronologies in non-Euclidian parallel realities in which only he could effortlessly jewel and tinker. Oblivion is a hack of a hack, an analogue Borgesian Zoom webinar made up of glitchy matrices and disturbing disturbances in the field. Hemley animates the palimpsests of all our encrusted sacred texts, and he pentimentoes every moment of every memoranda filed away in our misty mimetic mementoes. **Michael Martone,** author of *The Complete Writings of Art Smith* and *The Moon Over Wapakoneta*

'Only the living can manipulate facts,' Robin Hemley's bibliophilic friend Jozef warns us. In his latest literary experiment, *Oblivion, An After Autobiography,* Hemley does just that, becoming a mythological dybbuk, except Hemley's intentions here are not malicious, but delightful and sly. Kafka will roll in his grave, perhaps in laughter. **Dinty W. Moore,** author of *To Hell With It*

*Oblivion* is a book about expectations and disappointment, ambition and envy, self-obsession and self-doubt. It's about family legends and real lives. It is about a contemporary American writer's encounters in the afterlife with Franz Kafka. This book is a magic trick, and the sleight of hand is Robin Hemley's curiosity and vulnerability. The book is smart, imaginative, thought-provoking, and witty. And brilliant. **Judy Goldman,** author of **Child: A Memoir**

The premise of *Oblivion* is literally one to die for – it is a speculative memoir that imagines what might happen after its author's death… And the execution is just as extraordinary. Inventive and electrifying, *Oblivion* is a tragicomic ode to the power of art and ambition to shape a life; an intoxicating cocktail of melancholy, playfulness and mystery. It is the kind of a book where you just don't skip any lines, because surprises abound. Simply put, Oblivion is one of the best, most memorable books I've read in the last decade. **Lee Kofman,** author of *Imperfect and The Dangerous Bride*

I have never read anything else quite like *Oblivion, An After Autobiography*. I can more easily describe my reaction to the book than I can the book itself. I was startled, delighted, puzzled, riveted. But above all I was entertained. I suspect that if Franz K were around to read Hemley's small masterpiece, he would share in my admiration. I would not have wanted to miss this one. Nor should you. **Steve Yarbrough,** author of *The Unmade World*

Oblivion: An After Autobiography is a valiant, masterful act of imagination, a re-creation and visitation of Franz Kafka's life, and that of Hemley's literary forebears, in early 20th century Prague. In prose that is brisk, spare, and exceedingly funny, Robin Hemley takes us down corridors of literary oblivion, guided by the wry resolve of a narrator who finds his voice (and worth and audience) only after his own death. **Mary Cappello,** author of *Awkward: A Detour and Lecture*

What a relief to know that the afterlife is a hotbed of ambition, envy, and obsession, a referendum on one's earthly literary status as well as a goad to further writerly pursuits. Count me in! Robin Hemley's Café of Minor Authors is a funny, brilliant portrayal of the writer's terror of insignificance and boredom and the ego's imperative for the sweet spot of possibility… *Oblivion* is a think-piece with beautiful prose and a throbbing heart! **Patricia Foster,** author of *Girl from Soldier Creek* and *All the Lost Girls*

# OBLIVION:

## An After Autobiography

Robin Hemley

ISBN 978-1-63752-781-8
Copyright © 2022 Robin Hemley
Published by Gold Wake Press
Cover design by David Gee
Book interior by Paul Brooke
Oblivion 2021, Robin Hemley
goldwake.com

How everything can be said, how for everything,
for the strangest fancies, there waits a great fire
in which they perish and rise up again.

Franz Kafka's diary, September 23rd, 1912

In Memory of Kevin Heisler, Karen Stolz,
James Hughes, and for Jozef,
wherever you are. Please write.

# TABLE OF CONTENTS

# PROLOGUE

## IN THE CAFÉ
## OF MINOR AUTHORS

As we sat drinking our cappuccinos, my old friend Jozef told me that the only way to escape Oblivion was to steal Franz Kafka's typewriter. Not in so many words, but this is what I took him to mean in his cryptic fashion. Jozef had hailed me almost immediately in the afterlife and brought me to this café, just like the old days. I imagine many people have had friends like Jozef: friends by default, jovial boors who can talk at length on almost any subject and do so without interruption if you allow them. I should add that Jozef was both a stranger to me and not one at all. We had known one another when, in my twenties, after graduating from The Iowa Writers Workshop. I drifted to Chicago and landed a job, though one without any glamor or influence, at *Playboy Magazine* in the "Modern Living" section of Editorial. I thought at the time – really until the moment of my death – that I was destined for great things and, disappointed by my lowly position at *Playboy* (I merely logged in products to be featured in the magazine as they came in and shipped them back out when the photographers were done with them), I sought other ways to make my mark.

I met Jozef in Chicago one day through a mutual friend I had gone to school with, and he told me about a magazine he worked for with the horrible name, the odious name, *Hoot & Holler,* where he was the Book Review Editor. There was no pay involved – it was run by two socialites with bad taste and money to burn, and soon I found myself the Senior Editor of Hoot & Holler (without pay), toiling after work every day, thinking that I was going to make my mark here – if I could convince the owners to change the name. Jozef agreed with me that the name had to be changed and we lobbied for a year to make this happen, but Dorothy, one of the co-owners, had founded the magazine based on a dream in which the name appeared to her and which she treated as divine revelation. When Jozef and I saw that our cause was hopeless we both quit the magazine – which folded not long after – but we remained friends, sort of. We would meet at coffee shops almost every day in Wrigleyville where we both lived, me on Roscoe, he on Cornelia, and chat about rare books, art, ancient history, philosophy. Actually, it was Jozef who did most of the chatting, leaning across the table, cigarette in one hand, smiling with his yellow teeth, his accent a mix of Polish and Chicagoan, replete with "deses" and "dats." While I listened, I tried hard not to look as distracted as I felt. Jozef had a girlfriend named Vicky who was twice as boring as he was – she had been a volunteer reader at Hoot & Holler – and when the three of us met on occasion, the conversation was so dry you could have started a campfire with it. Slowly, I extricated myself from these friendships I had never really wanted in the first place, a process that involved leaving Chicago in a time before social media made it easy to keep in touch with all one's "friends."

The downside of this was that for some reason Jozef had always thought of me as destined for greatness, too. He was my Max Brod. As with Kafka's great friend, admirer, and fellow writer, Jozef collected everything I published and many things I hadn't published. He was a dealer in antiquarian books. Everything else that excited him was a hundred years old or more. He'd often sift through the stacks of the Northwestern University Library and find rare books that shouldn't have been in circulation. At one of their library sales, I remember, he even bought for fifty cents a signed first edition of Carl Sandburg's poems. "Most people don't know the value of what they have," Jozef told me after making that score. Now, as I contemplated the afterlife in the café with him, these words returned to me, and I thought perhaps I had not valued Jozef enough. If I had made a little more effort to cultivate his friendship rather than doing everything I could to alienate him, maybe he would have been a useful ally. A now–forgotten Pulitzer Prize–winning poet once told me that someday I'd get fan mail from crazy admirers and that I should never answer them. Now I thought he was probably wrong. In an age of declining readership, what author can afford to lose even the most deranged admirer?

Jozef, who cut a slight figure, was clunky and old-world in his fashion sense. He favored an assemblage of wide ties, rumpled sports jackets with lapels half as wide as Dumbo's ears, and loafers with heels worn down to the brink of complete uselessness. His mouth held a complement of crooked and stained teeth and a never-ending procession of cigarettes in constant contact. Only his wan laugh, his slender wrists and fingers, his narrow face, and perfectly groomed moustache offset his befuddled senses of fashion and health. The limitations of his fashion sense could be explained, I reasoned, by his bookishness and his relative impoverishment his entire life. When I knew him, he had made his meager living not only in the antiquarian book trade, but also by freelance editing, and book-binding. None of these provided steady incomes and none demanded any real need to care about his appearance. As far as I knew, he spent most of his life alone. In his sexuality, I wasn't that interested. I assumed he was straight – I saw him holding hands with his boring girlfriend Vicky, once, though I never saw them kiss. But if he had told me he was gay, I wouldn't have been shocked either. I had never really been concerned with anyone's sexuality but my own.

The café was crowded and smoke-filled. Not smoke, so much as mist. The mist seemed almost a living thing, curling around the ankles of some customers, obscuring entirely the features of others. There was a clamor of voices and spoons, the café full of men and women as far as I could see. Still, the place retained a cozy atmosphere, perhaps a result of the mist. A cappuccino sat in front of each of us, foamed perfectly, two dark drops dotting the foam where the espresso had flowed through. When I picked up my cup and tasted the coffee, the sensation was unlike any I had ever felt. My lips made no impression on the foam and nothing liquid entered my mouth, but I still had the sensation of drinking a perfectly-brewed cappuccino.

Some passing acquaintance, former student, colleague, or friend sat at nearly every table I could see. The afterlife, it seemed, was not unlike the annual Associated Writing Programs Conference, full of smart, unfulfilled people such as me. Not all the tables were two seaters. Some seated as many as a dozen people, sipping their coffees and chatting amicably. At one such table, I spotted my friend Maudy, who smiled and gave me an animated wave, and I waved back. I had last seen her at the AWP conference years before my death – a year before a heart attack took her. She was one of the sweetest people I had ever met, and we had been conference buddies for nearly thirty years, though we rarely saw one another more often than once a year. Still, I felt some modicum of hope that at the very least, I now had all the time in the world to catch up with my old friends. I motioned to her with my index finger toggling between us that we should catch up and she nodded back, her face bright, and then I returned to Jozef, who looked at me in a slightly bemused way.

"So I was wondering, _____," Jozef said, "if you remember the discussion we had about Milosz when you lived in Chicago, specifically his book, *The Land of Ulro?*"

"I vaguely remember the book," I said. "I reviewed it for *Chicago Magazine,* but I didn't like it. I don't think I understood it."

"You should look at it again," he said. "I think you might have a different view. Ulro, as you know, is the name that Blake gives the realm of existence beneath Beulah."

A conversation with Jozef was always like someone holding a

bunch of strings out to you. Eventually, you were going to pull them, one by one, half out of curiosity and half because he would just keep holding them out until you gave up and pulled. To me, Beulah was merely an old-fashioned proper name from the South, not a place. *Would you care for a little more sassafras tea, Beulah?*

"Is that where we are now, in Beulah?"

Hunched over the table, squeezing the life out of his cigarette, he chuckled in his familiar way, so soft it was almost a whisper, an amused light playing in his eyes.

"You wish," he said.

"So where are we then?"

"We're merely in Oblivion. Not so terrible. We still have hope. At least we're not dybbuks."

Even while alive, Jozef had always spoken in riddles, one of the many annoying things about him, including his cigarette habit. I was never good at hiding my annoyance. I nodded this time. "Oh sure," I said. "Dybbuks are no fun at all."

"You've read Blake?" he asked, ignoring – or more likely not even registering – my mockery.

I'd read almost nothing of Blake (all I could remember was the line, *Tyger! Tyger! burning bright*) but I gave an exasperated sigh as though I had done my dissertation on him.

"I actually need to reread Blake," Jozef said. "He's a comfort and a caution both."

"So, we're allowed to read here?"

"Yes, of course," he said. "You can do almost anything you like here, within reason as well as outside of reason. You know, _____, the dead can haunt the living, the living can haunt the living, the living can haunt the dead, but the real revelation is this: the dead can haunt the dead."

"What does that mean?" I asked.

"Ah, well, you'll see," he said in his obscure Jozef fashion, raising a hand, palm outward towards the multitude of writers in our midst as though serving me something on a platter.

"What did you mean by hope?" I asked.

"Hope?"

"You said we have hope."

"Look around you," he said. "We're not alone."

I considered this and wondered if the company of others truly constituted hope. Hadn't so many of the really great writers struggled in isolation? Could it be said that any of us were not alone – did the others in this café care one whit for anyone but themselves and their dead careers?

I took a sip of my never-cooling cappuccino so that I wouldn't burst into ethereal tears. I wanted none of this. It was over, all over, nothing more I could gain or lose in life, and that took some getting used to. Only reflection remained, endless reflection, and what did any insights matter now? Nothing I did or said here would have the same weight as when I had been alive. No weight at all, because there were no choices left, nothing anyway that would affect the future, that would even leave the faintest mark.

So much of my writing career had been about hanging on to my dreams of glory. These could be sustaining on occasion, though when they failed to pass, there was the inevitable hard fall from my imagined grace. The way I died was especially regrettable. The worst author death ever. Worse than Richard Farina who died in a motorcycle crash after a book party for his just-published novel, *I've Been Down so Long it Looks Like Up to Me,* which became a bestseller after his death. Worse than Sherwood Anderson, who swallowed a cocktail sword and died of peritonitis. Worse than Tennessee Williams who choked on a bottlecap. Worse than Frank O'Hara who was run over by a dune buggy while asleep on the beach on Fire Island. Even worse than Aeschylus who died when an eagle dropped a turtle on his bald head, mistaking it for a rock to crack open the shell. I was at lunch with my wife when I received an email from my agent telling me that the auction for my new book was in the stratosphere. "This is going to change everything for you," she wrote. I hadn't even realized that there was going to be an auction. I gave a little yell and told my wife what my agent had written, then wrote back to her asking who was bidding? And how much? Ten minutes later, I received a text from her.

"_____, I'M SO SO SORRY," she wrote. "That was meant for another client. No takers on yours, I'm afraid. But don't give up hope yet!" That's just what I did. I fell into my dessert, an enormous, celebratory slice of pecan pie with French vanilla ice cream, and died of a massive heart attack. I was sixty-two.

A fortune-teller had told me at the age of twenty-two that I shouldn't become a writer, and I saw that in the long run she was right, though I had laughed at her at the time. After all, I had just been accepted to the famous Iowa Writers' Workshop. How much more wrong could she be, I thought at the time: but what had all this brought me?

A life of small victories and large disappointments, and an afterlife filled with mirrors of myself, all trying to put a good face on our collective obscurity.

"You look so down, _____. Don't be too hard on yourself," Jozef said. "You had a respectable career. A small circle appreciated you."

He produced – out of nothing – a sketch pad and a piece of charcoal, and he started to draw while looking at me intently. I shook my head and gave him my most baleful look, which made not the slightest impression on him.

"Illustrations," he said. "For your biography."

"Why would I want a biography," I asked. "No one would read it."

"That's not necessarily so," he said. "It might even get you the recognition you think you deserve. Who knows?"

"Recognition? Here?"

"Among the living."

"The living?" I asked. "That's impossible."

"Yes, you're right. It is."

"So that doesn't happen."

"No," he said. "I'm afraid not." He drew a decisive line with the charcoal, my jaw line perhaps? "It has happened," he added with more deliberation. "But it's exceedingly rare."

"Who?"

"Hold still," he said, rubbing the charcoal back and forth – my hair, I assumed. "There have been cases," he said. "But you shouldn't …"

"Who?"

"Carl Winterhoven, best-selling author of *The Blackhawk Exchange,* for instance?" The way he said that. Daring me not to recognize the name.

"Oh," I said as though I was impressed and amazed. I had never heard of Carl Winterhoven, best-selling author of *The Blackhawk Exchange.*

"So I take it you've read the Blackhawk series?" Jozef asked.

"Of course," I said.

"Do you find him derivative of Highsmith as Rushdie did in the TLS or do you consider him his own man as Chernoff opined in the Post?" He let out a long, smoky sigh. "He's sort of a hero of mine," he added.

"Well, you've always had good taste, Jozef," I said. From years of practice, I was an expert at pretending to have read books I hadn't even heard of. "But how did he do it?"

"Turn," he said. "The other way."

I turned. "Like this?"

He nodded. "It's complicated."

He held my portrait at arm's length and examined it, then tore off the page and tossed it into a pocket of air. "Let's try this," he said and propped his hand beneath his chin. "Thinker pose."

"No," I said. "Stop it. You're making fun of me."

"I'm quite the Winterhoven buff. Little-known fact. He wrote the vast majority of the Blackhawk series after he passed. Saffron Segovia's another. I thought I had a vague memory of that name, but I couldn't place any of her work. You don't forget a name like Saffron Segovia."

"A wunderkind." Jozef said. "You must have run into her at literary events, though maybe you travelled in different circles. She was a bit more outré than you, hung out with writer/artists like Sophie Calle, Paul Auster, David Shields."

"I believe I met her at a party once?" I probably had met her at some conference or another. I had met pretty much everyone at a party or a conference once. All I had were vague recollections of most of them. There were so many, too many, and most of them were here in this café, but Jozef always made me feel as though I were the least well-read writer on the planet. "She struck me as a bit self-obsessed."

"Well, she was so young when she died," Jozef said. "At least thirty years our junior. Did you see the movie they made out of *Anatomy of a Mass Extinction*? Shortened to *Extinction* for the film."

I nodded.

"Can you believe she ended up here at first? A death unrecognized by the literary establishment, but she's universally revered now. We used to sit together all the time and chat, just like we're doing now."

"She and Winterhaven –"

"Hoven," he said. "Winterhoven. Your work reminds me of early Segovia," he said. "Before she found her voice. After her death."

He started to draw again. "I've met your father." He paused. "A warm soul and quite learned," and I heard in the space between his words an unspoken *unlike you*. "We've even discussed you before. Would you like to meet him? I could call him over to the table. Or you could go to him yourself. Or visit any part of his life you desire."

"My father?" I wasn't ready. I had last seen my father when I was seven, the night he had a massive heart attack when he was only fifty-one. Known largely as Nobel Laureate Isaac Bashevis Singer's editor and translator, my father had also been a poet and novelist, and one-time president of the Poetry Society of America. In his day, he had been well-known and well-regarded, but now only his association with Isaac Singer's greatness brought him any attention at all.

"What about others?" I said. "If I wanted to speak to, say, Abraham Lincoln, could you call him over?"

Jozef made a sucking sound and winced. "I'm afraid this café is for minor authors only. We're a bit segregated, you know, though Lincoln did write some bad poems in addition to some magnificent speeches. But if you wanted to visit his life, sure, you can do that. For research. If you wanted to write a new biography or an historical novel. Of course, it won't be published, but you could self-publish it and you might be able to get some of the other habitués of the café to look at it. I'd be interested. I didn't realize you had a fascination with Lincoln."

"I don't," I said. "What about Kafka?"

He took a puff of his cigarette. "Kafka" he said, with reverence. "Are you asking if he's here?"

"I know he's not here. I'd still like to meet him."

You can't actually meet him but I can show you around his life. I've visited many times. It's always surprising."

I had thought he was going to say, "enlightening" or "inspiring." What could be surprising about a life devoted single-mindedly to the production of words? I had read Kafka first when I was fifteen, for a book report. I chose *The Trial*. Another show-off chose *War and Peace*. Ever since, if anyone played one of those games where you could meet anyone in history, my mind always went immediately to Kafka. But he wasn't my hero. He was my obsession, just as he was the obsession of a lot of writers and readers, but not everyone's. To many who only have read his most famous story, Kafka is just that dead white guy who wrote the weird tale you had to read in high school about a man who turns into a cockroach. And when you mention that, someone is bound to add, "Well, cockroach isn't actually an accurate translation." At least in my circle. To others, his work distilled the nature of the entire 20th century (the individual's obliteration by the bureaucracy and heartlessness of the State), though he died only a fifth of the way through it. No one was his equal. I was a fan of *The Metamorphosis*, but also of "A Hunger Artist" and "In the Penal Colony," largely, I think, because of their high irony. They're gruesome, it's true, but they're also funny. Cosmic jokes with cosmic punchlines. In a different time, a different country, Kafka might have been the greatest stand-up comedian ever. When he read his stories to his circle of friends, they thought he was hilarious.

Still, there is hardly a writer more publicly misunderstood than Kafka. His life a muddy myth, he is a mass-produced postcard of a solitary figure strolling, his back to us, along a cobbled street of Prague. He is a coffee mug sold in Prague tourist shops. He is the clichéd adjective, *Kafkaesque*. He is the stereotype of the tortured artist who supposedly never saw any literary fame in his lifetime. As Borges once wrote: "Fame is a form, perhaps the worst form, of incomprehension."

I knew that there was a void between the way Kafka saw himself and the way others saw him, especially perhaps his biggest admirer, Max Brod, who thought of Kafka as "chosen." But to be chosen is to be passive, and writers can't afford passivity. I read once, perhaps in Brod's memoirs, that Kafka had loved a painting by the French artist, Jean Huber. It depicted Voltaire, dressed in his nightshirt and nightcap, stepping out of bed and hurriedly putting on his pants as a terrier sports at his heels and a manservant waits, quill in hand, at a nearby desk, ready for the day's dictations. Had the man been sitting patiently by Voltaire's bedside all night long awaiting the master's direction? Voltaire couldn't wait to start writing. He could barely keep his balance as he struggled with his pants, but his gaze was fixed firmly on the seated man with the quill. The painting is not a great painting, but it expresses greatness. Others would stay in bed. Others would take the dog for a walk. Others would continue reading the book propped on the nightstand. Others would answer the call of the open window where morning light streams in.

"You said Winterhoven and Segovia wrote something that changed their literary fortunes. After they died. In theory, I could do this too?"

"If you think it was difficult getting noticed when you were alive, look around you," Jozef said. "There are multitudes. Even tapping one key on Kafka's typewriter would be a miracle for you." When he seemed to notice my expression, he added, "For anyone among us. For me, the pleasures are now vicarious. Here, all pleasures are vicarious, which makes them less dangerous. The sooner you understand this, the happier you'll be here. Read. Write. Rediscover yourself. Think of this as a never-ending writing retreat. Think of your life as simply a promising movie with a disappointing ending, but not worth another worry. Any other life can now replace your own – all you have to do is let go and imagine. Relax."

How I hated that word. How unrelaxing the word "relax" is. When my first wife and I were going through Lamaze classes together before our first child was born, the coach told me when my wife was in labor never to use that word. Instead I should say, "release," which is a far more relaxing word. *Release. Release. Release.* Oh, how I wanted that, though it seemed impossible.

"The Eternal One is whimsical and His answer to every un-answerable question is inevitably, *Because I can.*" Jozef said this in a deep voice, obviously quoting.

"Blake?"

"Come now, _____. You don't recognize your own words? That's a direct quote from your Pushcart Prize-nominated short story, 'Another Harmless Poison.' One of your best."

The story actually *won* a Pushcart, I reminded him. It wasn't just nominated. His expression, a wince and a slight tilt of the head read, *My mistake, but who cares?* True. If I'd had the opportunity, I would have burned the story. It felt so dated, as though someone else entirely had written it. It felt unfelt, inauthentic like most of my work. Pale imitations of others, though the saddest part was that I hadn't realized I was imitating anyone else. I didn't hate everything I had ever written, merely most of it, and "hate" was too strong a word. I was disappointed in my writings the way a child who has only been given love and opportunities disappoints a parent with their lack of direction and conviction.

"I guess that to escape Oblivion you have to be good enough for Eternity to fall in love with you again," he said. "'Eternity is in love with the productions of Time.'"

"Yoko Ono?" which was my way of saying, *Just tell me already and stop showing off.*

"Blake again," he said, looking wistful. "As for me, I'm mostly done with ambitions, though a few still linger. But if I'm being honest with myself, I've given up on the productions of Time, which means no more intoxicated moments, but no more toxic moments either. I had a few intoxicated moments in my writing life, but I was unable to hold on to them. Did you have many?"

"Like drunk?" I asked.

"Not drunk. I'm talking about the intoxicated moment versus

the toxic moment. Sometimes one becomes another. The toxic moment is when you let yourself get carried away by the promises you think the world has made to you. The intoxicated moment is that moment in which the writer has tapped into something, well, there's really no direct translation. It can't even be said."

Good. Better left unsaid. It was a ridiculous term. Kind of woo-woo. Not quite as bad as *Hoot & Holler,* but almost. Hopefully, he wasn't simply referring to "inspiration" because I didn't believe in inspiration, divine or otherwise. I believed that you work towards inspiration – it's not something you wait for. If you wait for inspiration, you will be waiting an awfully long time. A few creations in our lifetimes are gifts perhaps, approaching greatness, but these can't be relied upon. To expect inspiration instead of the daily struggle simply reinforces romantic notions of writing that make people think it's somehow divine. Ask any writer his or her advice, and you'll most likely get the same stock answer, "Read a lot and learn to fail. Take risks and learn to fail." "Find your own voice" is another, but that's too vague and a bit too terrifying to be practical. What if you've lost your voice or have no idea where it is? What if it's a scratchy voice that people find unpleasant and don't particularly want to hear? What if you've got multiple voices?

Nothing felt intoxicating. All felt toxic. Maybe Jozef was right, but it was not easy, even here, to surrender my ambition. If I was to find any solace, it would have to be in someone like Kafka, for the sheer pleasure of his transcendent mind. "Maybe I should visit Kafka," I said.

"Yes, his would be an excellent life for you to visit, I think, especially since your great-grandmother knew him."

"My great-grandmother knew Kafka?" I said, looking around as though this might make others see me differently.

"I was doing some research myself and I stumbled on this. You knew she was an actress in the Yiddish theatre, didn't you? It's quite exciting really. She was with Yitzhak Lowy's troupe from Poland, and she even served as the inspiration of the greatest Yiddish drama, *The Dybbuk.* In a roundabout way."

My lack of recognition alarmed Jozef. "Really? You haven't heard of *The Dybbuk?* _____, what are we going to do with you?" Amusement edged his voice as much as alarm. He clearly thought I was an idiot. Perhaps he'd always thought this.

"I know what a dybbuk is," I said.

"Not a dybbuk, *The Dybbuk,* Ansky's seminal play. I tell

you, you won't find Ansky here. I know. I've looked for him. Your great-grandmother inspired the part of Leah. Didn't you know any of this?"

"Why didn't you tell me this right away?" I asked.

"I'm telling you now," he said, flapping his hand at me, the universal don't-make-such-a-big-deal-of-it gesture. "I was just waiting to tell you. Don't you think there should be some surprises in death?"

"My great grandmother knew Kafka," I said.

"Just casually, I'm afraid," Jozef said. "Don't get your hopes up. He's not your real great grandfather or anything of the sort, though he is rumored to have fathered a child."

"I wasn't getting my hopes up." Slightly.

What I had grown up with was a distilled myth of the woman. Yes, my great-grandmother Hanna had been a star in the Yiddish theatre, as my mother told it, and I knew that Kafka had been a devotee of the Yiddish theatre, but no one had ever mentioned Kafka and Hanna in the same breath, and they most certainly would have done so in my family. My mother, also a writer, was proud of the fact that we were related to Houdini, and she would have been over the moon to know this about Kafka. She had grown up in Bensonhurst, and she was quite close to her grandmother. Even though Hanna died long before I was born, I grew up with stories of her. Her mother had died in childbirth, so she was suckled much like Romulus and Remus, not by a wolf, but by a goat. Her father, a village mystic named Abraham, remarried, and Hanna grew up on a farm outside of Vilna, riding horses bareback, her long red hair flowing. When she was seventeen, her stepmother decided to marry her off to an old widower. Headstrong and independent her entire life, she ran off instead and made her way to Warsaw, where an older brother lived. At first, she worked in a factory, then she joined a Yiddish theatre troupe there. She toured around Europe until she met my grandfather Yitzhak, a shoemaker. They married, had their first child, my grandmother, in Holland and then emigrated to America.

On the day of my brother Jonathan's wedding, my great uncles, Morty and Leon sat with me and my other aunts and uncles, telling me stories about Hanna and teaching me Yiddish curses. In most of the stories, she was characterized as headstrong and independent. Invited to the wedding of a younger brother who had settled in Cleveland, she made the decision to fly there from New York – for the times, an unorthodox choice. Prior to this, most of her rebellions had been small ones according to my mother: the occasional cigarette or glass of wine. But flying alone to Cleveland? Such a distance and flying was in no way safe. My other relatives tried to dissuade her, from her children to her husband, my great-grandfather Yitzhak. She ignored them all. On the day of her flight, a passenger plane crashed upstate and all were killed, but even that didn't shake her resolve. Dressed entirely in white, she posed on the steps of the plane for photos with her children who were certain they would never see their mother alive again. She hushed them all, dried their tears and told them she'd see them in a week.

On the way to Cleveland, the plane hit bad weather, and Hanna took charge of an infant whose mother was terrified, but in the end, the plane landed safely, and she saw her brother married. Honeymooning at Niagara Falls, her brother and his bride gave her a lift back to New York, and she never flew again.

In later years, she became embittered by the loss of her husband's business during the Depression. He and a partner had had a successful shoe manufacturing business, but the partner embezzled the company funds and fled to South America. Yitzhak could have kept solvent personally, but he insisted on paying back all of the company's creditors. The story was told as an example of Yitzhak's honesty, but my mother told me that Hanna never forgave him for losing the family fortune. Sometimes there's nothing more annoying than a saint. Or was he a saint? Perhaps Yitzhak was a tyrant in other ways and paid back his debtors out of a kind of egotism, a desire to show his moral superiority. Perhaps he wanted her to suffer, and he didn't mind suffering too, if she suffered more. It's hard to tell when it comes to motivations. I didn't know either of them as Hanna died first of an aneurysm, and Yitzhak followed six months later, dying from a heart attack about fifteen years before my birth. Only outcomes are easily read unless the person in question writes honestly about their actions and some fraction of all that transpires inside them.

The reason I never kept a diary is that my personality does not mesh well with the personality of many diary keepers. I lived in an age of nearly full disclosure. Privacy was not highly valued – if you had a thought, no matter how personal, you shared it. For this, we had blogs, memoirs, and social media, and most writers functioned as their own personal Max Brods. But even in our seemingly most honest moments, we were constructions of a sort. I wrote and published two memoirs in my lifetime, but they could have been written by two complete strangers, their tones were so different. Both were aspects of my personality, but neither encompassed my entirety, an impossibility for all but a handful of writers. Even Proust needed multiple volumes to dredge the minutiae of existence into a comprehensive whole. I once read an intriguing book by Thomas Mallon in which he presented a concise history of people and their diaries suggesting that even the most private diarists intended a future audience of some sort, whether a descendant, a future self, or posterity. Given that Kafka wished adamantly that his diaries be burned, and only started a diary on the advice of Max Brod in the first place, it's unlikely he expected them to be read by anyone but Brod (because he knew that Brod was insatiably curious about anything to do with his friend). *"I won't deny you the opportunity to take a peek, still I would prefer it if you wouldn't, and in any case, no one else may be allowed to peek."* Kafka would never have wanted you or me to read his diaries or his letters to Felice Bauer, to whom he was engaged twice before breaking it off for good, but they're all out there.

Thousands of people have peeked – more than peeked. Many of us have taken a little bit from his soul as seen in these diaries and lit it, unheeding of his wishes. In his self-doubts and despair, we've recognized ourselves, in our grand ambitions whether spoken aloud or not.

*The tremendous world I have in my head. But how to free myself and to free it without being torn to pieces. And a thousand times rather be torn to pieces than retain it in me or bury it. That, indeed, is why I am here, that is quite clear to me.*

In my life, I don't think I met a writer who felt otherwise, whether they put a good face on it or not, the gregarious people, like the poet Billy Collins who sipped Tullamore Dew as he sliced golf balls into Puget Sound or the children's book author, Norma Klein, who seemed when I met her, smiling and full of warmth and intelligence, the last person I would imagine to take her own life, though that's exactly what she did. Success in any form provides little escape when you're being torn to pieces from the inside and simultaneously trying to convey the tremendous worlds you have inside yourself.

"Let's say," I said, to Jozef, "for the sake of argument, that I was able to write something –."

"Intoxicated?" he asked, as though urging a young child to repeat a difficult-to-pronounce word.

"I was going to say 'worthy of posterity,' but 'intoxicated' if you like."

I had never heard anyone laugh like Jozef, and I hadn't realized how much I missed it until I heard it again in the afterlife. His laugh was soft and sorrowful, tender, yet slightly mocking. An enigmatic laugh that would have infuriated a playground bully and would have initiated – and probably had in Jozef's youth – a thrashing. Yes, there was a kind of superiority inherent in his laugh, but timidity, too.

"What if one day I wrote something so good that Eternity would notice and admire it, and I would finally know that I had succeeded?" I asked. "Succeeded" was such a bland word, but I couldn't take the thought any further. I wasn't sure I believed in anything written, not even Kafka's words, lasting forever.

The full gamut of Jozefesque emotions were captured in that thin smile of his. "Okay, laugh," I told him. "But that's what I want. Intoxicated moments. Days. Months. Years. Maybe I'll write about Hanna and Kafka and in my retelling, I'll be their love child. If Segovia and Winterhoven can thwart Oblivion, why shouldn't I at least try?"

"All these questions," he said. "Why won't you believe me that you'd be much better off without them?" His voice was as testy as I'd ever heard it. "Just be satisfied." He didn't add "for once," but it hung there without needing to be said. "There are a lot of people who made out a lot worse. I didn't even have your stature." Ha, he admitted it. I had really rattled him – well, finally.

He closed his eyes and sat still. He straightened his wide tie and ran a hand through his hair, though it was a gesture with no effect. Before opening his eyes again, he seemed to push an internal reset button.

With a sip of coffee, he narrowed his eyes at me over the rim of his cup.

"Okay, go ahead and try," he said. "But finish your coffee at least. It's good, isn't it?"

# CHAPTER ONE

## AT THE GOGO

Jozef wouldn't tell me where we would spend our first hour in Prague, or the exact date, only that it would be surprising. On that word, "surprising," I found myself and Jozef on a broad boulevard lit by electric lampposts lining the avenue, with a wide sidewalk and buildings of a modest height, several stories each, stretching in orderly fashion and dominated at the end of the boulevard by a large domed building. I recognized this building immediately, but the name I couldn't remember. I spent some time staring at it, though it appeared only as a dusky shadow with a few lights on in its interior, otherwise shrouded in semi-darkness. I was in Wenceslas Square but what was the name of the building?

The Number Five tram bore down upon me. I screamed as Jozef shoved me out of the way, and the tram passed through him. "Old habits die hard," Jozef said after the trolley passed.

"Spirits, too," I said, and we both laughed. If I'd been alive, I would have owed him my life, and he would have died. I suppose it was reflex on his part, but still ... the implications. Did he think I was worth the sacrifice? And when I say he shoved me out of the way, it took the form of a shove, but it was more like a fan blowing smoke in a different direction. Even so, I felt a kind of muddled gratitude I didn't exactly know how to express.

The moment for thanks passed. Jozef, acting as though his action was nothing, which strictly speaking it was, asked me the obvious question, if I knew where we were.

"Vegas," I said. "1965. Let's go find Sinatra."

But after a couple of seconds, I stopped. I couldn't move, not because I was unable, but because walking struck me as so astonishing. I remembered with amazement swinging my arms, feeling the sidewalk or street beneath my feet. Not that I felt them now, but I felt as though I felt them. I saw them. I sensed them. I missed hurrying and ambling, too. After a bare minute, I felt hopelessly attracted to every small thing. Waves of unfiltered and inexplicable stimuli crashed upon me. A horse cart passed slowly by. The driver, a man in a rumpled suit, glanced over his shoulder and spat, the spittle landing at my feet. I considered it in a way I never would have bothered while I was alive. The spittle glowed there slightly against the grey cobblestone, a healthy dollop of foam, though even the most greenish diseased splotch would have struck me as beautiful in that moment. I bent over it and studied it – how alive and airy it seemed, not unlike the cappuccino in Oblivion.

"That was meant for you," Jozef said, glancing at me and flicking his ash, though it didn't fall. He looked away and made as though he was sucking in his breath in wonderment, I assumed, at the sight of this city boulevard, though he himself was less than the air he pretended to inhale.

"He saw me?" I asked and pointed to the driver, whose horse was leaving a trail of manure behind it.

"He sensed you. These early 20th century Czechs," he said, "are quite superstitious."

"Superstitious? How is it superstition if we're real?" I asked, but Jozef was already walking away, more like the kind of jump flying I remembered from dreams – not flying but not walking either, a kind of barely-tethered-to-gravity-loping. He loped, and I loped, too. Over buildings, through windows and dark cellars, past empty market stalls with straw strewn on the cement floors, past stoops with men smoking, couples chatting, a lone old woman sipping a bowl of soup, into a steaming kitchen and a bedroom with two sleeping children, onto a tiled rooftop, a church spire, a mulberry tree draped in sticky cocoons. I stopped at a bridge and followed a man with a cane, not an old man, wearing a straw boater and a butter yellow jacket over striped white and yellow pants. Also, mustachioed and whistling some tune I'd never heard before. I matched him step for step and unlike the horse cart driver, he seemed to have no intimation of me at all, though I was pressed to him almost cheek-to-cheek. A heavy–jowled man with a bowler and waistcoat gave the young man a dyspeptic look, like *what do you have to be so happy about,* and glanced away. I wondered too what made the man in the boater so cheery. Love, I imagined, poor schmuck. In that moment, he had no sense that all his dreams would soon be nothing, that I, dead as I was, wouldn't even be born for another sixty years or so. I felt I should warn him, the happy fool. "You might as well throw yourself off this bridge," I whispered in his ear, but he kept walking. He tipped his hat to a girl wearing a bonnet, a shop girl, I guessed, but she didn't meet his gaze. Three dogs, two small and one large, with a bald spot between its ears, barked greetings to the evening. Another tram passed and I stood in the middle of the bridge – not the Charles Bridge, which I would have known by its famous statues – but a lesser bridge in some grey district of Prague I didn't recognize, though of course I knew the river. A kind of super-nostalgia for life stuck me to the spot. Four drunk laborers, sharing a bottle between them, passed through me and one tossed the empty bottle in the river. It sank immediately and I had the desire to join it at the bottom, to follow it as though it were alive, too.

I felt Jozef at my side. I spat, though nothing came out, to rid myself of Jozef like the man in the horse cart had rid himself of me.

"So, this is where you ran off." he said in mild exasperation and bemusement, the closest he ever ratcheted to anger. "Maybe we should return to Oblivion," he said. We need to acclimatize you to Time before we plunge in wholesale. Everyone reacts a little differently."

I managed to nod, but my thoughts were all jumbled: despair, desire, and Time mixing in a combustible way that had me hatching a plan to give Jozef the slip, find a boarding house in Prague and just write. Wouldn't that feel good? I wouldn't need much, not even food. Some feeling in my fingers and a typewriter. That would be entirely sufficient.

"Does everyone return to the living?" I asked.

Jozef took a draw from his cigarette and blew out the spirit smoke. "These are great," he said, looking at the cigarette. He gave me a wary look, but his voice remained cheerful. "You should take up smoking again, _____." He flicked the cigarette to the pavement, but it hadn't left his hand before it slipped into an envelope of air. "No, this isn't for everyone. Most people aren't as adventurous as us, and if you weren't adventurous in life, you're not going to suddenly reform when you're dead, are you? But I don't see why this place isn't crowded with dead tourists. If I were more entrepreneurial and money meant anything in the afterlife, I'd run a travel agency. This kind of travel is such an education."

"Where is he?" I asked. "I want to be with him."

"You'll see," he said. "He's out with friends."

"No," I said. "I mean, where did he go after he died?" Maybe Kafka, Toni Morrison, Marquez, Blake, Dickinson, Milosz, Kawabata, and Sappho were in the first-class Lounge while I was forever stuck near the boarding gate, still vying for a seat, still trying to get somewhere worth getting.

"Out with friends, I suppose," he said, regarding me with undisguised pity.

I felt a kind of buzzing, like Dickinson's fly, a spiritual headache, a feeling that made it difficult for me to concentrate. I wondered if there was some spirit equivalent of aspirin that Jozef might be able to give me to rid me of this headache-like state, but I worried that if I said anything, he might carry me back to Oblivion straight away and I'd never leave the café again.

"How are you feeling?" he asked.

I assured him I felt just fine.

Jozef spent the next thirty minutes or so bringing me from one tavern to the next and telling me their various sordid histories. Racing Jozef around the ancient city of Prague was like a manic and creepy stag party, but without violence, vomiting, or STDs. We visited such dives, all notable, he assured me, as the Mimosa, the Battalion, and the Green Frog. The names of these places were all in German, but I could read German okay and understand it, though I couldn't speak it – all a holdover from my undergraduate major in comparative literature, making my liberal arts education more useful in the afterlife than it had been while I was alive.

At a bar with the notable name "To Hell," Jozef told me at great length the story of Duke Wenceslaus of Bohemia who was found passed out drunk under a table here in 1378 by his chamberlains. They had gone looking for him to tell him he was now Holy Roman Emperor. A typically pointless history lesson told in mind-numbing detail by Jozef. Much more fascinating was the bartender who seemed to see us without seeing us, who shivered and gave out a low whistle when we stood by him. Even as insubstantial beings, we had been felt, and didn't that alter Time just a bit?

Jozef claimed such disturbances didn't matter much as they had been explained by skeptics for centuries as the product of overactive imaginations. And imagination, unacted upon, alters nothing.

At a place called Café Melantranch, a bartender stood at the polished bar, the lights of the place blazing its emptiness, talking in low tones to a "famous bouncer," Honza Luft, who looked like a young version of my uncle Morty, bulbous-nosed and with long-suffering eyes. The bartender pressed money into the bouncer's hand while the big guy let out a sob and thanked the other man. Some drama of long ago, the light of another faded star. There were no more customers in the tavern, only another spirit like us, a woman dressed in nothing but beige undergarments and a red hat adorned with a peacock feather, singing to herself at the bar. She was another story.

There were just too many stories, and they kept on going, even past the bounds of life.

"We should probably get going," Jozef said softly by my side. "But it's fascinating, isn't it, from our perspective?"

"I thought we were going to meet my great-grandmother and Kafka." The annoyance in my voice would have been apparent to anyone but Jozef, with whom it didn't even register.

"They haven't even met yet," he said in a cheerful way. "You don't recognize this place, do you? Eighty years from now it will still be a bar, and will incorporate the brothel next door, one of Prague's oldest, and it will be visited by none other than...drum roll...yourself."

"What?"

Jozef laughed again. "Don't deny it. I was there with you."

I must have looked stricken. "Don't tell me you had no inkling? I'm sure you must have had some notion. I know that I often felt like someone was watching me when I was alive."

"You were watching me?" I asked.

"Don't be angry," he said.

"Don't be angry? You spied on me and ..." When I'm angry I become aphasic. I lose speech entirely. I could only think to call him a voyeur, which seemed too mild, too French, something he might like being called, and I was right. He smiled as though I couldn't have called him anything nicer.

"Cheer up. It's all for research. For your biography. I should think you'd be flattered. At this point, I probably know you better than you know yourself. I've been to all your major life events and many of the minor points of your life, too. I was there when you met your first wife and when she left you. I was there when you scored a basket in sixth grade playing half-court basketball for the opposing team. I was with you at your sister's funeral and your mother's. And when you stole your sister's Cleopatra necklace she bought in the Middle East and gave it to your girlfriend, Melissa Houk. I was there when you learned that your friend Donald fell through the ice of a creek and drowned. Of course, I haven't relived your entire life. A few things should stay private, not that I'm an expert on such things like you – when you visited the bathroom to masturbate, as you did quite often, I didn't cross the threshold, though I heard you in there."

At that, I went right through the front door of Café Melantranch and out into the alley. But Jozef stuck with me. I thought of a mentally-ill man passing out flyers on a street corner in Chicago in the early 1990s, when I was a young man. Cameras were following him everywhere, he claimed. Maybe he'd been right, but they weren't cameras, just nosy spirits like Jozef.

I suppose one of the biggest differences between my personality and Jozef's was that I tended to expect ill will before goodwill, while you could not convince Jozef that anyone meant him anything but the best. While I had long been aware of my paranoid delusions, that didn't make them go away. My self-knowledge simply muted my paranoia and left it, more often than not, unvoiced. But if my wallet was missing, I immediately assumed someone had stolen it, while Jozef was the kind who assumed it would turn up. In my experience, optimists like Jozef were more often right about such things. Usually, missing things turn up. Usually, people aren't out to get you. But that only makes the Jozefs of the world that much more annoying.

His delight in showing me around, in talking in riddles, in quizzing me, I saw as torment, as a way of besting me, displaying his intelligence and my ignorance. He seemed to see himself as playful, without malice. He constantly smiled, but I didn't trust that smile – how could I? In my hour back in Time, he'd simply degraded and shamed me, bringing me on a tour of Prague's brothels and telling me he'd spied on nearly every meaningful moment of my life, sparing me only from watching me on the toilet. The devout always say that the Eternal sees everything – perhaps, but maybe not directly. Maybe through a Secret Service of ingratiating souls like Jozef.

"You're awfully sensitive," Jozef said. "Maybe we should go now."

I smiled as brightly as I could. "I just need to be alone for a bit. Could I just wander the streets, take in the night air? I won't go far. I promise." I had seen a boarding house nearby and I considered which direction to take.

Jozef regarded me the way I used to look at my children when they asked me to give them something that was well beyond my means. "I'm afraid not," he said. "But the good news is that this was all just a prelude for the pièce de résistance of the evening, the crown jewel of Prague brothels, the Gogo."

"The Gogo?"

"Indeed," he said, raising his eyebrows, and there we were in front of a door that looked more like a theatre entrance than the entrance to a brothel. An otherwise nondescript building, the Gogo was set in an alley no more than a five-minute walk from Old Town Square. A set of double doors with frosted panes of glass and radiating suns of gold filigree suggested something special lay behind the doors.

"Here we are at U Goldschmied, known otherwise as the Salon Gogo by its illustrious patrons, which included," and here he ticked off the names on his fingers:

"Gustav Mahler, Otto Von Bismarck."

"And Kafka?" I said, tired of his games.

"Wait," he said. "His Supreme Majesty, the Emperor Charles the First of The Austro-Hungarian Empire." He said this in a rising voice.

"And Kafka," I said.

"Franz Werfel, Max Brod."

"And Kafka, obviously." I drifted through the door into a front parlor, the picture of elegance with its enormous crystal chandelier and a sweeping staircase. A woman in a dark-blue empire waist dress, her blonde hair piled elegantly, glided down the staircase as though she owned the place. Men of all ages sat in chairs, around wrought-iron tables with marble tops, some of the patrons sitting in bathrobes or smoking jackets, with plates of food, beer and flutes of champagne, laughing and chatting away, others receiving pedicures and manicures and reading papers. The place was filled with smoke I couldn't smell and food I couldn't taste, and sensations I couldn't feel.

"Patience was never your strong suit, _____," Jozef said. He nodded towards the staircase as I watched the young woman with the piled blonde hair, not the only one observing her graceful descent. I was trying to remember what it felt like to lust, but it was like clicking a lighter with no flint left.

"It's said that Otto Von Bismarck, after winning the battle of Sadova, raced up these very stairs six times that night, each time with a different woman," Jozef informed me. "I've been meaning to check on that, but I haven't found the time and I'm not sure of the exact date of the visit."

I gave him a sideways glance. "Five women, six women, or none at all. Who cares, Jozef?"

Jozef looked wounded. "You'd be surprised. There are quite a few people who care about such things. It's important, for accuracy's sake. Facts matter."

"Not when you're dead," I said.

"Even more so. Only the living can manipulate facts. The dead are too easily taken advantage of." He led me to a table where three men sat. "Do you recognize anyone?" he asked.

Only my idol. He sat at a table with two other men, one well-fed and baby-faced, the other mustachioed, sporting pince-nez glasses. Kafka, his hair swept back, looked like a teenager, though I found out later that this day in 1911 he was in his late twenties. A half-finished beer stood in front of him in a dimpled glass, the beer bottle beside it, the label a brand I had never heard of, Schwechater. I wanted nothing more than to sip Schwechater beer from a dimpled mug alongside him, not only for the pleasure of drinking a beer again, but to taste something that he had also tasted, to partake in conversation with him. He took a sip and his face settled into pleasure and his shoulders relaxed and his Adam's apple bobbed as he swallowed. I remembered reading that when he was dying, in the advanced stages of tuberculosis, hardly able to swallow, he, too watched others drinking with a similar vicarious satisfaction. But that wouldn't be for another dozen or so years. Now he laughed at something the larger man had said. And wiped his mouth. He didn't look like the sickly artist of the popular imagination, but tall and slender, not painfully thin, enjoying his youth with friends. I understood very little because they spoke in German and my German was rusty, and of course the noise made it all the more difficult to follow, so I concentrated on everything non-verbal. The man with the pince-nez glasses talked on for a couple of minutes without interruption, though the larger man tried to interrupt. Only Kafka seemed interested in truly listening.

I didn't care whether I understood them or not. Gazing at Kafka was enough for now. But of course, Jozef couldn't keep quiet. As always, he had to show how much he knew. "This man is Franz Werfel," he said, pointing to the larger man who wore a white scarf over his dinner jacket. He wrote poetry as well as novels and plays, and in his time was much more famous than Kafka. Have you read anything of Werfel's, _____?"

I ignored Jozef's question.

"Surely, you've read _The Song of Bernadette?_" Jozef said.

Surely, I hadn't. But I didn't want to give Jozef the satisfaction of revealing my bottomless ignorance of everything he considered indispensable. Werfel, flourishing a cigarette in an ivory holder, raised his voice in an operatic baritone and sang out so loudly that patrons at other tables turned their heads. I thought it was a snatch of Verdi. I do know something about opera. Kafka and the man with the glasses whom I assumed was his great friend and admirer, Max Brod, clapped, though a blush rose on Kafka's cheeks. Jozef ignored all this.

"_The Song of Bernadette_ was Werfel's most famous novel, the one I assume you've heard of, though everyone agrees _The Forty Days of Musa Dagh_ is far superior. They made _Bernadette_ into a Hollywood movie, but at this point, Werfel won't write it for many years. He and Kafka and Brod are celebrating tonight because Werfel, about seven years the junior of Kafka, has just been released from his compulsory service in the Austro-Hungarian army, and he's about to move to Leipzig to work for the publisher, Kurt Wolff. And he's just published his first book of poems, *Weltfreund*."

"World Friend?" I said.

"Friend to the World," Jozef said in his patronizing way. He stretched out his arms as though he were going to break into an aria, too. "My only wish is to be related to you, O Man," he declaimed in a booming voice that was a pretty good approximation of Werfel's. "It's pretty schmaltzy stuff by our standards, but in 1911 it slayed them."

I should have felt enthralled, but I felt something else in addition to my headache, a heavy pressure on my ethereal chest, a familiar pang. I could easily see why so few of the dead wanted to revisit life, why so few of us were tourists. It was torture enough to be alive and feel life's possibilities, hopes and dreams ebbing year after relentless year.

Jozef gave me a sad smile. "You feel envy?" he asked. "Kafka feels it, too. Werfel is well-known and Brod is already famous. He's already published several well-received books, but Kafka? He hasn't yet written "The Metamorphosis." He won't write anything of value for another year. See how uncomfortable he looks? See how he twitches a little bit and rubs his hands? The world is passing him by. No accomplishments – he works a dreary job at The Workers Accident Insurance Company, and he doesn't even have a girlfriend yet, though he definitely doesn't want one. Sex with prostitutes is one of his outlets, though sexual diseases terrify him. Marriage terrifies him even more."

"It's more nostalgia than envy," I said, though I hardly knew what I was saying.

"Ah, well, then," he said, giving me a pitying look. "That's serious, too. In the 19th century, nostalgia used to be a medical diagnosis. The Swiss were especially prone to it and people were even said to die from nostalgia."

If Kafka had died on this night, he would have died unknown and unfulfilled. I might have met him in Oblivion and not cared. We might have spoken of all the worlds inside us that had never found release.

Jozef peered into my eyes and must have seen desperation.

"Let's get you back," Jozef said, taking my arm. But I resisted.

"Just a little longer," I said and tried to breathe in the scent of the place, but I could smell nothing. I tried to see Kafka and his friends with such clarity that I would never forget them and they would always be my companions. Jozef looked distressed at my refusal to budge, but I ignored him.

"Let's go, _____," Jozef tried again, his voice high with notes of panic.

Jozef, tugging on my insubstantial sleeve with all his insubstantial might, could never have made me leave. He pleaded like the babysitter whose charge has wrecked the living room when he wasn't looking, the parents due back any minute. But Jozef, I grudgingly understood, had showed me kindness by bringing me here at all. And so, finally, I didn't tug back.

# CHAPTER TWO

# A PLACE THAT IS NO PLACE

Even in Oblivion, one has a hard time shaking the habit of referring to time passing. But time only passes for beings of substance, and we in Oblivion have none. There are no calendars, no days, no nights. There is company and there is solitude and mostly we choose company though solitude is perhaps the key to escaping Oblivion. To live with yourself in death the way you could not live with yourself in life. I have talked this over with some of my friends and most of us have tried it, but solitude in Oblivion is the equivalent of starvation in life. Undoubtedly, there is a point past sustenance when you don't feel your own starvation anymore, or your aloneness, but I have never come close to this point and neither have my friends.

Kafka wanted human society as much as anyone. He loved the movies. He rode a motorcycle and enjoyed beer. He sometimes visited brothels with Max Brod and others and travelled with his friend around Europe. He took up carpentry. But he had protectors and champions who gave him the space and permission to create – Max Brod was only one of them. Even Kafka's boss at the insurance company he worked for recognized that Kafka needed protection from the world. At the onset of World War I, Kafka wanted to volunteer for the Austro-Hungarian army, but his boss wouldn't allow it and argued successfully to the government that Kafka was indispensable to the business. It's hard to imagine Kafka as a soldier. But after my initial shock, it wasn't difficult for me to imagine him friends with my great grandmother, she strong-willed and talented, he charming and attracted to serious women who would understand the struggle to create.

After my first visit to Kafka's life, I went to the café and brooded at a table alone, nursing a cappuccino that never cooled. I stared at the foam and wished for it to cool, but it never did. Part of my foul mood had to do with Jozef. I should never enter Time alone, he warned me upon my return. His words were surprisingly harsh and he chastised me for having poor judgment, for wandering off by myself, for refusing to leave. I could get into real trouble if I ever went back alone. Time and I did not mix well.

What kind of trouble, I wondered, could I possibly get into? What could be worse than serving out my afterlife in a thinly-disguised storage facility for self-obsessed writers?

"There's a real chance of losing yourself entirely," he told me. "If your envy gets the best of you, next thing you know, you start inhabiting people and disrupting everything, and then it's all over. You're a dybbuk and you're doomed."

"Dybbuks?"

"Dybbuks to us," he said. "In Islam, 'Ifrit.' In the Hindu religion, a 'bhoot.' In the Philippines –."

"At least it would be more interesting than this," I said. If I hadn't interrupted him, he would have kept going until he'd rattled off the name of every demon equivalent in every society on earth, including those of uncontacted tribes in the Amazon.

"Don't even joke about it. You must promise me."

"Yep, okay, what does it matter?" I asked no one in particular, but Jozef took the question seriously.

"This would make a good topic of discussion between you and your parents," he said. "What does it matter? What is the meaning of the Afterlife? Your parents spend a lot of time together in the library. They do want to touch base with you, of course, but there's no rush. Eternity tends to make most people more patient than they were in life." He emphasized the words *most people* so that his meaning was clear. I got it.

Patience, was it? My parents only wanted to touch base with me? But I felt no great urgency either. I didn't miss my family terribly or even at all (not my parents, not my children, not my wife, not my grandmother, not my siblings, none of the people I had loved in life). This was curious as I had spent much of my life missing people. I was always away on fellowships for extended periods of time or giving readings or locked away in my office while my children played outside or had sleepovers or went without bedtime stories while I wrote. I had often lashed myself emotionally for my selfishness in having children and neglecting them and swinging inevitably to the companion thought that I never would have wished a life without them: thinking how much they must have suffered as a result of being a part of my life. But in Oblivion, I felt none of that, which was curious but not painful. Were the cappuccinos laced with ethereal Xanax that alleviated anxieties and regrets selectively? My anxieties and regrets about my writing still lived, but these others had vanished. Was this a mercy? I hoped my loved ones were all having nice days and when their nice days were finished, having nice afterlives. But beyond that, I suffered no one's absence. I wondered if the other habitués of Oblivion felt similarly – perhaps I would conduct a poll on the matter.

When I was a boy, I had a lot of sentimental and peculiar notions about the afterlife. I believed that no matter how bad that someone was, they would be forgiven if someone remembered and cried for them. My grandmother, daughter of Hanna, looked like she wanted to spit when she heard me say this, though she didn't. She lived in New York, not the *shtetl*, and she asked me who put such a crazy idea in my head?

"No one," I admitted. My mother, who was there for this pronouncement, too, started ticking off the names of horrible people, Stalin and Hitler to begin with, who were probably mourned by other horrible people.

Later, when I started to write, I modified my original idea. I imagined that forgotten authors would somehow live again if you read one of their forgotten books. This notion spurred me to pick up all sorts of books from various ages at antique stores and garage sales, setting up a kind of Red Cross of literary has-beens. In this way, I read some pretty interesting books: *The Journal of a Spy in Paris During the Reign of Terror,* the war correspondence of Richard Harding Davis during the Spanish-American War, and a book called *Ghosts I Have Met* by John Kendrick Bangs. A famous writer in his day who was virtually unknown in mine, Bangs was a humorist. While I was visiting the writer Robert Olen Butler in Florida once, Bob told me he was a fan of Bangs, too, and presented me with another of Bangs' volumes. Unfortunately, I neglected to read it until the Afterlife when I decided to revisit Bangs and his delightful stories in *Ghosts I Have Met.* I retreated to the library to be alone and catch up on my reading, especially all those classics I had pretended to have read when I was alive.

In the library of Oblivion, everything intended to be a book is a book, published or unpublished, half-finished, scrawled on loose-leaf notebooks, typed on typewriters and laptops, self-published. Not all of these are poorly written, or amateurish, though there are hundreds, thousands. A fire pops in the fireplace of the den, a calico cat curls on a sheepskin rug in front of it, the ceilings so high you can't even see them, walls of built in bookshelves soaring above the height of the tallest building in the world. The books that you want are always closest to eye level, or stacked companionably by your easy chair or on the marble stand beside the chair. Here, you can drink a couple of bourbons, neat, which you may set beside the books without a coaster and stare as long as you like at the condensation on the glass, the ice cubes melting. The bourbons taste as perfect as the cappuccinos. They meet your expectations in every way except they have no effect. They make nothing more bearable.

As I sipped my bourbon in the library I felt less alone. I found myself, if not in conversation with Bangs, then in some kind of harmony with him, especially when I read these lines in *Ghosts I Have Met:*

> My scheme of living is based upon being true to myself. You may class me with Baron Munchausen if you choose; I shall not mind so long as I have the consolation of feeling, deep down in my heart, that I am a true realist, and diverge not from the paths of truth as truth manifests itself to me.

Standard notions of realism had always struck me as too confining. What about speculation? People, it seems to me, are obsessed with facts though speculation and daydreams make up the better portion of our lives.

Bangs had been a gregarious person in life and had known many of the other literary luminaries of his day. He'd once run for mayor of Yonkers and had lost by only a couple hundred votes. On Mark Twain's seventieth birthday, he wrote an homage to the great man in *Harper's Weekly,* where he also served as an editor. But his work was uneven and only sometimes recognized. What he was most known for was the term, "Bangsian Fantasy," which is a kind of exploration of the afterlife with famous personalities. In a sense I was living (afterliving?) a Bangsian fantasy myself, except that it was sub-Bangsian. I wasn't famous, and neither was Jozef.

My musings were interrupted by a blonde boy wearing light blue shorts and a Chicago Cubs t-shirt. The boy was no more than five years old, skinny and freckled, and he glanced at the calico cat and then at me as though he was seeking permission to pet it.. He had intense blue eyes and was moving from side to side with the aimless energy of young children. I thought he might be lost.

I leaned towards him as he withdrew a pack of cigarettes from his pocket. "Mind if I smoke?" and at the same time I recognized Jozef's voice. The boy unfolded like a lawn chair and became a full-grown man, who took a seat beside me.

"Go away."

"Jozef smiled. "Oh, come on, _____, don't be such a kill-joy. I was just having a little fun. It's a pretty common prank here."

Not to me. Most of the time I presented as a man about thirty-six, what I thought of as my prime. Never any younger than that. I didn't play tricks like Jozef, dressing up as a child.

I wasn't in the mood for his games, and I didn't want to engage him in conversation. In this place that was no place, Jozef always seemed ready to pounce on me. I had assumed that it would be easy to refuse his company, the way you might refuse a call. But that wasn't the case. With Jozef and with others, I felt alone and together at once, co-existing the way people coexist on a call, a heterotopia, tethered but far apart. The only difference between a discussion in Oblivion and a call on earth is that time is not of the essence – it is not an essence, not an option. You are never on hold. You are merely held. There is nowhere. There is only you. Still you.

This didn't seem to deter Jozef in the least in seeking out my companionship.

His eyes sparkled. "Guess what these are?" he said, waving his hand in front of me.

"Fingers," I said. "In a fist."

"Have you lost your imagination entirely, _____? These are, or would be, if they had ever been issued, tickets for a performance at the legendary Café Savoy of the classic Yiddish play, Shulamith, not starring, but including in the cast, none other than the ingenue, Hanna Reimer, and attended by Franz Kafka and Max Brod. The Cafe didn't actually use tickets. People paid at the door, but you get the idea. We leave when I say, okay? And you must behave."

I held up my hand. "Say the word and we leave." This was his peace offering, I understood, fully intending to play by the rules.

"Okay, then," he said. "Let's play."

# CHAPTER THREE

## THE CAFE SAVOY

CHAPTER THREE: THE CAFÉ SAVOY

The Café Savoy as it existed at the end of my life was not the Café Savoy of Kafka's time. The Café Savoy in the Prague of the twenty-first century was a high-ceilinged Belle Époque restaurant with filigreed confections of fondant and chocolate and marzipan, not exactly the place you might imagine itinerant troupes of Yiddish actors putting on plays. The difference between the new Café Savoy and the Café Savoy that Kafka visited is the difference between say, Eastern European Jews and German Jews. The German Jews considered themselves far superior to those dirty Eastern European Jews living in their *shtetls*. In my own family, this conflict played out in the marriage of my grandmother Ida and her husband, Nelson. Ida, daughter of Hanna, was of Eastern European stock while Nelson's family was Hungarian. The Hungarian Jews in my family were horrified that Nelson would choose a woman whose parents were from Lithuania and Latvia and did everything they could to stand in the way, including, according to my mother, kidnapping her and her brother Allan for a couple of years so they would grow up in a more sophisticated environment. The two families lived only blocks apart in Bensonhurst, and during this time, my mother was never called by her first name, Elaine, but by her middle name Sylvia, the name of a deceased relative on her father's side. These dramas between German Jews and Eastern European Jews were played out all over the world until Hitler came along and neglected to make such fine distinctions between Jews. So many Jews of German descent perished precisely because they fooled themselves into thinking that Hitler meant those *other* Jews, not them, when he railed against *die Juden*.

My great-grandparents on Nelson's side probably would have loved Kafka, at least superficially, though he most likely would have found them boorish. He worked for an insurance company, a good German Jew from a respectable family. But Kafka detested the bourgeois values of his father, Hermann, the owner of a successful dry goods store. The two found one another utterly incomprehensible and the idea of attending the Yiddish theatre would have been foreign and distasteful for Hermann, just as becoming a partner in something as banal as an asbestos factory would have seemed a waste of time to Kafka. But Kafka indeed was the partner in an asbestos factory with his brother-in-law, Prague's first such factory, the money put up by Hermann as a way to entice Franz into something practical and profitable. Kafka rarely visited the factory, and it failed, adding tension to an already tense relationship. But if it hadn't failed, maybe Kafka would never have written "The Metamorphosis," which he wrote after his sister Ottla, his one consistent ally, sided with the rest of the family in this case in urging him to be reasonable. This betrayal, as he saw it, threw him into despair, but out of that despair came one of the most important stories ever written.

A pimp named Leon Migdal, who moonlighted as the Savoy's bouncer, stood at the entrance of the Café Savoy and Jozef pretended to introduce him to me. Even if Migdal could have seen me, I didn't want to make his acquaintance. In life, I would have given him a wide passage: a man with a chubby face, sweaty bangs that formed dangling commas across his wide forehead, small eyes that were deader than mine, a wide moustache and a lower lip that protruded like a constant challenge. He had his arms folded across his massive chest and it was hard to imagine anyone as sensitive as Kafka making his way past this monster.

"He's a teddy bear once you get to know him," Jozef assured me, but as usual, I couldn't tell if he was kidding or not.

The café had rather low ceilings with dozens of moths flying around the dusty chandeliers. I tried in vain to smell the old beer, cigarettes, and mildew that I knew such places as this harbored. Even such rank scents would have delighted me now that I could smell nothing anymore on earth. The place only held about thirty tables, bare except for watermarks that exposed the plywood under the dark varnish, dirty ashtrays, and candles stuck in green beer bottles in an apparent attempt to make the place elegant. The tables faced a rudimentary stage no more than nine feet long and nine wide, so small the actors were bound to tread on each other's feet. A single light dangled upon the stage where dust and more moths danced like a warm up act.

My hearing was better than it had been when I was alive, and by hearing, I don't actually mean hearing. I was little more than a vibration myself, but I understood. I co-mingled with other vibrations, softer and more powerful than me. Mice, unseen like us, scrabbled in the loose plaster walls, beneath the floorboards, hoarding, nibbling, listening and waiting for the empty hours when the café would be theirs again. A red satin curtain ran the length of the stage and past it to a hallway that led to the back room of the café where the actors, by the sounds of their muffled voices, were getting ready. Where the curtain stretched past the stage, there was a gap where I imagined actors waited to go on, their legs visible to members of the audience. The curtain ruffled and the floorboards creaked as furniture was moved and an assemblage of voices spoke in Yiddish, German, and Czech. One of the actors sang some kind of mournful song that I supposed was part of the production. I couldn't speak Yiddish except for the curses that my uncles taught me, but I could understand it a bit as far as its resemblance to German went. Still, the song, though it rose sweetly through the dingy café, was muffled by the voices of the other actors, the braying laughter of a man, the pop of a light bulb as it blew (our doing, I'm afraid, one of the consequences of having spirits in the house), then the curse of a bald man wearing a white apron who had seen the light bulb blow and now had to find a stool and replace the light bulb. Jozef, who had obviously seen performances here before, said the waiter's name was "Roubitschek." He looked as dour as the bouncer. "Don't ask me his first name. I don't think he has one. Everyone just calls him Roubitschek." Muffled voices filtered through the stage curtain, floorboards creaking. I made out the name "Solomon" in the song, but that was all.

Kafka had not yet entered the café, and while we were free to go backstage to spy on Hanna, I felt a bit shy about the possibility of say, encountering her naked while she was dressing. She was, after all, my great-grandmother, and I also wanted to experience my first meeting with her the way an audience member might encounter live the star he's seen only up to this point from afar.

I had felt Hanna's presence throughout my life. Did this mean that she, too, had spied on my life as Jozef had done? Would she approve of her great-grandson or would she feel completely alienated from me? I believed we were similar, both artistic and in our own ways, adventurous. But I felt jangly in the Savoy, as though I would be performing tonight, not her.

As people started to trickle in and take seats, I could characterize them in three groups: the dabblers, the devotees, and Friends of the Bouncer. The dabblers were eight young people, university students or of that age, who had joined three tables and who seemed, by their slightly terror-struck but enthusiastic taking in of their surroundings, on a kind of field trip into the far reaches of the Jewish cultural jungle. Two of the eight were women, and they all ordered beers immediately, toasted, and started murmuring cliquishly at their tables, laughing wildly, and then subsiding into whispers. The women had their hair pinned in buns, and dressed in puffy blouses, old-fashioned to me, but the height of modern fashion to them, the boys wearing pantaloons and colorful striped shirts –pretending to be artists or Bohemians (in the land where the term "Bohemian" was born) in training.

The second group was made up of a dozen men, and they were dressed rather formally in suits. Some of them had beards and some of them didn't, a few though not all, wore yarmulkes. These men, Jozef told me, made up the Association of Jewish Office Workers who were sponsoring the small Yiddish troupe. They were quieter than the students, but they joked too and drank mostly beer. Jozef also pointed out another suited gentleman who sat at a table by himself. A man whose tired eyes and deep lines made him look supremely bored or in despair, taking in a melodrama perhaps before throwing himself off a bridge; he had nothing in front of him, no drink and no food, and I might have mistaken him for an invisible being like ourselves had not Jozef told me he was a government official who had to watch all the shows to make sure they weren't lewd and did not advocate the overthrow of the government or disrupt public order. "I mean," said Jozef, "despite the shabby surroundings, these are mostly Biblical morality tales, though sometimes the warm-ups get a little risqué. If you like women bumping men with their big rear ends, then you'll love the warmup acts."

Burlesque was not actually something I particularly enjoyed, I told him, and he told me to loosen up. "You want a beer?" he asked.

"Yes."

"Too bad," he said. "You can have an Oblivion Lite when we're back." This cracked him up.

The third group, what I thought of as the Friends of the Bouncer, were the kind of people who go to a show to throw things (chairs and tomatoes) and yell at the actors if they displeased them. Jozef said there was no danger of that tonight as the bouncer made everyone check their rotten produce at the door. These were men of all ages with the grime of their workday on their clothes, still wearing boots, and older women in wrinkled dresses with moth holes, some wearing scarves on their heads, all of them conversing in Yiddish, unlike the college students and the Jewish Workers Association, who spoke in German.

I wondered what the lives of the café's patrons were like, where they lived, who they loved, and what had happened to them. I wanted to sit at every table, listen to every conversation, hear their stories, learn their names, make friends with them all in the afterlife.

A lone student who looked like he came from a Yeshiva, wearing his yarmulke, with a beard and sidelocks, sat at a table hunched in the far corner, about the only male in the place besides the waiter not smoking. Surely, he would have been reprimanded to be discovered pursuing such a pastime, even if the plays performed here had some spiritual themes. I excused myself from Jozef, who was people-watching like me and joined the Yeshiva boy, who called over Roubitschek in an overly loud, almost desperate voice (*Kellner, Kellner*) that cracked, and said in Yiddish inflected German, "May I trouble you for a beer?"

Roubitschek cleared his throat. "If you can be troubled to hand over the cash for it," he said and left.

In walked Kafka and Brod, Kafka bending under the low ceiling though his head cleared it by a foot at least, even with his bowler on. He carried with him a bouquet of roses. "For Hanna?" I asked Jozef. I imagined an indelible moment, the rare privilege of watching one of the greatest writers ever presenting my great grandmother, star of the Yiddish stage, with flowers.

"Maybe," he said. "Let's wait and see."

Brod had his homburg hat in his hands and looked around for an empty seat, chose the table Jozef already occupied, and sat on him. Jozef laughed as though he'd been tickled, but stayed put. He blended in with Brod, like a double exposure, but he didn't actually possess the famous writer.

I was too shy to sit in Kafka's lap, as it were (a sentence I never imagined myself writing before this), so I sat on the chair beside him where Brod had placed his hat. Brod, laughing, said, "Where are your manners?" and took off Franz's bowler for him in the teasing way that close friends have with one another. He set the bowler beside his homburg. Kafka laughed and ran a hand through his hair as though a second bowler might be lurking there ready to pop up. But he was just checking to see if his hair was in place. Kafka, vain? I hadn't imagined. But he was a beautiful man, twenty-eight though he looked about seventeen, thin but athletic, with shoulders squared unlike Brod who was slightly hunched. I won't say anything about his eyes. Or not much. Enough has been written about Kafka's eyes. But I'd like to settle one dispute once and for all: their color, which has long been debated. A greyish blue.

Brod called over Roubitschek, who was suddenly meek in front of the famous writer (Brod, not Kafka) and hurried over, bowing slightly in a way that made the ridges of his forehead, by far his most prominent feature, even more creased than ever.

"Yes, Mr Brod."

"A beer for Dr Kafka and do you have any of the dark or are you still out of it? Oh, never mind. Just bring me some schnapps and two glasses of hot water, and are you hungry, Franz?"

Kafka, who was regarding his friend with chin on hand, made a barely noticeable grimace, as if to say, "Not for anything here."

That was something I had noticed but hadn't thought about it until Brod asked for two glasses of water. Everyone seated had not one but two glasses of water beside them, no matter what else they had ordered. "It's the custom," Jozef told me. "All of the Prague cafés give you two glasses of water, though the proprietors don't like the tradition at all. People like to linger at cafes and the reasoning goes that two glasses will last longer than one and thereby justify your lingering without having to reorder."

"That seems kind of dumb," I said.

"To you," Jozef said, slightly offended. "But for the denizens of café culture in Prague in 1911, this was how things were."

"I would like onion soup, like the kind we ate in Paris," Kafka said after the waiter left. "Someday, in the future, perhaps fifty years from now, you'll be able to order onion soup as the French make it by snapping your fingers," and he snapped his fingers at Max. "Whether it's on the menu or not. And it will appear in front of you instantly, piping hot."

"Indubitably," Max said with an indulgent smile, but then gestured to Kafka as if handing him an invisible box. "I'm begging you. Werfel has issued her an invitation and she's agreed to come to Prague next month. I'm giving you plenty of notice, plenty of time in which to mentally steel yourself. We'll be in a group. You won't even have to do anything but shake hands with her."

"Why me? Who am I?" Kafka said.

"She's fun and lively, and her poetry has moments of brilliance," Brod said. "She's unique."

"Unique" was a word I had always hated, especially when people said something was "very unique." But it sounded a little better in German. "Einzigartig" or literally, "one-of-a-kind." How, I always wondered could something be *very* one-of-a-kind. It either was or it wasn't. Kafka gave Max a look as though Max had just made his point for him, a slight roll of the head downward while lifting his eyebrows. He repositioned his chair and wobbled the table, which was crooked.

"A one-of-a-kind urban mind twitching erratically. That should be the title of her next volume of poetry. *Erratic Twitches.*"

He was looking down at the faulty leg as he uttered this. Jozef laughed quietly in Brod's lap while Brod threw back his head and sputter-laughed.

The faulty leg seemed to bother Kafka as much as the writer about whom he was gossiping, and he wiggled it back and forth, as though he might convince the table to fix itself simply by demonstrating to it its lack of balance.

"Not one authentic gesture."

He finally looked up, still clutching the table. "Can we move? I can't sit here. I won't be able to enjoy the show."

"There's nowhere else to move. We can just call over Roubitschek and ask him to put something under it," and he called to Roubitschek, but this time the waiter, bustling by with some beer bottles on a tray, either ignored him or didn't hear.

Max withdrew a handful of matchbooks, one unused, the other two almost empty, from his jacket pocket and placed the new matchbook and one of the empties under the faulty leg, so that it was approximately the right height and the table barely wiggled. He took a deep breath and sat back in his chair.

"Werfel sent her some of your work and she recognizes its strength. She says she wants to meet you again."

"But I can't suffer her even in groups. I know there are plenty of people who adore her."

"I can see your objections, believe me," Brod said.

"And I can see her appeal," Kafka said, his voice resigned.

"You'll do it then?" Max said.

"Do I need to wear a costume?" Kafka asked. "Should I greet the Prince of Thebes in my attire as Julius Caesar?"

Jozef's eyes lit up and he put a finger in the air through one of Max's ears.

"Aha," he shouted. "I knew it. Else Lasker-Schuler. The poet. She's coming to town."

"Caesar doesn't suit you at all," Max said. "Perhaps the blind prophet of Apollo, Tiresias from Thebes, would be more appropriate. But I think he turned into a woman for seven years. You might find that disruptive to your routine."

"Not at all," Kafka said. "Just as Lasker-Schuler can be the Prince of Thebes, why can't I be a prophetess from that same ancient city? I imagine I'd find being a vessel of the gods refreshing. At least I could move from my parents' flat to my own temple. My first revelation," he said, placing his hands lightly to his temples. "I predict that after the Prince of Thebes has finished defrauding the audiences of

Prague, he'll return to his pure state, that of an unstable habitué of Berlin café society in search of her next meal."

Max smiled and shook his head. "It's not like you to be so unkind."

"You know what's like me and what isn't, Max? I certainly don't," Kafka's mouth upturned in a slight smirk.

"That's like you," Max said. "So, you'll do it?"

"Let's wait and see," Kafka said. "One thing I know about myself is that I don't like to be pushed into things."

I had no idea who Lasker-Schuler was and would have questioned Jozef further, but we were distracted by the appearance of a man who popped his head through the red satin curtain. In his late twenties or early thirties, he had a narrow boyish face, light brown curly hair, a high forehead, and a thick layer of pancake makeup. He looked as though he had never before seen people gathered in such a space or at least didn't expect them tonight. His glance rested on Brod and Kafka and he gave a small wave, then disappeared behind the curtain again. A small group of actors in makeup and costume poured from behind the curtain and to our table as though they in turn were going to watch the show of another troupe of Yiddish actors and they couldn't all fit backstage. Jozef looked up smiling from Brod's lap as though they were greeting him, too.

One of the actors was a statuesque woman wearing an elaborate costume of white flowing robes and her hair curled into tight dark ringlets to give her a girlish look though I guessed she was in her thirties. She walked barefoot but with an elegant, unhurried speed, her smile somewhat aloof. Kafka could barely take his eyes off her.

"Is that her?" I asked. "Is that Hanna?" I had thought my great-grandmother had red hair and this woman seemed a bit too old.

"That's Millie Tschissik. 'Madame Tschissik,' Kafka calls her. He has an enormous crush on her, and now that she's beside him, he can barely look at her. 'To look at her,' he wrote, 'would be to admit that I loved her.' She could do a lot worse than be admired by Kafka. 'She pulls invisible trains around her in the folds of her dress,' he also wrote."

That didn't sound very attractive. I imagined someone yanking a bunch of toy trains around with her. Jozef, noting my perplexity, added in a soft, embarrassed voice. "Trains as in a bridal train. Not trains as in locomotives. He thought she was mysterious, otherworldly."

"I knew what you meant," I said.

Kafka sat there like an adolescent at his first dance.

Yitzhak Lowy, the same young man who had first poked his head through the curtain, stood beside Millie Tschissik. Lowy was thin, but he had a pillow stuffed under his shirt and he was wearing a bald-cap and a kind of eyebrow extension made of yarn dyed the same color as his eyebrows. Seeming to sense Kafka's unease, Lowy pulled a long face, grabbed the flowers off the table, sniffed at them extravagantly, brandished them like a torch, pretended to scrub under his arms with the flowers, and handed them back to a blushing but laughing Kafka with a wide grin.

"How thoughtful of you," Kafka said.

A young woman with a cascade of red hair drew back the curtain, her face made to resemble a cat's, charcoal whiskers and a cat-like chin and eyes. She was not dressed like any of the other women in the room, but wore a leotard that immediately focused the attention of most of the men. The workers at their tables gaped. The university students stopped mid-laugh and gazed in reverent silence as though she were their generous mother, their alma mater, personified. The men at the tables of the Workers' Association looked at her with stern and suspicious appreciation as did the previously bored official who put on his glasses and scribbled something in a notebook. The Yeshiva student gripped the table as though it were a ledge and farted.

As if the force of their gazes were physically groping her, she startled and stumbled off the stage, a book and a pen dropping from her hands. She gave an apologetic smile and bent to retrieve the pen which had rolled under Kafka and Brod's table. Kafka looked up as though she'd flown away, and Brod stood slightly, alarmed that a cat woman was wriggling under the table. Yitzhak Lowy gazed at her rear end, its shape accentuated by the brown leotard she wore. With a kind of comic intensity, he waved his hand as though he had burnt it. A monarch likely couldn't have made the workers at the next table leap to their feet as quickly as they did for this cat woman. They hooted and clapped as the woman stood, ignoring them.

"That's your great-grandmother," Jozef said. "She knows how to make an entrance at least."

This young, as-yet-to-be-formed Hanna, asked if she could trouble Brod for an autograph. She stuck out the pen and the book virtually under Brod's nose and she gave him the smile of a young person who thinks everyone is their friend, and that no one wants anything in return, her face exuding an almost insane pleasantness that I mostly associated with people I had met in my lifetime from the Midwest and Utah.

"You're familiar with my work?" Brod asked.

"I gave her two of your novellas to read, which she devoured," Lowy said. "Then she moved on to your masterpiece, Nornpygge Castle." I glanced at Kafka to see if he registered any envy, but I could detect none. He smiled with gratitude, it seemed, as though he had written this apparently famous book which I had never heard of in my life.

"I especially admire your novella, 'Death to the Dead,'" she said.

"You must understand, this is several years old already," Brod said, stroking one side of his pencil moustache. "An artist matures."

"*Admire nothing. Admire everything.* These are words to live by. I believe in this Indifferentism of yours to my core. What else could Gottfried Tock do but kill himself?" And here she struck her breast as though pledging herself to the memory of Gottfried Tock, whoever he was.

She seemed anything but indifferent. I wanted words to live by, too, no matter how contradictory. A little youthful passion, to feel something like that again would have seemed almost divine.

"If I won't have any children, sir, you are the reason. At least, it's your words that will make me childless," she said, which made Brod attempt to sit up straighter in his chair and adjust his pince-nez glasses.

"Now you've really flattered him," Kafka said with a burst of laughter that turned into a cough, which he stifled with a sip of beer.

Millie Tschissik raised her eyebrows and excused herself while Lowy took Hanna by the shoulders and spoke as if to a feverish child. "There, there," he said. "Maybe after the show you can explain to the great author why his words have left you barren. For now, you need to get ready and let them be in peace."

Thankfully, she wasn't stupid. She knew when she was being patronized and she gave Lowy a sharp look and wriggled from his grasp just as Brod handed the book and pen back to her. "Thank you and I'm sorry," she said.

"No need to apologize," Brod said as she hurried off and Lowy made a quick courtesy visit to the tables of the Workers' Association, thanking them for their support and shaking hands all around.

"Odd girl," Brod said, "but pretty."

"Too coquettish for my taste," Kafka said.

The show kicked off with a series of jokes and songs from various members of the troupe. I couldn't understand most of the jokes as they were in Yiddish, but half of them ended with Millie Tschissik and Flora Klug, the other older woman in the company, swinging their rear ends, made prodigious with extra padding, with the precision of crane operators, at various male members of the cast. This didn't strike me as funny, but the room was otherwise filled with raucous laughter. Even Kafka, to my amazement, found these little skits table-slapping funny, guffawing (a word I've always hated) in a full-throated way I would have thought impossible for Kafka before this night. Jozef chuckled his annoying little laugh as always.

When the men didn't return the crane operators' advances, the women shouted curses at them, which I *did* find funny because Yiddish curses are unequivocally funny. A few of these I remembered from the lessons I received from my uncles on the day my brother was married, and a few others Jozef translated for me: *Lie with your head in crap and grow like an onion; May you have two beds and a fever in each* and the men striking back at the women with equally painful suggestions: *May you give birth to a trolley car.*

Many of the songs were of a different order, melancholy and slow, sung usually by a solo performer, occasionally a duet between Millie Tschissik and her husband Manny.

The songs dealt with luck, mostly bad, and fate, mostly bad, and women, mostly bad. Jozef translated these under his breath for me as though the audience might hear him and be disturbed. There was no chance of that even if we had suddenly materialized – the songs hypnotized one and all except for the government official who sipped a beer and flipped through the pages of his magazine while the performers sang and joked. Some of the workers wept and nodded as Manny sang a song about being driven to drink by a woman. Kafka seemed especially enraptured by a waltz sung by his great crush. She stood in her white robes in the center of the small stage, her arms pulling those invisible trains:

> Now I'm standing and thinking what a
> powerful might Fate has for everyone. Here it
> jokes, there it becomes furious. It can punish
> you and also bless you.
> If it was up to me, if I could only change your
> I would free you now, I'd begin your life again. And I'd
> pray for your happiness.

Kafka seemed deep in thought as he listened to this, one finger teasing a thorn from one of the roses he had brought. He pressed it as though it were a button over which he was hesitating, then sat back in his chair and folded his arms across his chest, gazing at the performer on stage, as if she were giving him a singular message from Fate itself.

Her words spoke to me as well, especially the lines about changing "your strange fate, I would free you now, I'd begin your life again, And I'd pray for your happiness."

I wondered how many people in this café felt similarly, wishing they might free themselves from one strange fate or another without imagining the strange fate that lay in wait for them. Had some of them survived this calamitous century and lived mostly happy lives? None of them had any notion of what lay in store. Not just one world war, but two, and one only three years off that would probably kill every able-bodied man in here or make them something other than able-bodied. Most of them probably felt safe tonight, and that was so, but only for a very short while.

After this song, the entire troupe of twelve filled the stage and led the room in a number of rousing songs dealing with luck, mostly bad, fate, mostly bad, and women, mostly bad. These songs involved clapping and shouting and singing along with the chorus. Everyone had their turn leading the audience in song and clapping, all except for Hanna, who was stuck in the back of the crowded stage with the chorus, her face usually obscured by someone else's shoulder. I tried to distinguish her voice from the others, but I wasn't even sure she was singing at all and her movements seemed confined to back-of-the-line swaying.

"I can barely see Hanna," I said to Jozef, as though he were responsible for her placement on stage. "I thought she was a star."

"I never said that," Jozef said.

"Well, my mother said it."

"Give her time," Jozef said. "She's the youngest member of the troupe by seven years at least."

Some of the workers rose from their chairs and danced or simply pounded their feet, like an army marching, and even the Yeshiva boy sitting alone at his table clapped and sang along. Even Brod. Even Kafka. But not me, because I had to wait for Jozef's translations, which he gave me in a spotty fashion, half of the time simply forgetting my presence, clapping without a sound, singing without a voice, and dancing without presence, but as joyful as I'd ever seen him, alive or dead. Two old men sat at a table in front by the stage, their faces dry and raw with age, their beards matted. One of them, his left elbow on the table, held his right arm crooked in the air, as though holding up a curtain to see the action. The music did its best to help him out of his chair. Flora Klug, seeing the two old men, stood at the front of the stage and held out her arms to them.

"Dear fathers," she said. "Come on and sing."

The noise level at the Café Savoy, by the time the main play commenced, was like that of a school lunchroom. But everyone quieted down when the curtain was drawn back again to reveal the modest set that had been pushed into place during the intermission. The most impressive piece of the set barely fit, a palm tree that rose as high as the ceiling (not that high, but a little over six feet or so).

Jozef said that the play, an operetta actually, was one of the most famous in the Yiddish repertoire, *Shulamith*, by the father of Yiddish theatre, Abraham Goldfaden. A love story set in ancient Israel, the drama told the tale of the young maiden Shulamith, who, while wandering in the desert, falls into a well. The well was a circle of wire and straw where she crouched, and in the way of such productions, it didn't matter to anyone, human or spirit, whether the setting was realistic. It was the emotions that mattered, the sense of panic and dread Millie Tschissik, playing Shulamith, conveyed with her neck stretched to heaven with a hopelessness that seemed utterly convincing. For long moments, the lights lowered, she crouched at the bottom of her well, arms clutched around her knees, rocking slowly back and forth as she hummed a faint tune. The audience stayed silent and someone, a woman from the audience, perhaps a plant from Lowy's troupe, yelled out in a stage whisper, "Save her, someone," and as though her character had been inspired by this perhaps spontaneous outburst, Shulamith called above her and sang in a plaintive voice in a minor key, "Someone save me. Oh, please save me."

Two figures appeared from opposite ends of the stage, one, a turbaned man, with a long black beard, Prince Absalom, played by Susskind Klug, the husband of Flora, and dressed in white pants and a white shirt embroidered with gold thread, one hand shielding his eyes, the other clutching a sword. The other figure was my great-grandmother dressed in her cat costume, who cavorted in front of the well. Her cavorting was not so much cat-like, or not a cat comfortable in its own skin, but kind of twitchy and jerky, making all kinds of movements with her head and back as though she were infested with fleas. In her hands, she held two rocks, and both Shulamith and Absalom seemed to forget themselves, staring openly at her. Hanna started to hop on one foot and bang the rocks together.

"An interpretive dance?" I asked Jozef.

Jozef shrugged.

Absalom seemed to remember his quest and turned to the audience, a hand shielding his eyes from the desert sun. His voice was clear and yearning, the notes similar to the sound of Jewish prayer "What do I hear? The voice of a spirit?"

His words seemed to excite the cat, who pranced across the crowded stage as much as possible, did a kind of wave in front of the well, legs planted wide apart, arms in the air, tongue extended as though she was about to perform the Haka. A smuggled tomato landed with a squashing sound at her feet.

She began to twirl, rocks still in hand. For a good fifteen seconds she twirled and then she lurched backwards, stepped on the tomato, lost her balance, and fell against the palm tree. The palm tree leaned forward as Millie Tschissik shrieked, her hands shielding her face as the palm toppled across the well, dented it, and then bounced off.

Millie held out a hand to the audience as though forbidding them to laugh or hurl any other objects, which they had started to do, and sang, "Who is there? I will bless you. Rescue a young girl who is trapped. Have mercy and save me from this deep darkness."

As though deciding that self-reliance was the best course of action, she stepped out of the well and crooked a finger at the cat, who had stopped all movement entirely, and stood frozen. Hanna put down her rocks and approached Millie Tschissik, abandoning all attempted cat-like movements. Prince Absalom went to her side as well and together they righted the palm tree and put it back in place, Absalom and Shulamith singing all the while.

"Are you a demon or spirit in the well, calling to trick me and trap me?" the Prince sang.

"Please believe me. I'm no demon. I am not yet a spirit," whereupon she, still singing, climbed back into the well, knelt down, and became helpless again.

I started to feel dizzy.

Jozef, noticing my distress, peered at me in a doctorly manner. "We're leaving," he announced.

"A while longer," I said. "We can't leave so soon. Fifteen more minutes. Go ahead, time me."

"Then prove it," Absalom sang to Shulamith. "Prove you're no demon. Say the name of the eternal."

Here, Jozef and I exchanged glances. As spirits, this part of the drama had a special relevance. Jozef's mouth hung open and his eyes dulled at hearing these melancholy lines sung. We could not pray. We could not say the name of G-d. What can the non-existent ask for besides existence? I can't say that prayer was denied us so much as impossible, the words scrambled as soon as we tried to speak. All I can say is that the sense of communion I'd always felt I derived through the artistic process was wholly absent in Oblivion. This absence was so conspicuous as to be painful, like some kind of dry socket where a tooth has been that was barely noticeable until it was yanked out.

"Here is your sign," Shulamith sang out. "I call on the name of G-d."

"Swear to me."

"I swear by the name of G-d. By G-d, by G-d, by G-d, I swear to you."

Jozef seemed to be undergoing some transformation, his form wavering, his ethereal lips quivering. He hung his head and wept.

His tears were contagious and I soon wept, too. Our tears were like smoke, like foam, they did not perform like human tears. As we could not pray, we could not properly weep any longer. I would like to say that our tears were our prayers, but they were certainly not that. They were small silences that fell from our eyes, pearls of desolation, inconsequential as a grain of sand in the imaginary desert.

"Oh, it's a maiden," said Absalom. "Young as a spring flower, as bright as the stars. What mortal could refuse to save such a child so that she might live? Don't worry, I'm here to save you, the fortunate soul who heard your cries in the desert."

He lifted her from her dented prison of wire and straw and twirled Shulamith, her feet off the ground, around the stage. Both of them instantly fell in love. I felt it was I being twirled, too, though not in love.

I wasn't sure why Hanna was there, her main role seeming to be to dance in front of the couple and serve as a mute witness to their vows that they would soon marry. Her dancing was as stiff as before but at least she had toned it down and she didn't hit any more props. My mother had always told me Hanna had been a star of the Yiddish stage. I could only hope that she had improved after this performance.

Absalom and Shulamith traded vows to be true in front of the cat and the well ("My dear one, my loved one, my diamond found in the desert") and then Absalom went off to Jerusalem and left Shulamith in the hands of his servant, Cingitang, to be brought back to her father Manoach in Bethlehem. Played by a short actor named Mano Pipes, Cingitang was a half Chinese stereotype, half Arab, a genie who only ate pork and people, whom Absalom had freed from a bottle and had to do his bidding.

As soon as Absalom was back in Jerusalem, he met Princess Abigail, completely forgot his vows to Shulamith, and married Abigail. Shulamith, meanwhile, fought off all suitors for years by feigning madness, true to her vision of the well, the desert cat, and Absalom. Away from her father and her suitors, including a pot-bellied rabbi played by Lowy, she sang a lullaby to an imagined future child of hers. The song, "Raisins and Almonds," the most famous lullaby in Yiddish, according to Jozef, was sung to me by my mother when I was an infant.

"My grandmother?" I couldn't remember my mother ever saying or singing anything in Yiddish despite the fact that she was one of Isaac Singer's translators.

"Your mother. In this production, Lowy has Shulamith sing it as a kind of dream of motherhood, but in the original, the playwright Goldfaden, who at the end of the day was a Zionist, played it differently. Absalom sings it in full battle gear as a reminiscence of his mother. The song is about a widowed mother in a corner of the Temple, telling her baby that he will travel the earth selling raisins and almonds before returning home a rich man. Everyone understands it as a metaphor for the Jewish Diaspora and Zionism."

> In dem Beis-Hamikdosh
> In a vinkl cheyder
> Zitst di almone, bas-tsion, aleyn Ihr
> ben yochidle yideln vigt zi keseider
> Un zingt im tzum shlofn a ledeleh sheyn.
> Ai-lu-lu

I didn't.

"Look at Kafka," Jozef urged, poking him in the arm with his spectral cigarette. Kafka bent forward on his elbows, his glass of beer in the triangle that his head and elbows formed on the table.

Kafka produced a pencil and a crumpled piece of paper from his trousers, leaning forward again, precipitously close to knocking over his beer. He glanced under the table at the leg as if someone else might have crawled under it. He wrote without looking at the words, as though we were guiding his hands. Jozef kept burning Kafka's forearm with his cigarette, and Kafka scratched the spot, but kept writing. Brod noticed him writing, too. Brod wouldn't have been able to see what was being written even if it wasn't dark, as Kafka used his elbows as a shield, as though Brod were trying to cheat on a test. Again, he scratched the spot that Jozef was burning invisibly, and Jozef raised his eyebrows and lifted his head proudly, glancing at me sideways as if to say, "Are you impressed or are you impressed with what you're witnessing?"

"Does he feel ...?"

Jozef waved at me before I could finish. "Yes, very perceptive, _____. An intoxicated moment."

What? I had meant the cigarette. Did he feel the cigarette? Jozef glanced at the stage, and I reached for Kafka's pen before Jozef could notice. Kafka's hand wobbled, and he paused, then resumed scribbling again. I couldn't be sure if my touch had caused the wobble or if this was just coincidence. Had I felt anything, the touch of the pen? I couldn't be sure but I felt I had felt it. When Jozef turned back, he saw me staring at my finger but he seemed to think I was pointing to Kafka in awe of his artistry, his commitment, or just his Kafka-ness. Yes, of course, I felt all that, but not at that moment. I was in awe of my finger.

Jozef clambered onto the table, facing Kafka, Kafka's beer an ethereal enema.

"This is a documented intoxicated moment, _____. Kafka experienced almost two hundred and fifty in his lifetime. Most of us get maybe four if we're lucky. You had seven, I believe."

"There's a record of intoxicated moments?" I asked. "I thought you just made it up."

"In 'The Metamorphosis,'" he said. "You've read it, haven't you?"

"You know I have," I said.

"Gregor Samsa is specifically offered raisins and almonds, but ..."

"Good, grief, Jozef, I didn't come here for textual analysis." I said this perhaps a little too harshly. Jozef looked stunned with hurt, and he returned to Brod's lap and didn't look at me for much of the rest of the play. I was well on my way to alienating Jozef in the afterlife as I had in life. He was just too annoying, too pompous, too pedantic. Why did everything have to be a lesson? My annoyance with him wasn't that he spoke too candidly – he definitely had filters. He wasn't the type of person who just says anything and everything without censoring some of his thoughts. On the contrary, he was the most difficult person to read. I could never be sure of his true intentions, if he actually admired my writing or if I was just an instrument he played out of boredom. A writer friend of mine from Guangzhou had once told me a Chinese proverb, "Settle all accounts after harvest." It meant that you should reap whatever benefits from a person or a situation while you can before discarding them. Perhaps I just amused Jozef, and when he had harvested enough, he would reveal his true opinion of me and make sure my own sense of insignificance stuck for eternity.

And so we stayed, Jozef convinced (enough at least) that I could hold my Time in the way that people who have become accustomed to alcohol can hold their drink. Still, the production was long, and Jozef, so engrossed in the play, seemed to have forgotten that I had told him we could leave in fifteen minutes. I was feeling quite full of myself, heavy with existence, a different kind of intoxication. How does a phantom reinvigorate his phantom limbs? This was my dilemma, my dislocation, my dream. The author Isaac Babel's grandmother, when he told her he wanted to be a writer when he grew up, told him, "Then you must know everything." But I didn't want to know everything. Not Kafka, not even my own great grandmother could capture my full attention that evening as much as my own finger, which I had hardly given a thought to when I was alive. I was in love with this finger and would have sung a song as endearing as "Raisins and Almonds" to it if I had only known the words. It's hard to tell a drunk that he's not making sense – for him, that only confirms the wisdom of his drinking. That was me that evening, though I had enough sense at least to hide how odd I felt from Jozef.

Absalom's bad choices soon came back to haunt him. One of his children with Abigail was bitten by a wildcat and died. The other fell into a well and drowned.

I had made many bad choices, too. Choosing to become a writer was top of my list, probably the worst because it had landed me a spot forever in that dumb café surrounded by people I hadn't especially liked in life, who probably hadn't liked me, whose work I rarely read and who had rarely read mine, drinking divine lattes that were so perfect they made me want to puke. Jozef hacked on one of his cigarettes, which in itself was strange – he had no lungs – and then when I tried to float up to the ceiling to pop another lightbulb after Shulamith finished her song, the only applause I could offer, I could barely lift myself off the ground. I sank under the table, where I found great comfort there under the crushing weight of existence, studying Kafka's shoelaces. These are the shoelaces of a great artist, I contemplated for the longest time. Kafka's shoes were black and white, white tips and black bodies, stylish probably for 1911, but the leather was cracked and I read those cracks like the lifeline of a doomed man. Things could not end well for this pair of shoes. They reminded me for some reason of the forlorn pile of shoes I'd seen behind glass at Auschwitz when I'd travelled to Poland to make a short documentary.

I have no memory of the play's ending, but Jozef told me the "happy ending," that Abigail released Absalom from his marriage and he returned finally to Shulamith, two children and a wife lighter, to marry the one he had been destined to marry all along. I couldn't see it as a happy ending, exactly.

By the time I emerged from under the table, the cast had just finished its bows and the curtain was drawn again. It started to open and then it closed again. It started to open and then it closed. Two more times it did this before Lowy's head appeared from between the curtain and he said, "Ladies and gentlemen. We hope..."

Here he stopped, and the curtain started to boil with activity behind it with indistinct shouts. He appeared again. "Tomorrow, the immortal classic ..." Again he stopped, pulled his head back in like a frightened tortoise and the entire curtain collapsed to reveal Lowy on his knees being yanked by Mano Pipes, the "savage" Cingintang, servant of Absalom, shaking him in a rage. Jozef told me later that Cingitang in the play had reformed along with his master and gave up eating people and pork for Kosher gefilte fish only. But Pipes, taking a cue from his former bestial nature, was biting Lowy's shoulder. Behind them, Millie Tschissik was hugging Hanna, patting her on the back. "And we who profess to teach morals from the stage," she declaimed, as though this were the true last line of the play she had just starred in.

I asked Jozef what was happening.

"Some kind of fight, I guess," he said. Normally I would have thanked him with a heaping portion of sarcasm for stating the obvious, but I was too preoccupied with my own strange sensations: bobble headed and dumb, the way that marijuana had made me feel when I was alive. I never understood why people said it made them feel high. It made me feel as though I was sinking in mud. I felt low.

Pipes, sporting a black eye, grabbed Lowy by the head and the two twisted off the stage, crashing onto the table of the two old men with matted beards. Almost the entire audience rose, and as quick as they could, moved away from the two combatants. Only the laborers remained seated. The Yeshiva boy fled as fast as he could.

I poked my head through the table to get a better view.

"Fair warning," Jozef said, standing between Brod and Kafka, who had risen too and clutched their chairs as though they might have to use them as weapons. "If you keep your head like that, it might stay that way. You haven't had enough exposure to Time. You might remain for forty years or a thousand with your head planted in that position, however long that table lasts, and by that time, you'll be a lost cause." Jozef coughed and looked at his cigarette, then tossed it aside.

By this time, Roubitschek and Migdal the bouncer had made their way through the terrified crowd. Migdal took care of the two troublemakers, yanking them to their feet and frog-marching them both simultaneously out the door. The Jewish Workers Association was in an uproar and the government official just wanted to leave. Roubitschek put his hand on the man's shoulder in a way that was controlling if not threatening, sat him back down, and handed him a shot of something.

I started to lower my head back through the table, but around my chin, I found myself stuck, unable to lower myself further. "Jozef?" I said. I thrashed from side to side, but only succeeded in lowering myself to the bridge of my nose. "Get me out," I said, and I thrashed some more – the table wobbling, Kafka's beer toppling.

He and Brod took this minor earthquake as something caused by mortal disturbances rather than otherworldly ones. But they decided it was best for them to leave.

Soon after, I was left alone at the table with Kafka's abandoned roses and spilt beer. *In* the table. I could smell it all, the stale and sweet. Jozef had disappeared, returned to Oblivion without me? This was me now, the ghost in the table. This was my punishment, a thousand years or so locked in a stockade of sorts. Where the table went, so would I. Would the table survive World War I? Would it survive World War II? Would it wind up in a junkyard, buried under tons of the detritus of urban Bohemian life? I guessed I would find out. At least, there was solace in knowing that the table had its own life, its own drama, and perhaps its own table dreams. If I ever were able to escape and make my way to the right side of a table, any table or desk, I would write this table's story, its biography. "Everyone has a story worth telling," I told the table. "Even you."

"Are you ready to go now?"

Was the table rejecting me? It was Jozef, speaking from beside me though I couldn't see him.

That night, we were the last customers to leave the Café Savoy. Only when Roubitschek and the other waiters had finished wiping the tables and mopping the floor, only after they had turned out all the lights and locked the door and I had slipped through the table centimeter by centimeter, did I think there might be a chance of escape. Oblivion was better than this, but I felt the heaviness of existence pulling me back. I tried to stay focused on drawing my head through the table as Jozef calmly muttered instructions in my ear. He told me I might have to leave my scalp embedded in the table, that we might have to come back for it later, but I told him no, either I went whole or not at all, and maybe he should just go back without me. No sense of both of us being stuck here, but he said he wasn't leaving until I was freed. I was grateful, of course, but in the end, it did little good. For some of us, no matter how many chances at calm, if not peace, we're given, we always somehow choose the maelstrom.

# CHAPTER FOUR

# EVERYTHING CAN
# BE SAID

Jozef was smoking as usual and reading a German-language newspaper with heavy letters, BOHEMIA.

"Anything interesting happening on ..." I peered at the newspaper's date, "November 10, 1911?"

"Ah, _____," he said, shaking the newspaper in a fussy way, but folding it rather haphazardly and putting it aside. He sighed and offered me a cigarette as though he didn't already intimately know all my likes and dislikes. "If there were tomorrows here, I'd say that perhaps tomorrow you might like to take up smoking again." He tilted his head like the mischievous boy he was at heart.

He knew I would want to return, but he didn't know the real reason why. He thought that I wanted to observe Kafka, that I wanted to be a tourist in his life, a mere acquaintance, as my great grandmother had been. No, I didn't want to be part of a family legacy that included a line of forgettable bohemians who met great people, even worked with them, but were themselves, pale reflections. Yes, I wanted to know more about my great grandmother and her path from the Yiddish theatre in Europe to the unremarkable streets of Bensonhurst, but that wasn't compelling enough in and of itself. If I'd wanted to study the life of a relative and that alone, I probably would have started with my father's life, as I had barely known him. If I was ever to escape the maelstrom of my dissatisfaction, I needed to get out of here. Knowing me, maybe Jozef thought I wanted to be Kafka. But he would have been wrong. I didn't want to be Kafka. I wanted to write something worthy of him. What I really wanted was to be Carl Winterhoven, best-selling author of The Blackhawk Exchange or Saffron Segovia. Why I didn't visit their lives was simple. They had produced their greatest work in their afterlives, not their actual lives. Even if there had been something worth gleaning from their lives, I would have avoided them just as I avoided their works in the library of Oblivion, just as it was so difficult sometimes for me to walk into a bookstore when I was alive. The books of my friends and acquaintances were inevitably stocked, but most often not my own. In hindsight, this was self-defeating and petty, but my inability to be in the proximity of the work of a successful peer was almost phobic in its intensity.

"I'd like to experience another one of Kafka's intoxicated moment again," I mumbled.

"A what moment?" he asked. "A precious moment?"

I said it again.

"A *Hoot & Holler* moment?" he said in a fake Southern accent, lips forming an unnatural smile.

I crossed my arms and transformed into my sixty-two-year-old self. I'm not sure why except that it was my most tired and resigned visage. I wasn't going to grovel.

"You really want to return to Prague?" he asked. He pretended to suck air between his teeth. "I would hate to see you become a dybbuk," he said.

"I don't want to possess anyone," I said.

"You could have fooled me," he said. "You tried to possess a table back there." He looked at me not only with amusement, but with a certain admiration, too.

"I didn't try to possess a table."

"To become a dybbuk is to forfeit your soul forever. It is the afterlife's worst kind of madness."

I didn't want to possess anyone but myself. All I needed was a typewriter, my memory, and some feeling in my fingers. I had made the table in the café move. I had made Kafka's pen tremble. If I could do that then why couldn't I tap out a story on a typewriter? Even death could not rob me of my literary ambition.

"A table dybbuk," Jozef said, placing his hand in front of his mouth and convulsing with laughter. "Stay in Time long enough and you'll lose all self-control."

"I was merely poking my head through it," I said. "I thought it would be harmless."

"Harmless?"

"What about you?" I asked. "You're dying to return to Prague." I pointed to the newspaper.

"What about me?" He picked up his paper as if to resume reading and put it down again. His voice was still soft. "I know how to pace myself. I have self-control." I was just checking to see if there was anything worth seeing the weekend of November 10, 1911. Some cinema perhaps. Or perhaps a reading. The famous German author Else Lasker-Schuler arrived that day at the Prague train station for her first reading. Brod and Werfel and even Kafka were there to see her, as well as a crowd of admirers, including your great-grandmother. The arrival of the poet caused quite the stir. I was just reading about it."

"Elke Laker Shorer?"

"Else," he said. "Not Elke. Lasker-Schuler. Kafka hated her, which was really quite unusual for him. He hardly ever said a bad word about anyone. Werfel, on the other hand, loved Lasker-Schuler, but then he was a bit of a drama queen himself. As for Brod, he was fulsome in his literary hatreds and rivalries. They were like milk and honey to him. Kafka, though, he had other things on his mind. But of course, that wasn't covered by the papers."

I willed my face into a picture of perfect calm.

"Take me there," I said. "Please."

"I will never forget the sight of your head poking from the center of the table."

I could have gone on my own, but it was like learning to drive. I needed someone beside me to help me navigate these first times out.

"Take me back," I said.

"I'm afraid you need more preparation," he said. "I don't think you're ready to fully appreciate the experience."

"I've read pretty much everything that Kafka ever wrote," I said.

He tossed the newspaper he'd been reading aside and it vanished into the same pocket of air that his cigarettes always disappeared into when he was finished with them. He reached beside the table and placed a book on top. "Have you read anything of Brod's yet?" he asked, pointing to the book, a hardback of blue leather with no dust jacket. "Go. Read a little Brod," Jozef said, like he was speaking to a disruptive boy told to play on the swings and leave the grown-ups alone. "I think you need to read Brod. You haven't read Werfel but at least you should read Brod. You and he even share the same birthday."

I started to protest though my impatience was not rational. It resisted all evidence that there was, in fact, no hurry to get anywhere as the time I finished reading Brod would be the same time I started. "Jozef," I said. "Please don't treat me like a child." But he grabbed another newspaper, this time a *Chicago Tribune* from 1977, and stuck his head inside. Soon he was chuckling softly to himself and seemed completely uninterested in my presence. "I love Mike Royko," he said, it seemed, to no one in particular. "After he died, the *Tribune* was never the same."

So I returned to the library and read the novella that my great grandmother had spoken so rapturously about, *Death to the Dead* or *Tod Den Toten* in German. In the process, a number of things she'd mentioned about Brod made more sense.

At the beginning of *Death to The Dead* was the maxim, "*nil admirari!*" and at the beginning of another novella in the same collection, *Indifferentismus,* was the competing maxim, *"omnia admirari!"* Admire nothing – admire everything. It was all the same. Not that I believed this self-cancelling manifesto. I believed there were things worth admiring and things that didn't deserve admiration. Wasn't that in fact one of the main directives of humanity, to try to sort these things out, who or what deserves our admiration, artistic or otherwise, and who doesn't? But I admired the passion of Brod's youthful contradictions, just as my once youthful great-grandmother had admired them. I, too, if I had lived in Prague at that time, might have been Brod's Brod, his greatest admirer and champion.

I found it sad that Brod was mostly remembered, if remembered at all, only as Kafka's literary champion and executor. Wasn't he a great writer in his own right? My parents, too, had suffered from this kind of life, in the shadow of a great writer. In the early 1950s, my father was at a party thrown by Dan Talbot, the famous independent film impresario and owner of The New Yorker Theatre. A new issue of the influential magazine *Partisan Review* had just appeared with a story by an unknown Yiddish writer, Isaac Bashevis Singer, translated by Saul Bellow. Talbot stopped the party to read aloud to the assembled guests this story, "Gimpel the Fool." My father was wild for the story and asked Talbot to meet Singer. And so began perhaps the most important relationship of Singer's career. It was good timing, too, for my father. He had recently co-founded an influential but chronically impoverished publishing company. Singer, as it turned out, was unhappy with the publication of his first novel, *The Family Moscat,* by Alfred Knopf. Knopf (at that time a person, and not only a publishing company) had cut the middle of Singer's book in barbaric fashion, according to Singer, treating the novel as though he were rendering fat to make soap, rather than crafting a narrative. My father and Singer decided to work together, and my father became Singer's main editor and translator. My father didn't know Yiddish, but Singer would make a rough translation, and my father, a poet and novelist, would work meticulously with Singer to create the works in English that were essential to Singer winning the Nobel Prize in Literature, a dozen or so years after my father's early death. In a way, I always thought that my father had won a shadow Nobel. As soon as he became involved with Singer, his own literary career was subsumed by Singer's. My mother, who also translated Singer's work, suffered a similar fate. Of course, no one put a gun to her head, as the saying goes, but guns aren't the only means of coercion around. This was the 1950s, and my father, while certainly not a tyrant, urged her to put Singer's career and the business of the press ahead of her own burgeoning career. At that time, she had published one novel and a number of stories in influential magazines, as well as in *The Best American Stories* anthology. The well-known editor of *The Kenyon Review*, John Crowe Ransom, considered her one of America's most talented short story writers. That slowly fell away as she had my father and Singer as well as us kids to take care of. She was never bitter towards my father or us, but she felt that Singer never fully acknowledged his "translators," and she didn't appreciate his attitudes towards women, especially his wife Alma, whom he either regularly ignored or insulted. One of Singer's favorite phrases was that "women are long on hair and short on sense." My mother didn't appreciate that either, but this was at a time when women writers had to champion themselves. Only a few among her favorites made it to the finish line: her friends Grace Paley and Tillie Olsen, both Jewish writers like herself, long on talent and fortitude (their hair not especially long), the Black writer, Ann Petry and the white Southern writer, Eudora Welty, with whom she briefly corresponded. Some writers, by dint of fortitude and persistence and luck, made it without a Brod or Cecil Hemley or a Jozef. But how many others were left behind because their voices weren't loud enough, or the dominant culture drowned them out or ignored them, or because they had no champion, or because they died before they could finish their book? Or all of the above?

In Brod's novella, *Death to the Dead*, Gottfried Tock, a billionaire in Berlin, hates old art because he thinks that to worship anything made by someone dead is to kill life's essence. Tock collects the most expensive and contemporary art as a means to discover what makes one piece of art worthy of acclaim and another unworthy. He arranges the artworks in a theatre, some onstage and some in the seats as both spectator and performers. But they're neither performers nor spectators, simply empty signs of Tock's delusional obsessions. Like most synopses, this doesn't do the book justice. It must seem silly. Paintings don't perform. We could have told this to both Tock and his creator, Brod, and spared them the trouble of the novella, no? But the story is more than its bare bones. We see a character here struggling with notions of value and meaning, and the form is innovative and engaging, a performance-like dialogue between Tock and another character, gaining in intensity until Tock, realizing he's no better than a statue himself, decides to blow up his collection and his home, and dies in the conflagration.

This type of story is what one of my teachers in graduate school,

Don Hendrie, Jr, used to call an idea story, which wasn't meant a compliment. Still, I always secretly liked idea stories. I didn't th ideas were necessarily such a problem. Narrative illusion, no mat... how well done, is artifice, after all, written by someone with ideas. Some of us like to coax ideas out of hiding, suggest that they should just be themselves. For such writers, we have essays, but some of us want both ideas and narrative. One of my favorite fiction writers, Jorge Luis Borges, penned such idea stories. A favorite and one of his most famous, "Pierre Menard, Author of the Quixote," tells of an author who is trying to create the world's masterpieces out of nothing. He's not trying to recreate the masterpieces, but to create them in the manner of the "infinite monkey theorem" which postulates that an infinite number of monkeys with an infinite amount of time pounding out on typewriters (this was before word processors) will create by happenstance all the world's masterpieces eventually, purely because they have all the time in the world to do so.

An idea story. But a great idea. And the narrator of Borges" story takes Menard's project completely seriously, reporting in a tone of admiration that Menard, in his lifetime, randomly typing, only produced a few paragraphs of the world's masterpieces. As proof, the narrator gives us a paragraph from Don Quixote alongside Menard's version. The two versions are identical, of course, proof of nothing. But they're different, too. Menard's version possesses something that Cervantes' version lacks: all the intervening history between the 1500s when Cervantes wrote the original and the 20th century when Menard randomly typed his own tiny "masterpiece."

At twenty-two, in homage, I wrote a story about a perfectionist dollhouse maker who eventually becomes part of his creation. I made up an epigraph for the story and attributed it to Pierre Menard. In our conference in his office, Don labelled my own tiny masterpiece an idea story. He asked me who this Pierre Menard was. I explained, and he gave me an irritated look. "Look, _____," he said. "Maybe one in ten readers will know what you're referring to and be in on the joke. Maybe one in a hundred or one in a thousand. Are you trying to reach an audience or just trying to show how smart you are?"

"I just like the Borges story," I said, feebly. "It's a great story."

He started to speak, but then he stopped himself and handed me back my typescript, red marks all over it. "Think about your audience," he said. "Who's your audience? Who are you trying to reach?"

These were questions that dogged me, and ones I could never

fully answer. They seemed akin to that famous and mostly unanswerable question, "Why do you write?"

Indeed, why do you write? Over the years, I had known many talented writers, some of whom went on to become well-known, some who stopped writing, who lost confidence, who focused on other things, who died young, who took their lives. One of my friends, James Hughes, with whom I spent seven months in my late twenties as a Fellow at The Fine Arts Work Centre in Provincetown, was perhaps the most talented short story writer I ever met. Funny and troubled, a Mississippi native, he was chronically in despair at the age of twenty-seven that life had already passed him by. James and I walked the desolate beaches and empty streets of Provincetown in the winter, me in awe of his ability to craft a sentence that was impossible to ignore, he constantly recycling his demons that prevented him from writing. "Open House," the first story he ever wrote, and at the age of twenty-one, he sent to *The New Yorker,* and they published it. His second and third stories, too, were snatched up by the best magazines. And then he stopped writing. Mostly. A few months after we left Provincetown, he sent me a new story of his to critique. To me, brainwashed by then by the dominant aesthetic of Iowa at the time that if you weren't writing like Raymond Carver, you were not writing short stories, James's story seemed like gibberish to me. The voice and language were gorgeous and hilarious at once – though I remember only one phrase, a character admonishing in Biblical rhetoric the "old Gingivites." The story had no narrative coherence, or at least it was not what I was used to reading. I sent James a thorough but conventional critique and received back from him a letter full of hurt and disappointment that my critique had been so uninspired and unoriginal. I was saddened, but I thought he was unhinged, and we never communicated again.

I have never been a big Charles Bukowski fan, but I found a quote of his in the library of Oblivion that I liked, and I recalled it every time I needed a lift from the depression that now beset me:

> There's nothing to stop a man from writing unless that
> man stops himself. If a man truly desires to write, then
> he will. Rejection and ridicule will only strengthen him.
> And the longer he is held back the stronger he will be
> come, like a mass of rising water against a dam. There is
> no losing in writing, it will make your toes laugh as you
> sleep, it will make you stride like a tiger, it will fire the eye

and put you face to face with death. You will die a fighter, you will be honored in hell.

In my youth, I was part of a little clique of poets at our university, who took all the same classes, went to all the same readings, edited the school literary magazine and memorized poems which we read aloud as though we were pouring one another glasses of sherry. Gerard Manley Hopkins, Ferlinghetti, Emily Dickinson, Sylvia Plath, the canonical poets of our decade. We fueled our dreams with the usual suspects: nicotine and caffeine, not pot so much, or alcohol, not in my case, at least. I wanted my senses clear, not deadened. One memorable night, my friend, Gary Katsarida, and I and another young poet, Jocelyn, went to a reading by Robert Bly. Jocelyn, poor soul, was in love with me, and I, in turn, was in love with her poetry. She, in fact, was the main reason I gave up on poetry because I never felt I could equal her. But after one small chapbook, which she dedicated to me, her "raison d'etre," as she wrote both ironically and completely seriously, she silenced herself. What do you do with a case like that? So unlike the showboats, the horn-tooters, like myself, the personality cults of one. Do you simply relegate her to the trash heap, say, well, she must not have been serious after all? I've never accepted that notion that the cream will always rise. I believe there are more Kafkas than we'll ever know, writers of exquisite beauty that were somehow missed, overlooked, or who simply didn't have the fortitude. Or those multitudes who possessed the fortitude but were still denied a place at the table because of their gender, their race, their ethnicity, their language, their time. But I had none of these impediments. I was of the privileged race, and spoke the privileged tongue. And in this, Robert Bly was my brother, stalking the stage in a witch mask, intoxicated by his own booming voice. After every poem, he asked, "Do you want to hear that one again?" The answer was always yes. Could it be anything else? Afterwards, the three of us walked home, arm in arm, Gary the most intoxicated by the words of Bly, recalling his favorite lines. We stayed up all night telling stories, heedless of our classes, of midterms. Gary told us of working in the steel mills of Youngstown, Ohio, a college kid working summers to earn some extra money while there was nothing else, no alternative for the lives of his co-workers, white and black, whose jobs were being phased out, exported, made redundant. Two years later, in grad school, I wrote a story based on what Gary told me that night.

After the fact, I asked his permission and he refused it, which shocked me.

"But you're a poet," I said. "You'd write the story so differently from me."

"It doesn't matter," he insisted. "It's my story, not yours. If you write it, I'll never speak to you again."

The choice at the time was easy, stories being much more valuable than friendships. I included the story in my first collection and Gary, true to his word, never spoke to me again, not in this life.

In the years that followed, I would see him on occasion at the annual Associated Writers Conference, sporting a beachball-sized do of frizzy hair that was out of style a year after we were freshmen. He cultivated that goofy hairstyle doggedly and irrationally decade after decade, his tower of hair bobbing atop a sea of literary small fries, and I would walk in the other direction. Always.

But enough of Gary Katsarida. He was, as it's said, history.

Back in the café, I wandered among the tables meant for two and the tables meant for four, among the larger round tables that held as many as wanted to take in a literary conversation or a reading. A sea of writers before me bobbed up and down on great waves of flattery, self-doubt, envy, and cappuccino foam. I sat down with some. I listened to some, asked some what they had been reading, what they were working on, and they inquired the same after me. I asked a number of them if they missed their families. They considered the question in a slightly baffled way, (chin in hand, or serious gaze into the Middle Distance, or face turned in profile, as though they had misinterpreted the question and thought they were meant to strike Author Photo poses), and then they took a sip of coffee or said they needed to be somewhere and moved to a different table or vanished. Eventually, I stopped asking directly, and sought a more roundabout entry point. Had they ever written about their families? This was a question that almost always produced a spirited response:

"No, I would never write about my family."

"My family was my greatest source of inspiration."

"It depends what you mean by 'writing about.'"

"Did I write characters based on my family? Absolutely."

"I'm sure in some sense I did, but only unconsciously."

And a million variations of this.

Our families lived in stories, in decaying books, on nonexistent pages, and in books we had always meant to write but never found a way to do so. But did we miss them? The question was a simple one, and yet, to answer it fully might have taken the rest of Eternity. It was wrapped up in so many other questions. Why do you write?

I had thought that the writing world was actually rather small, but when multiplied by all of time and history and a multitude of frustrated writers, it turned out to be about as many as the monkeys needed to enact the "infinite monkey theorem."

Still, there were many writers I expected to find in Oblivion who were nowhere to be found. I couldn't locate, for instance, my friend Jocelyn, whose poetry I had loved in my youth. I took her absence in Oblivion to mean that perhaps her greatness had been affirmed by the Universe if not on earth. Perhaps she sipped tea with other great but unrecognized literary geniuses like James who was also nowhere to be found. That seemed plausible for those two, but what of the others, especially the horrible poets whose interminable readings I sat through? It seemed to me, on reflection, that there were a lot of lesser-known writers I hadn't run across in the café. I would die all over again if I learned that they had transcended. Had other lesser writers graduated as Saffron Segovia had and Carl Winterhoven? Or had they never inhabited the café in the first place? If not, why not? I still didn't understand the rules, the playing field, and Jozef's riddles were no help.

There were a number of writers whose presence surprised me and seemed to flummox them. Some once-famous writers who shall go unnamed (why glorify the bastards?) made no secret of their disdain for the rest of us so we just avoided them. No sense fawning over them if they hated us so much. The criteria for a seat at the table in this café were not always obvious, but when have the mechanics of the universe ever been obvious? The question: who decides, baffled me as well.

Many writers were easy to find in Oblivion. They wanted to be found. Jozef always seemed too easy to locate in this place that was no place, ready to pounce on me.

I found him sitting with my graduate school friend Maudy, who had died about a dozen years before me. She had lived in Arab, Alabama where she taught five classes of business memo composition a term and the occasional creative writing course at Snead State Community College. Like so many of us, she tried to keep the guttering flame of her career alive, ten years after a novel of hers had briefly achieved bestseller status: *The Ladies Auxiliary Rassling Society of Sweet Jesus*. Maudy, when she first saw me, smiled that sweet sad smile I remembered from grad school – I never doubted that she was happy to see me. Like many of us, she was just not so happy to see herself.

After we had hugged, we settled down at her table and traded stories. I told her I had been so saddened by her death.

"I mean, condolences to you, too," she said, and we both laughed. Her beverage of choice was sweetened ice tea, not coffee.
She gave me one of the business cards she'd recently printed and asked me to keep her in mind if there were any opportunities I might know of. Her two book titles were written in gold embossed lettering on the back of the card.

I didn't know immediately how to respond. I just looked at the card as though she'd given me a miniature of the Rosetta Stone.

Even here, I thought. Even here. But I felt a creeping desire to have some cards printed of my own.

"I'll keep my eyes open," I said.

Jozef told Maudy that I was following the life of Kafka.

"Oh, are you going to write a biography of him?" Maudy asked. "I'm sure it would be fascinating, but he's never really appealed to me. I'm following the life of Maya Angelou. I just returned from a series of lectures she gave at the American Film Institute in L.A. in 1978. She told the cutest story about how, when she visits elementary schools, she requires –"

"The kids all bring a nickel to pay her," I said.

"Why yes," Maudy said. "How did you know?"

"I was there," I said. "I was a teenager. My mother was a Fellow that year at the AFI, and she brought me to those two lectures. I was the only one who took notes."

"That was you? You don't look anything like you did then. You were so adorable."

"I know," I said. "She called me 'everyone's little brother.' She gave me her address and told me to write to her but I never did."

"Aw," Maudy said. "Well, you didn't have to pay her a nickel at least."

"I doubt that nickel was the reason the children listened so intently in the first place. She was such a commanding presence."

"She was indeed," Maudy said. "I love that you were there and I didn't even recognize you."

I generally moved around the café as my thirty-six year old self. I could have chosen here to transform into the teen version of me, but I didn't want to come across as vain.

"I haven't heard those lectures yet," Jozef said. I had almost forgotten he was there and I cut him such a sharp look that he swallowed what he was about to say. He took a sip of his cappuccino and told his cup. "But they're on my to do list."

"You should definitely go," Maudy told him, countering my little rebuke with her ever-ready cheer.

That perked him back up. It never took much. "I'm writing a biography of _____, you know?

"A biography of _____?" she said in a tone of near shock. "How fascinating."

"Maybe I could find a biographer for you or write one myself," Jozef said. "I'm cheap. I get paid in lattes or cappuccinos."

"A biography," she said. "I never considered that."

"You should. I'm sure you led a very interesting life."

The real torture of the afterlife was this, that my petty feelings didn't vanish against the immensity of the universe. They seemed to intensify. Jozef was supposed to be writing my biography, not Maudy's. She had written two books. I had written fifteen. But my former colleague, David Hamilton, had correctly observed once in the corridor outside our offices that it wasn't the number of books that a person wrote that counted.

I must have made a sound, a clucking of disgust, because Maudy looked at me with obvious hurt, and Jozef took a drag of his cigarette and sighed.

I put my head in my hands.

"The transition has been kind of brutal on _____," Jozef told her.

"Brutal?" I said. "Rough maybe, but brutal?"

"Rough," Jozef said and nodded. "I stand corrected."

"No one's going to read a biography of me now," I said.

"I'd read it," Maudy said.

"You see," Jozef said. "An audience is an audience."

"But what's the point?" I asked in a reasonable tone. "We're dead."

"Everyone has a story worth telling," Jozef said.

This was exactly the problem: too many stories. By the time I died, the world was one big freaking story factory – writing wasn't special anymore. The café seemed too crowded.

"If we weren't worthy of biographies in life, how can we expect to be any worthier now?" I really meant "if you weren't worthy," but I said "we" to be polite.

Maudy said nothing, her smile frozen.

Maybe you should speak for yourself," Jozef said to me. "Do
[re]mber the poem 'Berryman' by W.S. Merwin?"

[Y]es, I remembered that poem. He hardly needed to say any
more to me. Not only did I remember it, but I quoted it back to him
and Maudy in full. In the 1990s the poet Sam Hamill gave me a
signed broadside of the poem which I promptly lost, to my everlasting
regret, but the poem had stayed with me, its last stanzas particularly:

> I asked how can you ever be sure that
> what you write is really
> any good at all and he said you can't
>
> you can't you can never be sure
> you die without knowing
> whether anything you wrote was any good
> if you have to be sure don't write

I wished that I had known earlier of Berryman's advice to the
young Merwin. I would have taken it because I wished I had never
written if it meant that it was all the same to the world whether I had
written or not. Why was I afraid of insignificance? That would have
been a good question for me to ask myself every day of my life. I might
have lived differently had I been open to the idea.

I wondered if Sam Hamill was in the café anywhere. Certainly,
Berryman and Merwin weren't. I doubted Hamill was here either. I had
only met him once, but I'd been intimidated by his intensity. A former
Marine and a former heroin addict, he'd eventually rejected both war
and drugs and had lived most of his life in Port Townsend where he
had co-founded a famous poetry press, Copper Canyon. When I met
him at the Port Townsend Writers' Festival, where I was invited to
teach a workshop, he didn't seem to like me much, or maybe he was
just gruff. About twenty-five years my senior and grizzled, he glowered
at me during a reading of a story of mine that had won a prestigious
prize, and which had an audience of a couple hundred people in stitch-
es. But not him. After I left the podium, he walked past me and said,
not congratulations, but, "Are you some kind of clown?"

No, he wasn't just gruff. He didn't like me. That's why he had
given me the poem, obviously, and that's why I had lost it. And that's
why I had memorized it, too.

It struck me that Jozef might have been there and seen my

humiliation, which I had never in life mentioned to anyone. I placed Maudy's business card back on the table between her and Jozef.

"There are no opportunities here," I said.

Maudy took her business card back and she looked on the verge of tears. I apologized and said maybe we could do a reading together. "I'd like that," she said in an equally unconvincing voice. She took a last look at her business card as though she were viewing a body in a casket, and she left it where it lay. She smiled. "I'll see you around then," and she vanished.

"Was that really necessary?" Jozef asked me after she'd left.

What had I done? Now I'd humiliated one of the nicest people I'd known. I should simply have taken the card and pretended in death as I had in life. "I'm not trying to be mean," I said. "It's just frustrating to listen to someone still trying to make a name when names mean nothing now. Printing business cards, peddling the same old books. If you can't reinvent yourself like Segovia or Winterhoven, what's the point?"

He raised his head as though it was on a pulley and regarded me. "I see," he said. "Now I understand. But I told you not to get your hopes up. It's a near impossibility."

"People always say Rest in Peace, but I don't want to rest."

He patted my hand. "A little rest might do you good, _____. Why get so worked up about something you have no control over?"

"Rest in Peace," I said. "We just drink fancy coffees and gossip."

"Yes," he said. "I take your point. Maybe we should cut down."

I drummed my fingers on the table. "I was just wondering. In your biography of me, do you mention my meeting with Sam Hamill in Port Townsend? I think it must have been 1997 or so."

"Why do you think I brought up the Merwin poem?" he said. "In fact, I think that's a very good title for the biography: *Don't Write: The* _____ _____ *Story.*" He read from an imaginary marquee, his hand blocking out the non-existent text in the air.

He said he was kidding, though if there were any way to strangle a spirit, I would have found it and strangled him. But I needed him. Jozef quizzed me on a few aspects of Brod's work. If I'd had proper teeth, I would have gritted them, but I answered his questions all the same. Afterwards, I seemed to have satisfied his preconditions for another visit, and sighing, he put down his paper and tried but failed to say a phrase that was merely a throwaway line on earth, something you say when you're going against your better judgement, a phrase taken for granted by the living: G-d help me.

# CHAPTER FIVE

# CLOSELY WATCHED TRAINS

I'm not particularly fond of train stations, though I've always been drawn to decrepitude, just not the particular kind of decrepitude of train stations. Certainly, train stations have more character than airports, but I find the chaos and whiff of menace of train stations more disconcerting than charming. The first time I visited Prague's train station was in 1990, not long after the Velvet Revolution. My first book of short stories had been translated into German and was being published by Goldmann Verlag and I convinced John Grooms, the editor of a local free weekly, *Creative Loafing,* to assign me a cover story on the Frankfurt Bookfair so I could meet my publisher. He couldn't cover airfare, but maybe Lufthansa, which had just opened a gateway between Frankfurt and Charlotte, North Carolina, where I lived at the time, might be persuaded to fly me there if I mentioned the gateway in the article. I called up their office in Atlanta, made my pitch, and to my everlasting surprise, they said yes. I hadn't travelled overseas in over ten years at the time, and I didn't like traveling alone, so I enlisted a friend and former student, Kevin Heisler, to accompany me. Kevin worked for an airline, the now-defunct U.S. Air, and was able to get a free ticket.

Kevin approached the world as though he were interviewing it for a profile of a very funny, sometimes inexplicable curmudgeon. He had little trouble charming even the curmudgeons of the world, partly due to his good looks: cleft chin, thin and slightly hawkish nose, intense eyes framed by dark eyebrows, and a rakish smile. Kevin was only attracted to powerful and smart women – not long after we travelled to Prague, he moved to New York where he married a well-known novelist.

He was the opposite of frumpy Jozef – Kevin with a thin, athletic build, always looked put together, and Jozef, well, he looked like a living sepia photograph from early-twentieth century Europe: stained yellow, from hair to teeth, and where his charm lay, it was hard to say. The difference in their voices and laughs was enormous, too. Jozef's voice was soft but not soothing: his was the voice of someone trying to sell you a suit you didn't need, dripping insincerity even at his most earnest. Kevin had a voice that was smart and smart-alecky at once, full of good humor, his accent mid-American though he had been raised in North Carolina. He seemed to find everything slightly amusing, and he loved testing your opinions by posing devil's advocate questions. Why couldn't he have been my spirit guide instead of Jozef? At least, Kevin really liked my writing – Jozef seemed always to be in search of new ways to cut me down to size.

In Frankfurt, we stayed with a professor and his family, Günter Nold, who had been an exchange professor a year earlier at my school. Günter and his wife Frieda loved antiques as I did, and their spacious apartment was full of them. When I asked if they were family heirlooms, Günter and Frieda grew quiet and finally she offered that heirlooms had never been a part of their lives. Günter's childhood home in Frankfurt had been bombed to smithereens and Frieda had been born in the Sudetenland, home to thousands of ethnic Germans in what was now Czechoslovakia. At the end of World War Two, her family was given twenty-four hours to leave their home and move to Germany. So no, they didn't possess any heirlooms.

I had no idea when and if I would ever return to this part of the world, so I decided to spend a few more days in Europe and travel to Prague by train from Frankfurt. Kevin was game, too, though neither of us had a good sense of the logistics involved. We didn't even book hotels. By our calculations, we would have no more than twenty-four hours in which to explore Prague and then return to Frankfurt and make our flights. What later became a six- to eight-hour journey took eleven to twelve hours at the time, largely because of the hard border between Germany and Czechoslovakia. Czechoslovakia had not yet joined the European Union or undergone the "Velvet Divorce" to become The Czech Republic and Slovakia. Or later still, "Czechia." Czech guards boarded the train and examined our passports and we were then made to wait to transfer from a sleek German train to a rusty green Czech train, where we crowded into a compartment with a dour Czech man who insisted on smoking the rest of the journey with the windows closed, and a young woman from New Zealand, travelling on her own. I had never met anyone from New Zealand and didn't know much about the country, so I asked about the "May-ori" as if I were asking after a distant relative of mine. "And how are the May-ori doing these days?"

"What?" she asked. "Who's that?"

"The May-ori. The tribe. Aren't they in ... "

"It's not the May-ori," she said with the force of a slap, and she pronounced it correctly for me. "Mowry." She turned to Kevin then as though I no longer existed and asked him if he had a condom. He laughed.

"Really?" she asked as though he couldn't possibly be serious.

"Search me," he said, but she didn't take him up on that and instead stood and left the compartment presumably to locate men as handsome as Kevin and better prepared.

Why had this obnoxious Kiwi woman not asked me for a condom? Not only was she not attracted to me, but not in her wildest dreams did the guy who asked her about the May-ori possibly have a condom on him. She was right. I didn't have one. Still.

These were the types of things I stewed over.

The Prague Station looked like a mausoleum magnified to a hundred times its necessary size. A neglected mausoleum, tinged with soot, the better part of its interior a utilitarian cavernous hall with people hurrying through. We made the mistake of having a meal in a café upstairs to plan our next move, where we ordered a soupy stew with three slices of translucent meat. From a table nearby, three men dressed in pea coats eyed us openly. We were obviously wealthy by comparison to almost everyone there. On our way out of the station, we stumbled upon a side room off the main hallway where tourists like us lined up to find accommodations. Now that Czechoslovakia was open for business, the government was rushing to meet the influx of tourists. The city had few hotels so private citizens had opened up their homes to tourists to make some extra money. The only decoration in this office was a poster of the musician Frank Zappa sitting on a toilet with his pants to his knees. The country was in flux, Soviet soldiers selling their belongings on Charles Bridge, shops nearly empty of goods, the country raided by the antique-seeking Günters and Friedas of Germany who, if they couldn't recover their own patrimony, wanted to purchase someone else's heritage at bargain basement prices. But I was only interested in one thing in this soot-covered city: Kafka.

He wasn't hard to find, or at least a semblance of him. Already, he'd become a mini-industry in a city of Czechs that was in its own way a time capsule, but so different from the city Kafka had known, its traces of Germanness and Jewishness preserved in its intact Jewish Quarter (Hitler wanted to preserve it as a kind of Museum to a Vanished Race). Still, you could buy postcard sketches that maintained the myth of Kafka as the sickly angst-ridden artist, walking with a cane down a cobbled street. You could even visit his birthplace in Old Town, though when we tried, it was closed for renovations and surrounded by a construction wall. Disappointed, I stood for a photograph by an advertisement on the wall for an upcoming concert by "Up With People," a bust of Kafka clearly poking from the building behind me like a literary gargoyle. When I returned to the city almost twenty years later, the Kafka industry was in full bloom and I could have visited the house, but I never did as I learned that his house wasn't really his house, but a house built on the spot where his house had once stood, before a fit of Austro-Hungarian urban renewal had demolished it and others in the years not long after Kafka's birth. It's so often this way with reconstructions, whether birthplaces, famous sites, biographies, or memoirs. There's always some embellishment, some ruse, some crucial information omitted.

If you wanted an authentic Kafka experience, you might as well book a room at The Intercontinental Hotel, around the fourth floor, overlooking the Vltava River and Prague Castle. The apartment where he and his family lived in the teens was pulled down after World War Two, damaged as it was by artillery shells. At least here you might see an approximation of the view he saw daily from the family's flat. But not many people in the world are the level of fanboy that I was towards Kafka – the chance to visit him (no, study him in person) almost seemed worth dying for to be given the opportunity.

In November of 1911, the Prague Train Station, only a few years old, looked completely different from the grimy hall I'd arrived at in 1990 with Kevin. The edifice was gleaming and colorful. Art Nouveau statues popped from the light brown walls. Suns sparkled with spear-like beams. Over grand archways, languid figures of bare-breasted goddesses and muscular gods lounged with lush faux-foliage of dark green draped across their shoulders.

A throng of perhaps a hundred men and women stood in front of a train much older but more elegant than the one Kevin and I had taken, black passenger cars with red roofs and red framed windows. The buzzing mercury vapor lamps that lit the platform reflected in the shine of the cars. A lanky boy of eighteen or so stood next to an older man with a greying beard, both in dark blue uniforms with gold buttons, red lapels, and black hats, leaning towards one another as they spoke Czech in confidential tones and observed the crowd that milled about one of the open doors of a docked train. The tint of their skin, a bluish green, from the mercury lamps, made them seem as if they had stepped out of some Berlin street scene by Ernst Kirchner (my favorite artist of the period).

An impressive banner of white satin with purple lettering proclaimed: "Prague welcomes the Prince of Thebes" and was held aloft by two women in their twenties wearing togas and crowns of white feathers. "There she is," one of the women shrieked as they hurried along the platform toward a car where a slightly built figure took a furtive step, seemed to think better of it, and moved back inside. Werfel stood out in red cape, knee-length boots and pantaloons tucked into them, and some kind of ceremonial sword strapped to his ample middle for good measure. "Theatrics," Jozef said. "She does call herself Prince of Thebes, after all. So, she needs an honor guard of sorts to greet her." Nearly every other man on the platform was dressed almost identically in grey or black wool jackets. Werfel raced to be the first to greet Lasker-Schuler, his sword clacking against him as he trotted along. Kafka followed Brod, hands in pockets, like a doctor following a mad patient acting out some far-fetched and unhealthy ideation.

Jozef and I hovered above it all from the impossible vantage point of dream or memory. If anyone dreamed about this event or remembered it many years hence, chances are they would see it as we had, untethered to law or logic.

Almost as soon as the crowd had reached the platform where the figure had briefly emerged, Werfel in position to welcome the poet from Berlin, she appeared in the doorway of the car behind them, where the crowd had originally gathered. A thin woman with short dark hair, she wore a black vest with gold brocade and baggy black satin slacks too thin for the chilly temperature, the wind billowing her pants. Around her neck, she wore ropes of green glass beads, and she carried a flute in her hand like a baton at the ready, as though forming a police line of one.

I was the first to notice her new position and I shouted, "There she is," but no one heard me and so I tapped Werfel on the shoulder and he turned. "There she is," he said. "Splendid."

Kafka turned his eyes towards heaven and groaned. "This night, promise me, must never be recorded in your diary or mine. On my deathbed, you may quiz me: remember the night you met the Prince of Thebes? Even then, I will deny it."

Brod said nothing but shook his head slightly.

"I know," Kafka said in a voice that was almost a whimper. "You and Werfel both think she's magical, so perhaps I am completely in the wrong."

Brod simply took him by the arm. "Let's play her courtiers for one evening only."

Kafka returned a weak smile.

Lasker-Schuler barely moved though she must have been freezing in her thin costume, as the group approached again and faced her.

From somewhere, a bouquet of spring flowers had found its way to Werfel's sausage fingers. He made a small bow as The Prince of Thebes nodded to him, her features softening as she accepted the flowers, held them to her bosom like a beloved child and sniffed extravagantly. "Ah," she said. "The flowers of life are but visionary. How many pass away and leave no trace behind. How few yield any fruit ... and the fruit itself, how rarely does it ripen."

Werfel grinned broadly. "Let me see. Yes. And yet there are flowers enough; and is it not strange, my friend, that we should suffer the little that does really ripen to rot, decay, and perish unenjoyed?"

"That's Goethe," Jozef whispered to me. "From *The Sorrows of Young Werther.*"

"I know," I said. "I read it in school."

This was only partly true. I never would have recognized the quote if Jozef hadn't told me. "If I remember correctly," Jozef said. "This was in Oscar Kenshur's class. You had trouble keeping up with the assignments and I don't believe you read Werther in its entirety. Didn't you stay up all night in the diner below your apartment, chain-smoking and flipping through the pages but mostly listening to the jukebox and chatting with the wait staff? That waitress you had a crush on, what was her name? You called her Janet Planet, I believe."

"Nothing could delight Yusuf, Prince of Thebes more than to be greeted by Franz Werfel, Prince of Prague," Lasker-Schuler said. She patted him on the cheek like a good boy and he took her hand and kissed it with reverence.

"She's in her forties, you know, though she hardly looks it," Jozef said.

"When she wrote to me, she called me the Prince of Prague," Max complained to Kafka. "What I want to know is where am I in the order of succession? I'm much older than he is."

"Perhaps we will have to lock up Werfel in the clock tower to protect your rights," Kafka said.

"No need," Max said. "I've arranged for Werfel to be pressed into a gang and shipped off to Shanghai."

Kafka's laugh was full of boyish delight, high and musical. "I can just imagine," he said. "Let's see what kind of Weltfreund he makes then."

Werfel suggested to Elsa Lasker-Schuler that she might like a brief tour of the old city while her valises (three large trunks: costume changes?) were sent on to her lodgings. Afterwards, they'd have a meal and then her reading tomorrow that he assured her half of Prague would want to attend. This all seemed agreeable to her and he led her and most of the party of well-wishers through the streets and squares of Prague, the procession attracting almost universal curiosity as it went, the notes of the flute she played as she walked cutting through the voices and ambient rumblings of the city. While Werfel led Lasker-Schuler as though she were a living trophy captured on safari, I tried to identify the wistful tune she played. I really could have used some kind of media device just then, but we were not allowed them in Oblivion and so I awaited the inevitable. I wracked my mortal memory trying to remember, so that I could beat Jozef to it, but I couldn't.

Behind them, the rest of the poet's fans flowed, chattering and laughing, in high spirits as they wondered where the various princes would lead them.

"Scheherazade," Jozef said. "Rimsky-Korsakoff. She's butchering it."

But I thought it was beautiful and wanted to weep, reduced as I felt to less than one plaintive note of Lasker-Schuler's flute, saddened that all I remembered from *The Sorrows of Young Werther* was that the book prompted a wave of suicides across Europe and the term *Sturm und Drang*. I had forgotten that Jozef had visited almost my entire life. I couldn't keep anything from him. I only hoped he'd leave that episode out of my biography.

"When will she die?" I asked, a question that was not rude in the present circumstances, and as common as "How are you?" among the inhabitants of Oblivion, though it was usually asked in the past tense.

"Jerusalem, 1945. A refugee, she grows increasingly eccentric, isolated and penniless, writing in German, a language that no one particularly wants to read, given the place and the war."

And it was either that odd feeling of seeing someone at the height of her popularity, knowing that she would die unheralded, or the brisk November air that I shouldn't have felt but did, inexplicably, that caused me to experience an unremarkable physical reaction sometimes caused by spirits but rarely experienced by them.

I shivered.

# CHAPTER SIX

## OBLIVIOUS
## READINGS

# CHAPTER SIX: OBLIVIOUS READINGS

Oblivion, according to Jozef, is like a half-sunk vessel within an ocean. The ocean has no discernible shore and pours over the decks of the vessel which sinks but is never sunken. In this way, Oblivion floats upon Time, half wrecked. New souls enter the sinking-but-never-sunken vessel, and Oblivion adds to its passengers. The reversal of this process threatens the collapse of the entire system. To re-enter the ocean alone is to be carried on a current that flows with pounding force in the opposite direction from the Order that is G-d's vessel. Plunge into its depths, stay underwater too long, and you remember breath, you remember hunger, you fill with unquenchable desires as your lungs expand with the effort but never burst. You grow now not as a child would grow into a healthy being, but into a vast collection of fibers and polyps, as Blake writes, down "into the Sea of Time and Space." Torment drops upon your head with such force that all you want is to find a place to hide from the floods, some shelter, the body of another who knows yet how to float. This is how you find that you have become a dybbuk.

Unless. He didn't verbalize this *unless* but I knew it was there. Segovia and Winterhoven had known it. Had I still been alive, I might have said that I lived for that *unless,* that all my hopes were tethered to that *unless.* Kafka had written in his journal that even the "strangest fancies" can perish in "a great fire" only to "rise up again." Even if Kafka wasn't with me, his words were my true guide, not Jozef's. I hoped that it was still not too late for this smoke to rise up.

As Time and I did not mix well, Jozef wanted to limit my forays back, and so after meeting Lasker-Schuler's train at the station, we returned to Oblivion to float in stasis within the wreck, a kind of decompression, if not healing. All I could think about were Winterhoven and Segovia. The greatest of escapes, to shake Jozef and return long enough to write, something brief at first, and then if that was successful, I'd attempt something longer. A classic the world never knew it needed, but needed so much that even death could not stop its production. I had read so much now in Oblivion's library my mind was bursting. If given enough time (and enough typewriters) who knew what I was capable of producing?

I contemplated reading some of Lasker-Schuler's poetry. If Kafka disliked her so much she must be the most appalling of poets. This was the first reading I would attend after my death, and I should have been excited for this reason, but I had died a thousand deaths at readings during my lifetime.

Once, in college, I had attended a reading by the writer, Tillie Olsen, who was well-known at the time for a novella, *Tell me a Riddle*. A graduate student who was doing his dissertation on Olsen delivered the introduction, which lasted half an hour. When he finally finished, Tillie Olsen went to the podium and thanked him but said his dissertation was a load of bull crap. The audience laughed and clapped at this – we thought the guy deserved it. Who wanted to hear half an hour of graduate student prattle?

Unfortunately, Olsen decided to read the entirety of *Tell Me a Riddle* that evening. With readings, shorter is almost always better. Olsen's reading was like climbing Everest, oxygen-starved and lost in bad planning and a blizzard of words. Halfway through the three-hour reading, she paused and suggested that the audience should stretch. Half of the audience bolted at the opportunity, leaving only the faithful and the masochistic like myself. I don't know why I stayed, but I almost always did.

Kafka tended to stay as well, suffering through readings like a *penitente*, whipping oneself while wearing a literary hair-shirt. At one such reading, given by Bernhard Kellerman, the audience kept filing out much to the reader's dismay. After he'd read only a third of his story, full of "mediocre passages," as Kafka wrote in his diary, Kellerman grew alarmed. "There's only a little more," he said, Kafka noting that he was lying. When Kellerman finally finished, almost no one clapped, but he still didn't want to give up. He thought he should read one more story, "maybe several." He took a sip of mineral water and half the audience fled. "I should still like very much to read a little tale that will take only fifteen minutes," he said. "I will pause for five minutes." And with that all but five people scattered. But Kafka stayed, and here, finally, were the passages Kafka and Kellerman had been waiting for, passages that "were justification for anyone to return from the farthest point of the hall right through the middle of and over the whole audience."

I'm sure though that even Kafka's bountiful patience and generosity would have abandoned him if he had attended a reading I wound up at in Chicago, at a bar where a drugged-out poet told the audience at an open poetry reading that he was composing the world's longest poem and he wanted to read some of it for us.

The poem consisted of couplets:

By the beard of Odin.

It's a drag.
By the beard of Sam.
It's a drag.
By the beard of Priscilla.
It's a drag.
By the beard of Rover.
It's a drag.

And on it went, the apparent aim to fit into this couplet, every name – man, woman, and pet, that had ever been uttered. As the reading progressed and the poet showed no signs of flagging, the crowd grew restless. His allotted time was five minutes, but at the fifteen-minute mark, the bartender turned off the microphone. The poet kept reading. At twenty-five minutes, he turned off the lights onstage. But the poet bent down, squinting, and kept reading. At half an hour, the reading was officially cancelled, which made no difference to the reader, not even as people started to leave. In my perverse way, I stayed and so did Jozef, who was with me that Sunday. All he could say was "Wow," smoke his cigarettes, and chuckle. But I finally gave up, too, giving one backwards glance as I left at a kind of postmodern Edward Hopper painting: the poet bent to his papers on the darkened stage, Jozef, the last holdout lost in thought, the bartender furiously wiping down the bar as he made preparations to close the bar for the day, perhaps quit his job, and end his life.

Sadly, I was more often Kellerman, the hapless self-promoting boob who didn't know when to give up, than Kafka, the hopeful genius waiting for intoxicating moments.

Not long after I published a "how to" book on writing, I was hired to teach at Fairhaven College in Bellingham, Washington. The circumstances of my employment were not pleasant ones for my predecessor, a woman whose contract had not been renewed. She was suing the university. My book was about using personal details of one's life in one's stories and novels to give them a sense of authenticity. Her contract had not been renewed because she allegedly spent much of her class time telling her students intimate details about her life, chief among them that her husband was a demon who needed to be exorcised. Her suit claimed that I was being rewarded by the university for the same things she was being punished for.

Elliot Bay Books in Seattle invited me to give a reading from my craft book not long after I was hired at the university. I should have given a workshop, but I took the invitation to "read" too literally. Who wants someone to read a manual to them? I drew a crowd of about fifty, but instead of simply discussing the ideas of my guide, I read to them the literary equivalent of a driver's education manual. In Tillie Olsen fashion, when I finished and asked them if they had any questions, they ran for the exits, all except for a cheerful woman with a copy of my book in her hands. I reached in my pocket for a pen to sign the book at the same time she asked me what I thought she must obviously already know. "Are you _____?"

"Yes?" I said as though I wasn't sure.

She handed me an envelope and told me she was the lawyer for the woman whom I had replaced at the university, and here was a subpoena. Then she put down my book on a nearby chair and left, though she did say that she had enjoyed my "talk."

The one good thing about death was that I thought I'd never have to give or attend a reading again. This wasn't something I needed to tick off on my after-bucket list.

While Kafka dutifully attended public readings by the dozens, he hated the thought of giving readings. Still, he read his work all the time privately to friends. Of public readings, he only gave one as far as I recalled: in Berlin, where he read his story, "In the Penal Colony," about an explorer who comes across an island of prisoners. The sadistic commandant of this island executes men by strapping them into a machine that tattoos their crimes on their flesh continuously until they die. According to the commandant, the criminals supposedly gain enlightenment in the moments before their deaths. At the reading, five or six audience members reportedly fainted. Kafka marked the event as an utter failure, but this was the only reading I would have gladly attended.

I decided to suggest we go to Kafka's reading instead of Lasker-Schuler's. Why was she so special? Kafka didn't even like her.

As usual, I found Jozef with ease. "If I'm going to go to a reading, let's go to the one reading Kafka gave in his lifetime," I said, "Wasn't it a disaster? Didn't Kafka read from 'In the Penal Colony' in Berlin in 1917? And a dozen people fainted?"

"One actually," Jozef said. "And two others vomited, and one suffered a mild stroke later that evening, though whether that can be attributed to the reading is debatable. And it was Munich, not Berlin, and 1916, not 1917. And he gave more than one reading in his lifetime. Another reading he gave in Prague was quite well received. One overwhelmed critic even wrote that the audience had been given a sample in Kafka of the 'future face of literature.' In any case, you're really not stable enough and I won't consent to it. You want to understand Kafka's genius? Why he was so favored? Then you should take it one step at a time. Lasker-Schuler's reading, too, was a momentous evening in its own way."

I pressed him for details, but he shook his head and smirked. "As your guide, I'm afraid I can't compromise value for crass expediency. It's not only the answers that are important, but how you arrive at the knowledge you've gained."

"That sounds like bad fortune cookie wisdom, Jozef. Come on, don't be cruel."

"My tour, my rules," he said. He disappeared and so did I, plunging back into the current.

# CHAPTER SEVEN

## YUSOF, PRINCE
## OF THEBES

# CHAPTER SEVEN: YUSOF, PRINCE OF THEBES

The reading took place in a lower ballroom of the Hotel Er-
zherzog Stefan in Wenceslas Square, the hotel facade another grand
art nouveau structure, painted orange and topped by enormous marble
statuary: three half-robed maidens holding an egg-shaped globe, two on
either side of the globe, one in the center on whose back the globe
rested, a marble peacock by her side. Jozef and I arrived just in time
for the reading to begin – the ballroom was packed with upwards of two
hundred people and we hurried to our seats excusing ourselves as we
passed through people in the rows of chairs that had been set out. We
took our customary seats, me in Kafka's lap and Jozef in Brod's. I had
not spotted my great-grandmother before the lights dimmed, but Jozef
had assured me she was present, so I figured I'd run into her after the
performance. Kafka was fidgety, tapping his foot, and rolling up the pro-
gram that had a photo of Lasker-Schuler in her Prince of Thebes outfit
surrounded by a filigreed orientalist script. He looked around as though
scouting for exits in case of fire. Brod patted his friend's thigh in a
gesture that seemed appreciative and tender, and Kafka gave his friend
an unconvincing smile. In my time, this smile might have been accompanied by an equally unconvincing thumbs up sign. But Kafka giving
a thumbs up – inconceivable. He once again made the gesture I had
first noticed at the Café Savoy, patting his hair in place, though now it
struck me as less a gesture of vanity than a kind of checking to make
sure he was all there, like someone who's hit his head, and touching his
hair, wonders whether he'll feel it slick with blood.

As Werfel hopped onto the stage, Kafka leaned forward, hands
planted on his knees. Delivering an expansive introduction to Lasker-Schuler that was as puffy as dandelion spore, Werfel reminded the
audience that when he had published his volume of poetry this year
at "the callow age of twenty-one" he had looked to the lyrics of Lasker-Schuler for inspiration. Had he known that his volume would be
such a literary sensation, selling out its first edition overnight, and had
it been possible, he would have happily given his acclaim to Lasker-Schuler because she deserved it more. He said he was envious of
those encountering her poems for the first time, for it was a singular
event, much like "Adam naming the animals."

I wanted to throw up, though to the dead, every physical gesture
contains beauty, even vomit. Brod and Jozef, wore almost identical
smirks. What a wonderful portrait that would have made – the dead

minor poet sitting in the lap of the once famous Max Brod, both equally bemused by Werfel's self-serving introduction. But Kafka seemed to take his friend at his word, nodding, lips pursed, as if reconsidering his entire taste in literature.

Werfel finally left the stage with a flourish to the wings as he summoned Lasker-Schuler forth. Not until the applause had died down so that the only sounds that could be heard were coughs, did Lasker-Schuler make her way to the center of the stage, striding out soundlessly in her slippers. Here, she knelt and lifted a bejewelled dagger to the ceiling. She lay it beside her, stood, head bowed, eyes closed. Raising her arms high above her head, palms up, she slowly twisted her hands so that the palms now were down. A small groan escaped from Kafka, and I turned to look at him. He glanced furtively at Brod, but then back at Lasker-Schuler. The rest of the audience seemed so rapt you could almost hear Jozef and me breathe.

"I am Yusof, Prince of Thebes," she said in a voice that was earnest, almost meek. She didn't try to mimic a man's voice, though her natural speaking voice was on the low side. "I have come here tonight seeking your attention, your counsel, your wisdom. I am a desert wanderer, and I have known both riches and deprivation. I have withstood great thirst, my spirit parched, my lips cracked, my tongue silent as the desert stars. The dunes I have traversed in my life have been covered in treasures that transformed into writhing snakes in my hands, and yet I have let them bite me. I have put them to my neck and willingly beseeched them to corrupt my flesh. I have withstood their fangs. I have absorbed their poisons and have transformed these snakes back into jewels, which I offer you humbly now. They contain poison. They contain honey. Will they kill you or cure you? Is everything mirage? I leave that for you to ponder."

The rest of the evening was given over to a kind of proto–performance poetry. Sometimes she would run up a step ladder in the middle of the stage and scan some fake horizon for a caravan before she would drop on all fours or slither and writhe on the stage. Occasional bouts of gibberish erupted from her with the suddenness of a gas pain, and flights of bad flute playing.

But her poems.

There was something undeniable about them – nearly all were love poems, brief lyrics that needed no elaborate costuming. The simple words, their humility and strength bucked the silliness of the performance. One poem in particular, which seemed to have been picked out especially for us, almost had Jozef and me in tears again:

> Can you see me
>
> Between heaven and earth?
> No one has ever crossed my path.
>
> But your face warms my world,
> All blossoming stems from you.
>
> When you look at me
> My heart turns sweetness.
>
> Underneath your smile I learn
> To prepare day and night,
>
> To conjure you up and make you fade.
> The one game that I always play.

I looked into Kafka's blue grey eyes as she recited her poems from memory. He scratched his cheek absently, withdrew his pocket watch, didn't look at it, but transferred it from hand to hand as if cooling it. He was elsewhere. He remained unconvinced, untransformed. But he was wrong about her. He was wrong.

Still, he clapped when she had finished and smiled like a Nobel judge at a talent show put on by ten-year olds. I still had not spotted Hanna in the crush of people filing out to the lobby where they had checked their hats and coats. Kafka and Brod had no notion of Hanna's presence at the event and probably wouldn't have made a point of looking for her even if they had known. They were, as usual, in a huddle of two, Kafka's shoulders hunched to accommodate the height difference between him and Brod and to hear better presumably in the clamor of conversation about them. Brod, who seemed to know everyone, had an eye out for acquaintances and waved to one, squeezed the arm of another, made little pips of appreciation for the reading or received them. *Marvelous evening. The perfect venue. That was transporting, no?* All the while, Kafka smiled and nodded and even said a cheery hello or two, but had the look in his shifting gaze, his hunched stance, and his nervous smile, of someone being smuggled across a border, maintaining a disguise just long enough to make it out the doors.

"You could have told me earlier, Max. Was that the only reason you lured me here? I would have given something even though I suspect her tragedies are of her own making."

"So what she read ... ," Max started.

"... did not stir me in the least," Kafka said. "But it's not your fault. I'm a hopeless case, I'm afraid." They seemed as close as a long-married couple who could finish one another's sentences and read one another's minds. I was stuck with Jozef, who didn't think my sentences were worth finishing. I guess we were like a married couple, too, but a different kind, the kind whose marriage is a test of endurance.

"Werfel is taking up a collection for Lasker-Schuler," Jozef said, observing this exchange, too. "Her second husband has just left her for another woman and she has a child to take care of. That's what all those fangs and poison and wandering in the desert is about."

"Kafka seems awfully hard-hearted about her," I said.

"A little," Jozef said. "More like uncompromising. He considered her a fake. But in the end, he'll contribute some money, too. Not a small amount, either. Typical Jewish guilt."

As they stood in line for their hats and coats, Hanna and Lowy appeared from one of the ballroom doors, making their way to the hat check line. She held onto Lowy's arm with both of hers as they walked. She wore a shawl and a magenta dress with white lace embroidery around the neckline. He wore a tan vest, a bow tie, and a high collared white shirt.

"Costumes," Jozef told me. "That's where all their money goes. The dress and his outfit are from a production of *Eyne Fun Yene,* by the Polish playwright, Paula Prilutski. It's another lost classic, a proto-feminist play about a prostitute among the gangsters of Warsaw. I've seen Lowy's production, but I wouldn't recommend it as one of his best."

Lowy lit up when he spotted Kafka and Brod, and shouted a greeting. Kafka seemed especially overjoyed to see Lowy, the two shaking hands vigorously. Hanna wore a dreamy look, her eyes heavy lidded, her face pale. She offered a smile that seemed a bit sad. Something was wrong. Was she ill?

"Miss Reimer has been going on as though she's just seen a true monarch," Lowy said, by way of hello. "You remember Hanna Reimer, the cat of the desert in Shulamith?"

"In my opinion, you stole the show, Miss Reimer," Brod said, making a slight bow.

Instead of laughing and blushing, and saying something like, "It's a wonder they keep me in the troupe," she seemed to take his compliment seriously. "Thank you. I'm glad that what I was attempting to do came through despite the tomato tossed by that vulgarian in the audience. It did come through, didn't it?"

Brod turned his head like a panicked robot, first sharply right to Lowy and then sharply left to Kafka. Both men were expressionless. He wasn't getting any help from those quarters. "Quite," he said in a soft voice.

"Oh, good," Kafka said. "I've been meaning to ask for your interpretation. What *did* come through for you, Max?"

Max opened his mouth but not a peep issued forth.

"Someday, our Hanna Reimer will be a great actress," Lowy said, saving poor Brod from Kafka's fun. "In five years, she will be playing the best theatres in Berlin, and who knows, maybe even London and New York?"

"There's nothing in this world I'd rather do. I just need a little seasoning. That's what Yitzhak tells me."

She lifted her chin and looked with adoration at the maestro, who at that moment wore an uncomfortable smile.

"Lowy's a luftmensch if there ever was one," Jozef said. "And she's got her head in the clouds, too, but they make a cute couple, don't you think?

"No," I said. This was my great-grandmother. They all were making fun of her and Lowy was taking advantage of her adoration. One look told the whole story. Even if I hadn't known how her life turned out, a child could have seen that it was obvious her dreams were hopeless. So much for family legends. I would have preferred to see her with Kafka rather than Lowy, even though he didn't have the best track record with women. Still, the scenario was worth consideration. How would such a match have affected both their lives, their careers? Would he have made her agnostic? Would she have eventually turned him into an observant Jew? Would he have turned into a Zionist as Brod soon became? Would Kafka have brought out the best of her talents or would she have dragged him down to her level of mediocrity?

Turning to Kafka, she said, "I'm sorry I've forgotten your name. I'm so forgetful when I haven't eaten."

"That's quite all right," Kafka said. "I forget my name sometimes, too. And I forget to eat."

"It's Dr. Kafka," Lowy said.

"Aren't you feeding her, Yitzhak?" Brod asked.

Lowy turned out his pockets and gave them a hangdog expression. "You can't possibly know what we have to put up with, the indignities of a travelling troupe. We make a fraction of what the German theatre companies make."

"German theatre?" Kafka said, stopping as though at a traffic light though the line pressed forward. "I don't care if I ever see another German play. There's no life in them. The urban Jews have forgotten everything. They have lost touch with this more fanatic Judaism."

"That's right," Brod said. "There's an unfeigned brilliance in Yiddish drama. I see it as the natural legacy of the frenzied mysticism of desert wanderers. Lasker-Schuler also embodies this, that's why ..."

"I couldn't disagree more," Kafka said. There's a world of difference between Eastern European mysticism and ..."

"Excuse me," Hanna said, looking at both of them as though they were speaking the gibberish that had punctuated Lasker-Schuler's Prince of Thebes shtick. "The line's moving."

A large gap had opened between them and the person before them in line. A white-haired man with a waxed moustache, standing behind them, cleared his throat apoplectically and stood so close that he seemed ready to join the conversation. Hanna spoke again as they moved forward. "We fanatic eastern Jews might impress you cultivated, modern Jews. But we'd also be happy to free ourselves from that desert. That's what my dance was about. A dance of freedom from false promises and the expectations of society." It was impossible not to hear the note of bitterness in her voice, though she said this in a playful tone and smiled.

Kafka and Brod stared at her as though a cat had indeed spoken and heaped scorn upon them. They seemed to have never considered that Eastern European Jews wouldn't find themselves exotic. Even if no one ever recorded the event, my great grandmother had just put two great writers in their place.

Lowy apologized. "We're both feeling a bit light-headed from all this wandering in the desert. After the last three days of nothing to eat, next Yom Kippur should be easy."

Brod and Kafka didn't seem to understand what he meant.

"You've fasted for three days?" Kafka asked, glancing at Brod as though to check whether he had heard the same.

"I wouldn't call it fasting," Lowy said. "The reading was free, so it was a welcome distraction."

"After this reading, I shouldn't have to ever eat again," Hanna said. "Wasn't she glorious?"

"Miss Reimer thinks it's an artistic statement to starve," Lowy said.

"We've had a bread crust or two and some water," she said. "I wouldn't want to lie."

"You see," Kafka said. "These are the artists who need a collection taken up for them, not Lasker-Schuler. She will always have her assorted princes like Werfel in the palaces of culture to see to her needs."

As it was just after the dinner hour at the Kafka household, 9:30 every evening, there would likely be some leftovers, Kafka told them. "Our girl," by which I imagined Kafka meant their maid, would fix them something in no time. The apartment was a mere fifteen-minute walk from Wenceslas Square. Lowy insisted they would be fine, but Kafka and Brod were even more insistent.

"Is that a good idea to show up for a meal at this hour?" Lowy asked. "I don't think your father holds Eastern Jewry in the same high regard as you. That's my impression at least from the last time I visited."

"I'm awfully hungry, Yitzhak," Hanna said. She looked pale, her eyes imploring.

"Don't worry," Kafka said. "I live for my father's disapproval. I'll protect you."

"And I'll protect you," Brod told Kafka.

They donned their coats and hats and stepped out into the November evening where it had begun to snow and carriages and cars were bearing away the wealthier patrons of the arts.

While Lowy seemed relatively smart and was definitely attractive with his curly light brown hair, his acrobatic and lean body, and a face with a kind of dog-like sweetness, his only lasting importance in the world was that he had been a friend of Kafka's. Hanna had taken up with the wrong guy, and obviously she was going to find out sooner or later as she hadn't married him, but another somewhat more boring but stable Yitzhak the shoemaker from Latvia. At least he kept her fed.

I wanted to teach Lowy a lesson for taking advantage of my great grandmother, for lying to her, for giving her unrealistic expectations. Not something that would kill him, but something a step down from that.

"How did Lowy ... " I started.

"Treblinka Extermination Camp," Jozef said. "1942 or 43, I think."

Maybe something fourth or fifth order terrible to teach him a lesson. Maybe only a prank. It's difficult to maintain a grudge against someone when a death camp is in their future.

They walked two ahead and two behind: Brod and Kafka still arguing over Lasker-Schuler's authenticity. When the group reached Old Town Square, I was assaulted by memories of things that had not yet transpired. All of the variations of Prague I had seen in my life many years later than 1911 rested upon one another like translucent curtains across which flickered the comings and goings of humanity. Across the large square, I saw an antique car show I had passed here in 2012 with dozens of cars from the 20s, 30s, 40s, and 50s, even one car from the early 1900s that looked more like a carriage. I stared as people from different times traversed the square through the carnage of time, some admiring the cars, but most walking through them, people from 1990, from 1911, from the 2000s: couples and quadruples and loners marching with a purpose towards a home, a tavern, a concert, a café, a date, or perhaps simply an evening constitutional, taken with regularity. What distinguished these crossed times, besides the way people were dressed, was the air, the syrupy atmosphere of summer meeting the crisp air of a November day in 1911. While I could not feel these atmospheric changes, I could see them, life made visible in clouds of breath. I tried to focus on these November people, the cloud breathers, the people rubbing their gloved hands as Kafka did, or holding hands as Lowy and Hanna did. Lowy and Hanna whispered to one another, she unmistakably in love, blessedly unaware for now that most of her choices in life had so far been the wrong ones.

# CHAPTER EIGHT

# THE BIRD THAT
# SWALLOWED THE CAGE

# CHAPTER EIGHT: THE BIRD THAT SWALLOWED A CAGE

The young maid, face as broad as a cabbage, shivered and crossed herself when Kafka entered the apartment with uninvited guests or maybe because of Jozef and me passing through her; it was hard to tell. Kafka's mother hurried into the foyer and took in the situation at a glance. "What's this?" she asked her son, almost under her breath, as though he'd brought home a school of dripping fish. I'd only seen Julie Kafka in photos that gave her a kind of stern flatness, a polite insensibility in the eyes, as though they were capable only of taking in surfaces. Photos will do that, but the photos seemed not too far off the mark.

Kafka kissed his mother on the cheek and told her there was no need to make a fuss, but they were all famished as they had just been to a reading. "Even I'm starved, Mother, and you know how poor my appetite is."

She gave him a mildly disapproving look but said nothing. Max, too, gave Mrs. Kafka a peck on the cheek and Lowy gave her a smile and an awkward hello and introduced Hanna as Miss Reimer from *Lite*. Jozef and I studied the family portraits on the hallway wall: the parents, and Kafka and his three sisters, his photo five to ten years old by the looks of Kafka's even more boyish face in them.

"From Poland?" Mrs. Kafka asked as though there was no such place as *Lite*.

At this, Hanna stepped forward. "It's a great pleasure to meet you," she told Mrs. Kafka. "I'm from Lite, which is not Poland." This seemed to be an important distinction only to her. Mrs. Kafka gave her son a puzzled look.

"Litauen," Brod told Mrs. Kafka, using the German rather than Yiddish name.

"Russia, Mother," Kafka said with a slight roll of the eyes.

"Very well," Mrs. Kafka said as though grudgingly admitting there was such a place. She told the maid to prepare some tea, some schnapps, and some pumpernickel, and was there any stew left? And maybe some of the stewed prunes from lunch? Or apricots even.

"Do we have any of the Goldwasser left from the wedding, Mother?" Kafka asked, mischief in his eyes, accompanied by a boyish smile that probably worked as well as a hypnotic trigger on his mother under normal circumstances.

She cleared her throat and looked at the woman from Russia/ Poland/ or wherever and that actor – I could practically hear her thoughts. She looked as though she wanted so badly to shake her head, to cluck her tongue, to give some indication that Goldwasser was not to be wasted on such people, to say that she was saving it for better people, people who you knew where they came from at least. But her manners won out and she said, "I'll get the proper glasses from the china cabinet. The girl doesn't always know which glasses are which, and that's very important."

"Does the girl have a name?" I asked Jozef.

"Sometimes," he said, lighting a cigarette. True to his word, he had cut down and this was the first I'd seen him smoke a cigarette since the Café Savoy and his alarming coughing jag. "Ah, delicious," he said. "Her name is Marie Wernerova."

Jozef asked me how I was feeling and told me to let him know the moment I felt anything odd at all. I assured him he'd be the first to know. He nodded slowly and looked me up and down. "You seem fine."

Brod asked Mrs. Kafka not to go to any trouble, but he followed that statement with an assurance that he loved Goldwasser. The group filed into the dining room, Lowy behind Mrs. Kafka's back as she gathered the proper glasses from the china cabinet, recalling, enraptured, the rouladen she had prepared "on the occasion of my last visit."

The room was crammed with museum pieces, the kind of objects that made respectable Jews with certain delusional social aspirations feel part of an empire: the china cabinet filled with tea-sets and hand-painted tureens, cut glass decanters, and gold-embroidered platters adorned with scenes of aristocrats gaily picnicking in the countryside, Greeks in the Parthenon, and lastly the kind of tiny gold-rimmed glasses one sips Goldwasser from. Foot soldiers were carved on either end of the cabinet, and feet like giant lion claws. An enormous matching credenza took up three quarters of the wall space in the room.

"The girl prepared it," she said of the rouladen. "But I'm pleased you found it to be a memorable meal. It was my mother's recipe. I'll instruct the girl to make it for you another time, if given some ... advance notice."

Three cages on stands dotted the dining room like floor lamps. Hanna made a beeline for the closest cage where a canary bobbed its head while skittering on its perch as Hanna poked a finger through the bars. "How do you do? I'm Hanna Reimer from Lite, which is not Russia either. So pleased to make your acquaintance."

Isaac Singer had kept birds, too, but not in cages. Like Kafka, he was vegetarian, and knew Lowy years after Kafka in Poland. Lowy spoke incessantly about Kafka and showed Kafka's letters to whomever wanted to see them. The difference between Kafka's birds and Singer's was that the birds in Singer's apartment in Manhattan were never in a cage. Singer let his birds fly free in his apartment and shit over everything. To my child's mind, when we visited, this, not literary fame, constituted Singer's greatness. Still, it took me a long time before I grew to like the man. When I was four, I captured a frog in a small pond at the publisher Roger Straus's house outside of New York and brought it to the patio where my parents sat drinking cocktails with Singer and Straus, thinking the adults would praise me and admire the small creature in my cupped hands. "Put it back, put it back," Singer yelled at me. "It belongs in nature." I had never been yelled at by an adult in that way, and after I put the frog back in the pond I returned to my mother's lap to quietly weep there. To me, he was just some mean guy whose face looked like a hard-boiled egg with tiny eyes and a pinched mouth. After that, he was always nice to me, but I never held him in the reverence others did because he was such a familiar fixture in my household. After my father died, whenever I saw Singer, he would tell me what a great friend my father had been, but my mother claimed that he never gave his translators enough credit. Maybe not, but he did dedicate a book to my father.

"What is your name, little one?" Hanna asked the canary and turned back to the others, her delight trumping her hunger.

"His name is *Tuchus*," Kafka said, and Hanna and Lowy laughed in surprise.

"Marie named him." The maid was setting down some bread on the table.

"I'm sure I don't know what you're talking about, Dr. Kafka," she said, though she smiled and shook her head in mild exasperation.

"Then Mother named him."

"I would *never* choose such a vulgar name," Julie Kafka said, snatching a copy of the newspaper, *Prager Tagblatt,* from the table as though the newspaper might overhear and record in its pages the canary's name in association with the good name of the Kafkas. Someone had been playing bridge before our arrival, and Mrs. Kafka also seized the unplayed hands and a deck of cards before Marie spread a fresh white cloth over the dining table.

"Then I must have named it," Kafka said, sitting down. He said all this without smiling, and grabbed a slice of the pumpernickel and slathered some kind of red cabbage spread on it. "Forgive me," he said, either to the assembled guests for starting to eat before them (though he indicated with his hands that they should all sit down) or to his mother for falsely accusing her of naming a bird "rear end," or perhaps to the bird itself.

"It's no name for such a beautiful bird," Hanna said. "To me, you're Little Yitzhak."

"I'm not sure how I should feel about that," Lowy said, rubbing a hand through his hair.

"You should feel flattered," Max said, "when a beautiful woman names a mellifluous creature after you."

"Though I'd argue the bird's not the only mellifluous tuchus in Prague," Kafka added, covering his mouth, "as we saw demonstrated tonight on stage."

"Dr. Kafka," Hanna said through her laughter. "You should be on the stage."

"Franz," Brod said, and he was not laughing. "You really give no quarter, do you, in this matter?"

Soon, they were all enjoying a meal of leftovers, seated around the heavy oak dining table, stained so dark it seemed to trap light from the chandelier above and make the room darker still.

I felt a pang of hunger, too, at first merely a twinkling ember in my nonexistent belly but growing as though someone were blowing upon it to make it burst with full force. Lowy heaped food on his plate and ate with his elbows on the table, drinking Goldwasser along with Brod. Kafka and Hanna drank coffee the maid served in gold and white demitasse cups, rather than tea served from a samovar like the one Hanna had handed down to my family, about her only possession brought from Lithuania, which is not anywhere else.

I was still stuck on *tuchus*. It wasn't a terrible word – he could have done much worse in Yiddish – but I had thought he was too ethereal, too intellectual to act so juvenile. I remembered him writing something much more high-minded to do with birds.

"Didn't he write, 'My mind is a bird in search of a cage?'" I asked Jozef. "How does the person who wrote that name his bird *Tuchus*?

"'I am a cage in search of a bird' is the accurate quote," Jozef said, unable ever to resist correcting me. "He means little Tuchus no harm, I'm sure. He loved animals, except for mice, which he was deathly afraid of."

"Allow me to just say this and I'll never utter another word about her again," Kafka said. "This is what I've come to understand. Mediocre literary works can gain some advantage by the sheer force of the personality of their authors while those authors are still alive. But when the authors die, their words, relieved of their impossible task, free themselves, seeking shelter in other, better books, until all that's left of the others are pages that might as well be moldering graves." The words were a little muffled behind his hand which he held in front of his mouth as he chewed. His tone was mild, almost apologetic.

Brod's face darkened. He dipped a fork in his goulash, speared a cube of meat and brought it to his mouth, carelessly soaking his moustache in the gravy. But then he withdrew a pen and a small notebook from his pocket and he jotted down, almost word for word (I looked over his shoulder), the ridiculously well-spoken observation his friend had just made. Brod's friend had just put him in his place, Brod had been angered by it, but he'd written down what Kafka said for posterity, regardless. That was just depressing.

"I really didn't need to hear that," I told Jozef.

The second depressing thing was the word, "moldering." The phrase in German was "zu schimmel wenden," which means "to turn to mold." I'd once run across a review of the stories of Ann Beattie in *The Chicago Reader* in which the reviewer, who was anonymous, said that Beattie's work would obviously stand the test of time while the stories of _____ _____ and Mark Richard, both of whom had at one time been ballyhooed as up-and-coming short story writers, already lay moldering on bookstore shelves. I was flummoxed that this critic had such animus towards Mark Richard and me, or that he considered me worthy of such an unprovoked broadside. I wrote to my friend David Shields and asked him if I should write a response to the paper, and he advised not, that that would only call more attention to it. But I wondered now if perhaps Jozef had written it. I could never be sure what his long game was.

"Me?" he said, when I asked him, and he changed the subject. "Notice how completely Kafka chews his food before swallowing. He was an ardent adherent of Fletcherizing. Fletcherists like Kafka believed in the health benefits of chewing each bite 32 times, once for every tooth."

I would have pressed Jozef, but Kafka was sniffing the air as though the devil belching sulfur was about to appear. I smelled it, too, which should have been a warning to me that I could smell anything at all. Kafka's father, Hermann appeared from the hallway, clutching a noxious cigar, not a pitchfork, and wearing a green smoking jacket. Head like a concrete block, groomed black moustache, grey close cropped hair, and tiny glasses, irritation and unhappiness crouched in his jowls, camped in his eyes, twitched in his nose. Mr. Kafka took everyone corporeal in with a sweep of his grey eyes, wished them all a good evening and locked eyes with his son, who said nothing.

"Did you see the papers I left for you to sign, Franz?" he asked. "They must be signed by tomorrow evening. Your brother-in-law has signed them, I have signed them. They await only your signature and then they can be sent to the attorneys."

Kafka stared at his father as if at a blank wall.

Jozef explained that Kafka's father, in his latest scheme to turn Kafka into the respectable businessman he had always wanted for a son, had opened the first asbestos factory in Prague and made Franz the partner of his brother-in-law Karl who had married, a year earlier, Kafka's eldest sister, Ellie – their wedding, the apparent source of the coveted Goldwasser. So far, the scheme wasn't working out too well for the elder Kafka, since his son had zero interest in asbestos or factories of any kind. Hermann Kafka gave Lowy a look like he was to blame for his son's indifference to commerce, and Lowy returned the look with a lopsided smile as though he sympathized, but what could you do? Some people just preferred to starve. This was the way of the world.

Hermann Kafka wished them a "good night" as though wishing them bedbugs and tromped back down the hallway. Mrs. Kafka disappeared after her husband with a slight bow and an abashed smile. Marie returned to the kitchen, eyes downcast as though she'd been caught at an illegal political meeting and banged pots in the kitchen to make up for her sweet demeanor, giving voice to the umbrage the apartment was supposed to feel at all these lowlife intruders.

It's always been difficult for obsessive writers to justify themselves to others. Even other writers do their best sometimes to discourage younger writers from following their ambitions. As a student at The University of Iowa, I let drop – or, okay, I bragged, that Isaac Bashevis Singer was a family friend, and the head of the Writers' Workshop at the time, Jack Leggett, asked me to call Singer to invite him for a reading. This was our conversation:

"Hello," he said.

"Mr. Singer. This is _____ _____."

"_____ _____. What happened to you?"

"Nothing. I'm at the Iowa Writers' Workshop."

"Are you married?"

"No, that's my brother, Jonathan."

"Which one are you?"

"_____."

"So how is your writing?"

"Great. I'm having a wonderful time here."

"And what is your brother doing?"

"He's in L.A. He's an electrical engineer."

"Is his wife there? Is she a nice girl?"

"She's there, and yes, she's very nice. I just called to say hello and ask if you might give a reading here."

"This year, I'm very busy, but I would like to in the Spring."

"That would be wonderful, Mr. Singer."

"Call my secretary, Deborah. She's a nice girl."

"Great."

"And _____, how old are you?"

"Twenty-two."

"Twenty-two. My Gott. How time goes quickly by. You know this thing your brother did, becoming an engineer, is very good. Publishing is bad these days. If you want, you should become an engineer like your brother."

The indignities. Had I become an engineer like my brother or opened up an asbestos factory or done something practical with my life, would I have fared better? Would I have been happier? Maybe I would have given my employees cancer and gone bankrupt from all of the lawsuits. Maybe I would have died and wound up in a fire-retardant Oblivion or an Oblivion made up of electrical engineers. Were there such specialized afterlives for other professions? An afterlife of accountants? An afterlife of baristas? An afterlife of literary agents? Were all the humans sorted in orderly fashion by profession after they died? What if you had more than one? Certainly, there had to be an Afterlife of Musicians. Whenever a famous musician died, you could count of someone saying something along the lines of, "She's gone to that great rock and roll band in the sky."

"Where are you going?" Jozef asked me as I wandered down the hall of the apartment. Wasn't it obvious? There was no way I could be in such close proximity to the place where the Master wrote his creations without taking a peek.

If you had asked me before my visitation whether Kafka's desk was neat or a mess, I would have told you with certainty that it was meticulously neat – that was my overall impression of him. I felt almost overjoyed to see that Kafka's desk was a complete mess. The writing desk, modest but elegant, was made of some kind of dark wood with tapered legs, two drawers in front, a cubby at the back with a small curved wooden panel that could be rolled closed or opened, and two small drawers on either side of this compartment. Hardly a spot of the green felt top was visible under stacks of letters, magazines, loose papers and in the center of it all, his typewriter, an Oliver 5, the lead type bars rising like the pipes of a church organ on either side of the nave, the type bars striking the paper to form Kafka's words when he tapped the white keytops. A shaving mirror sat on top of one of the recessed drawers, a ruler rested precariously on the ledge of the opposite drawer. Pencils with broken tips lay scattered about the papers, a collar and a bow tie beside the shaving mirror, a matchbox, a few mismatched cufflinks beside a souvenir paperweight made of marble and inlaid with semi-precious stones in the shapes of flowers and the word "Karlsbad" in the center.

I had, even in my afterlife, a collector's spirit, and I wondered what had happened to this typewriter, where his table had ended up. If a sister had inherited them or Kafka had moved with them – certainly he must have taken his typewriter when he moved out of his parents' flat. Had he ever purchased another or kept this faithfully until Dora Diamant, his last love, had thrown it out after his death of tuberculosis at age forty? I wanted it. I wanted it for myself. In life, I would have displayed it with pride, would have brought it out for dinner guests and let them touch it.

And that's what I did. I touched the letter "t" and my finger went through it. I touched it again with the same results. I thought to try it one more time before giving up. This time, I could feel the key's resistance. I tapped it a fourth time and the corresponding type bar flew upwards and smacked the platen. There was no paper in the typewriter, but that didn't matter. I tapped it again and the type bar made its resounding thwack, the sweetest sound I had heard in the afterlife. I wanted to write a word, any word. "The" would do. Even if it would be invisible to anyone who didn't look closely at the platen, it would still have made a mark. I contemplated if I had enough materiality to open Kafka's desk drawer, locate some paper and feed it into the typewriter. Surely not, but that moment of contemplation, a pause from my mindless banging on the empty typewriter, saved me. When I turned around, Jozef stood in the doorway with a pitying expression.

I didn't wait for him to say anything. "No, no no," I said. "I feel fine. I just needed a break," and I went back to the group in the dining room.

A woman in her early twenties, who looked like Kafka's twin, the same dark complexion but with brown eyes that seemed deeply compassionate and intelligent, had joined the company and was sitting on his lap in a heavy robe, her hair in a tight bun. This woman, Jozef told me, was "the fabled Ottla," Kafka's youngest and favorite sister. She was young enough to see a late-night eruption of strangers in her apartment as exciting, unlike her sister Valli, who stayed in their shared room. She handed her brother a tiny glass of schnapps but he shook his head and directed her with his eyes to place it in a cup of tea Marie had served him. She picked up a spoon and stirred the schnapps and said, "Careful, it's still too hot." Kafka nodded and she turned her attention to the guests. The brother and sister seemed the mirror images of one another. The smile, the eyes, the nose, all the same, though she was slightly heavier, but if her weight was a strain on him, he gave no indication that he was uncomfortable.

"Now that Elli is out of the house," she said, "my brother is eager to marry us off, too."

"That's not true," Kafka said, "though I wouldn't mind the extra space and a quieter apartment. And their room is better heated. Mine is always too cold."

"You see," she said, swatting at his shoulder. "You admit it. At least you have a room to yourself. Our parents are planning to move to a more spacious apartment later in the year. They would do anything for Franz, even grumpy papa. But I think Franz would be just as happy if we married and moved out. He hates disruption. Then he could roam the halls, writing wherever took his fancy. He'd practically have the place to himself."

"It would still be too cramped," Kafka complained. "And the walls are like paper. In any case, Ottla, I forbid you to marry. You will stay and take care of me as a dutiful sister for as long as required."

"What? You want me to be an old maid?"

"When did she ..." I started.

"Auschwitz, 1943," Jozef said. "His other two sisters, Elli and Valli, Chelmno, 1942."

"I wanted to know when she was married," I said.

At that moment when one sister was asleep in her bedroom, or pretending to be, and another was with her new husband, and the third,

Kafka's favorite, sat on his lap, entertaining guests in an impromptu brother/sister act, I didn't want to know.

But it was too late to unhear.

"Well, yes, her marriage," Jozef said. "She actually married rather late for the time, and unconventionally, a Catholic, a Czech nationalist, named Josef David, in 1920. Kafka's father was livid, his mother thought Josef too poor, too 'alien,' but gave in anyway. Julie Kafka wrote a sweet letter to Ottla, giving her blessing, finally saying she just wanted her to be happy. Franz liked Josef, though he hated the man's poetry, which Josef insisted on sending to Kafka. But Kafka was unequivocal in his support of Ottla. He wrote that marrying Josef was 'better than marrying ten Jews.'"

"This ... is a disturbing image," I said.

"Remember that he wrote it in a private letter to his sister," Jozef said. "He wasn't aiming for greatness."

Kafka nudged Ottla off his lap and told her to say goodnight to the guests which she dutifully did before striding off to her room. The movement down the hall seemed to awaken the beast within its depths.

"Lie down with dogs," a muffled Hermann Kafka bellowed from somewhere in the apartment, "Wake up with fleas."

Lowy, his spoon in mid-air, looked at Franz. "What was that?"

The guests all exchanged looks except for Kafka who seemed to collapse a little, shifting all his weight onto an arm he rested on the table. He cleared his throat a couple of times but otherwise said nothing.

Hanna, who had finished her soup, blushed, and asked Lowy to escort her home. But Kafka looked up and made a motion to stay. He asked her to tell them about herself, her life in ... Lite ... before making her way to Prague. Brod, too, asked to know the story of her life.

"There's not much to tell," she said, setting her soup aside, "But it starts before I was born." Placing her palms on the table, she looked at everyone in turn as though practicing the basic acting technique that Lowy had coached her on. Not to be overly critical of my great-grandmother, but I felt embarrassed by her corny delivery, like she was at story hour and holding a picture book for a bunch of three-year-olds, not the greatest author of the twentieth century and the greatest literary sidekick. Akin to the shame of an adolescent for a previously beloved parent, I felt that somehow if she humiliated herself, she would humiliate me, too, even though I was invisible, dead, unborn, or imaginary, depending on your perspective (In Oblivion, there's little difference between states of nonbeing). I seemed to be the only one with a problem

– the others gave her their full attention as they would give to a mature artist.

When her mother was pregnant with her, she said, her best friend was also pregnant and the two of them made a pact. If one should deliver a girl and the other a boy, then they would be betrothed and married when the time came. And so, from the moment she was born, she was engaged to be married to a boy two weeks younger than her named Solomon. They grew up together and their parents always referred to them as "bride" and "groom," which only drew them apart. When Hanna was six, her mother died and her father remarried, and her home life became miserable. But as she got older, she and Solomon grew interested in one another again, though her stepmother said she needed her around the house and would not allow her to marry.

It was a kind of Cinderella story. With three stepsons and one stepdaughter, her stepmother saw Hanna as the only one of them who had value as a servant. What was in it for her if she allowed Hanna to marry? Bupkes. She had enough sway over Hanna's father to prevent the marriage. Finally, at twenty-four, Hanna felt she had no choice but to run away to Warsaw to join one of her brothers, who had left to seek his fortune there years earlier. He encouraged her to come and told her she should bring her dowry money to keep safe from their stepmother who would surely steal it the moment she left. She told Solomon about her plan and he wept at their separation – she did, too. He would go with her; they would elope. No. She put a finger to his lips. She kissed his tears. But she could never marry if she married without her father's blessing. She would get it, too, but only by making her father miss her so much that he would have no choice but to overrule his wife, give her his blessing, and allow her to return to marry Solomon.

"I thought you didn't want to get married," Brod said, taking a delicate sip of his Goldwasser before adding, "because of my works and Indifferentism."

"That was later," she said. "In Warsaw, I met my brother. He was not happy with his wife and he took all my money and went back home to join the military, and I was left not knowing the streets or the people. After several months, my shoes were torn, my dresses ragged, and I didn't know what to do. I stood on a bridge looking below at the Vistula River and I thought of jumping in and drowning to get carried away with my troubles. As I stood looking and thinking, I felt a hand on my shoulder. I looked back in a fright. I saw a young man who knew my brother and asked me where he was as he owed him money. I began to cry and told him my troubles. He said I should come tomorrow in the place where he worked as a foreman and he would ask his master and maybe he would give me a job."

She was given a job sewing buttons on waterproof coats, but the thread was so heavy it made her fingers bleed. The other factory girls mocked her as a "greenhorn" and when the boss came over and asked what the matter was, the others said she didn't know how to work. She showed him her hands, raw and bleeding. Calling over the same foreman who had stopped her from jumping in the river, he told him to watch over her and show her the way things worked. In this way, she made ten rubles a week, of which she rented a room for two rubles and split the rest with her abandoned sister-in-law. She spent a year there and eventually worked her way to a position where she was in charge of the very girls who had mocked her. The "master," Willy Polanski, was nice, but he had a wild son who worked upstairs and would inspect the coats the girls delivered to him. Unfortunately, he wanted to inspect the girls, too, and they started refusing to go upstairs.

"One day," she said, "I took a package of pins and stuck the pins through cardboard under my blouse. When I brought up the coats, I went over to him, and when he caressed me I pressed both his hands against the cardboard. He screamed, and everyone came running."

"Look what she did to me," he yelled, but everyone laughed.

"The foreman asked me what was the matter and I told him the girls refused to take the coats up and I was teaching him a lesson. The foreman told the master's son that if he ever touched a girl at the factory again, he would make him wish he'd never been born."

"That taught the uncouth ruffian a lesson, I'm sure," Brod said.

"Not so much," Yitzhak said. "The uncouth ruffian went to his father who promptly fired both the foreman and Hanna. And that's how we wound up on the streets without a job."

"That was you," Brod shouted, slapping the table. "You were the noble foreman."

Lowy placed a hand over Hanna's and they exchanged the most sickeningly sweet smiles. "Noble, I'm not sure. But I had been dreaming of starting my own acting troupe and this was my chance. Within a fortnight, I had most of my troupe pulled together. Hanna didn't have much in the way of acting experience at the time, but what a performance with the master's son. Anyone who could pull that off, I thought, had a future on stage."

"I never would have believed it myself," she said, "if Yitzhak hadn't believed in *me* so strongly."

"Give it time, my darling," Lowy said. "In time, you are destined to do great things," and he patted her hands, which she had folded in front of her. "It's only a matter of time." It was as though he had just purchased a circus bear named "Time" and that he had it on a leash, and it would do his bidding if he just yanked hard enough.

My mother had told a version of this story, but far different from this. In her version, my great-grandmother had triumphed on her own. She had not been fired and the bad son had been warned by his father never to molest the girls again or else he would lose his job. The Yiddish theatre troupe was not a part of the equation in my mother's telling, the family legend of Hanna.

"It's a great triumph of the arts," Brod said, with only a hint of sarcasm, "but dare I point out the obvious?" With his eyes and an uptick of his chin, he indicated the wasteland of empty plates in front of them that they had devoured like a plague of grasshoppers

Kafka shook his head and raised his hands. "It is a triumph for the arts," he said. "Even if you starve to death you'll have won."

Hanna burst out laughing but Kafka didn't crack a smile. "What?" he asked.

Brod raised his glass and they all toasted. "To brave Hanna from Lite, which is not Poland or Russia," he said. "And to our noble Yiddish actor and foreman from Poland."

"Which is also not Russia," Yitzhak said, "despite rubles, treaties, maps, and other outward appearances. But Russian, Lithuanian, it hardly matters. We're Jews first to them, if not always to ourselves. A third of the people of Warsaw might be Jews, but ask a Pole if that makes us Polish and he'll spit."

"To forging our own way then," Brod said.

They all raised their glasses, though Kafka's was empty except for a drop which he let fall on his tongue with what seemed like great satisfaction, as though that drop itself was the vaunted Victory of the Arts. Not enough to make anyone drunk or overly confident. But no one was starving tonight.

"I'm working on a great drama now and basing it on some of what you've heard tonight," Lowy said. "No one has permission to steal it from me." He wagged a finger and laughed.

Brod raised his eyebrows and asked what it was about.

"Her early life, the promise that was made by her mother and the other woman that their two unborn children should wed."

He proceeded to tell them his idea that two women promise their unborn children to each other in matrimony, but one breaks the vow. He hadn't quite figured it all out yet, but the two women lived in different towns. One of them dies in childbirth and the other forgets her vow. Many years later, the daughter, escaping her awful stepmother, flees to the city where the other woman has married a very wealthy businessman. Their son is very devout, studying to become a rabbi, and his mother employs the young woman to whom he had been promised, as a maid. Neither knows the other's true identity, but it's bashert, and they fall in love. But the mother forbids their love. She has arranged for her son to be married to the daughter of the richest man in the city. She casts the girl out of her house despite the son's protests. It's then that the girl makes a pact with Satan and says that she will give her soul up if Satan allows her to be together with her true love. The woman performs a ritual which kills her.

"Sounds incredible," Kafka said. "But how does it kill her?"

"I haven't figured that out yet," he said. "I'll have to ask a rabbi."

"I would never make a pact with Satan," Hanna said. And here she covered her mouth with a hand and made three puffs of air that were like spitting. She tried to do it discreetly, but it was obvious to everyone, though no one remarked on it. "But otherwise, it's the role I was born to play. No?" They all laughed at her joke, and Brod gamely lifted a glass to her.

"It's not my life," she said. "Not exactly. But close enough."

"You wouldn't make a pact with Satan," Yitzhak agreed. "No matter how much you loved this young man." He snapped his fingers.

"Solomon."

"Solomon. And she hardly gives him a thought anymore, but of course, this is what an artist has to work with, the raw material of a life to transform it into something even truer than life." He said this as though it were an original thought, something for the ages. Brod and Kafka exchanged uncomfortable glances while Lowy continued. Neither said a word but Kafka had probably figured that one out in kindergarten and Brod would not have enjoyed being lectured about the transformation process in art from an untested playwright. "And Hanna's indifferent to marriage," Lowy continued. "She knows it's just another form of slavery. She's her own person." Here, she leaned her head on his shoulder briefly.

"And she dies? That's it?" Brod asked. "Kaput? It seems to be lacking something."

"How much have you written?" Kafka asked.

Lowy scratched behind his ear and nodded as though he had been caught at something. "I haven't really had the time to start," he said. "But I will soon, and I know everything that will happen. It doesn't end with her death. After she dies, she becomes a dybbuk and enters the body of her beloved. She refuses to leave him, and the mother and father of the young man call in a great rebbe to perform an exorcism on the man. In this way, the whole community learns of the vow and how it was broken by the greedy woman, the mother of the young scholar. The spirit finally leaves the possessed man, but in his sorrow and love for the young woman, he dies too, and the lovers are finally reunited in the afterlife."

"In Hell?" Brod asked. "I thought she sold her soul to the devil."

"I haven't figured that part out yet either," Lowy admitted.

"It's genius," Kafka said. "You must write it. Just don't talk about it. Don't tell another soul. You're calling it ... "

"I won't," Lowy said. "I just need to find the time. I'm calling it, *The Broken Vow.*"

"And I'm going to star in it," Hanna said. "Of course, it's more a role for Millie Tschissik," she said, which was someone's cue to contradict her, but Lowy just looked down at his hands and bit his lip, nodding almost imperceptibly.

"Not at all," Brod said. "It's your story. Who else could play it?"

"I do worry," Lowy said, "that you might be a little too close to the role ... there are some reasonable arguments for ..." and here he trailed off as he caught her glare.

"But of course it's your story," Lowy said.

"*The Broken Vow?*" I asked Jozef. I had never heard of it.

"Yes, it was a great idea," Jozef said. "Too bad he didn't finish it, though someone else wrote it. Can you guess who?"

"Duke Wenceslas of Bohemia?" I asked. "Emperor of the Holy Roman Empire?"

"Now you're just being silly," Jozef said. But he still took my answer on some level seriously, a further opportunity for more edifying lessons on drunken Duke Wenceslas and the history of Prague and its bars that he had begun on our first evening together in the city. "Duke

Wenceslas did as a matter of fact pen some poetry in his time, not all of it terrible. But no dramas that I know of. In some ways, the poems are surprisingly elegant and spare, reminiscent in content if not form of the Japanese poet Basho, though of course there's no way that Wenceslas... "

"Do you want to order a pizza?" I asked over my shoulder as I made my way back to Kafka's bedroom.

All I heard behind me was a deep groan from Jozef. I felt dizzy from all my mortal hungers. I felt like the bird that had swallowed a cage. Whole and without chewing even once.

My shoulders rose, and I breathed in by Kafka's open window, looking out at the river and its dark currents. Somehow, I was breathing in the night air. I shivered and wished for an overcoat.

"Help me with this thing," I said, turning to Kafka's desk, trying to lift Kafka's typewriter. But Jozef just stood there watching me. Despite my best efforts, I couldn't get a handle on it. I really thought if he wouldn't be so selfish, if he would just help me, I could have carried it off, back into Oblivion. In the end, I only succeeded in jiggling it and making its bell ring before I finally gave up.

# CHAPTER NINE

## THE STAMMTISCH
## OF STOLEN IDEAS

# CHAPTER NINE: THE STAMMTISCH OF STOLEN IDEAS

If I'd had breath to draw, I would have drawn it sharply when I spotted two people I knew at the Stammtisch that Jozef insisted on bringing me to once we were safely back in Oblivion. One was Yitzhak Lowy, and the other was the poet, Gary Katsarida. If I had known that Katsarida was going to be there, I wouldn't have agreed, and that's why most likely Jozef hadn't told me. The very same big-haired guy who had stopped speaking to me because I had based a story on him in grad school. Jozef hadn't known Gary in life – but he'd visited practically every moment of my life, so he couldn't play innocent. With Lowy, curly-haired and handsome in his cockeyed fashion, with his crooked smile and dancing eyes, it was a different matter. I felt a little shy. Why? He didn't even know me. It was just a reaction. I felt as though I had seen him naked or something, like some kind of pervert, a Time Molester. There was something really deviant about Jozef's and my particular brand of voyeurism, and the shame of it struck me full force when I saw Lowy again. The idea that he had no notion who I was made it worse.

Katsarida didn't look surprised to see me – he smiled in a way that seemed judgmental, almost cruel, the thinnest smile, the hardest eyes. Like, *Look who's here. Look who finally made it to Oblivion.* He still hated me.

We had entered the tavern through a massive wooden door attached to nothing. To be polite – appearances must be maintained –we went through it rather than around. A long table sat amidst the mist with an elaborately lettered sign that read "Stammtisch." I had never been invited to a proper Stammtisch, something I'd always been curious about since my college studies where I first encountered the word in German class. In Trieste, the sleepy Italian port that in Kafka's day had been one of the main harbors of the Austro-Hungarian empire, I had shepherded a group of students for a summer course. There, we had dined one evening at a German restaurant with a long wooden table in the middle, a sign above it reading "Stammtisch" where no one but a select group of regulars were allowed to sit.

"I thought you'd like this Stammtisch, because some of these guys knew Kafka," Jozef had told me before we arrived. "Consider this a healthy alternative to visiting Prague again. But I wouldn't mention anything about the typewriter incident. You know, they might take offense." His Chicago Polish accent was on full display and he almost sounded like a mobster. *Dese guys.*

"Deal," I said. "Don't tell them about my head getting stuck in the table at the Savoy either."

"Forgotten," he said. A smile crossed his lips and faded. The men made room for us at the table. I sat between Lowy and Jozef and across from Katsarida. One guy with a well-trimmed beard and a receding hairline sat alone at his own table writing in a journal and paying no attention to anyone else. He wore a tightly buttoned black jacket with a high collar and his hands twitched as he wrote at great speed. He hardly seemed to pause for thought. "Is that Freud?" I asked Jozef.

"Hardly," he said, and the people around us laughed, though Lowy coughed the word "Nazi" into his beer.

"That's Johannes Schlaf," Jozef said.

"A Nazi," Lowy said again in case I hadn't heard. Gary was smiling a closemouthed smile, staring as though Lowy had called me the Nazi.

I nodded at Katsarida and his eyes narrowed. He said my name as though it were a bug spray. Looking exactly as he had in college, he pushed across the table a foamy liter of golden lager in a fat mug dripping condensation. He offered me pretzels, too, and good mustard. I thanked him politely, suspiciously, though there was no danger of being poisoned. I was about to ask Jozef why he hadn't told me about this place earlier, but there was no earlier, no later. We were simply shared ideas sharing the idea of beers, pretzels and grudges in the collective idea of the Stammtisch. Footnotes having a get-together.

"You working on anything?" Katsarida asked me.

"No," I said. In death, I had so far suffered the worst case of writer's block ever. Not that I believed in writer's block. I had always liked poet William Stafford's famous response to someone who asked what to do about writer's block. "Lower your standards." He had died a proper writer's death, at the breakfast table, a last composition on the table beside him. "I'm between projects," I said. "You? Got something going?"

He made a sound almost like a beep and said, "Maybe," before taking a gulp of his beer. "I don't like to share my ideas before I write them. I've learned from experience. Not that it's so much of a problem here. Mostly, they're yakking in German, which I don't speak. I come for the beer."

Lowy, who didn't know the history between Katsarida and me,

leaned over. "Let me introduce you to some of the regulars." A man who looked to be in his early twenties, was introduced as Karl Muller, author of "The Remetamorphosis of Gregor Samsa."

"Actually, Brand is my nom de plume," Muller said.

I smiled and took a sip of my beer. It was good but not as good as the coffee. A little metallic tasting.

"What did you say?" Muller/Brand asked.

"Nothing. Pleased to meet you."

"Oh," he said, but kept looking at me as though he suspected I'd made some insult.

"So why is that guy a Nazi?" I asked Lowy in what I thought was a low tone.

"I don't know," Lowy said. "You'll have to ask him."

The man at the table stopped writing. "Ask me what?"

He removed his glasses and clasped his hands in front of him. "I hear you're interested in Kafka. I knew Kafka. He visited me on occasion, paying his respects. He greatly admired my theories on cosmology and showed an avid interest in them."

"You old gasbag," Lowy said. "Kafka was humoring you. He did that with fools. He was too kind."

Gary patted the table to get my attention. "This is what it's always like. The only word I understand is Kafka."

"He mentioned me in his diaries," Johannes Schlaf said. "Did he ever mention you?"

"All the time," Lowy said.

"That's what you say."

"Here," Lowy shouted. "Here." Holding up a copy of Kafka's diaries, he slapped the front cover. "How many times?" He could barely form a sentence, he was so livid. He read a passage about the Café Savoy, the very performance in fact that Jozef and I had attended. Jozef smiled and I made a shushing sound. Lowy put a hand to his mouth and said in a stage whisper, "He thought you were touching. He could listen to deranged people forever. Once when we were strolling through Königliche Weinberge..."

"He admired my ideas," Schlaf said, clutching the table as though he would hurl it at Lowy. "You know, I sent him my book in 1914, *Professor Plassmann and the Phenomenon of Sunspots* as well as my most important work on the subject, *The Fact of Geocentricism as a Direct Consequence of the Phenomenon of Sunspots.*"

"And?" Lowy said, cocking his head and raising a hand.

"They were a great influence on his belief system and shook him to the core. He told me so."

Lowy mouthed the word *Liar*. "He thought you were crazy and your coffee was bad."

"He admired me," Schlaf yelled, standing.

Lowy didn't stand, but spoke to me and Jozef in an unruffled voice. "He only admired your absolute certainty in your *meshugga* theories, the fact that you seemed happy despite your dwindling career." I was starting to pity the man, too. Oblivion seemed to have had a negative effect on Lowy. He had an edge to him now that I hadn't noticed before, though I remembered the fight at the Savoy between him and his fellow actor, Mano Pipes, whatever that was about.

Schlaf crooked a finger at me and invited me to sit with him. "I'll explain everything," he said, sitting and patting a seat beside him.

I started to rise, out of politeness, I guess, because I always had trouble saying no and causing a scene. But unlike Kafka, I was deathly afraid of people like Schlaf. They terrified me because they seemed to carry judgment in their eyes, dispensing it like lightning bolts. They saw through my cheerful exterior, to my soul. They exposed me because, like young children and animals, when they looked at me, there was nothing I could do to deflect their gaze. Dogs growled. Children flinched or hugged their parents. Kafka feared going mad, but I feared deranged people like Schlaf more than I feared my own hold on sanity, probably a result of some early traumas. I'd had a sister who was diagnosed with schizophrenia and who died at a young age, and she had seen ghosts all the time. There was nothing more frightening in my childhood than her sudden change of focus. She'd stop mid-sentence, swivel her head to some empty corner of the room, and start talking to invisible beings, usually arguing with them. "Get out, get out," she said once, and began yelling as she shielded me against some unseen force, her words and actions so distressing on that occasion that I actually blacked out. Now of course I wondered if she'd really seen something. The utter confidence of delusional people consistently terrified me through my life. Their certainty in their delusions could make me doubt almost everything about my own existence.

"Don't get up for Schlaf's sake," Lowy told me. "Besides being an idiot who thought that he could overturn Copernicus in the twentieth century, he was a Nazi. In 1933, he signed the Gelöbnis treuester Gefolgschaft."

That, I didn't understand completely, and I turned to Jozef.

"The vow of most faithful allegiance," he said. "To Hitler. One of ninety or so writers who belonged to the new 'cleansed' Prussian Academy after Hitler came to power."

That changed matters. I sat back down. Schlaf made a sound of disgust and returned to his scribbling. For him, I no longer mattered, not that I had ever mattered to him.

"Why is he allowed here?" I asked Lowy. "And if you hate him so much, why do you stay?"

"To remind him," Lowy said, "when he looks up from his nonsense, that it matters what you sign your name to. For that, I should always be here. The rest of the fellows are good companions, even poets with *meshugga* hair, isn't that right, Gary?" and he clapped Gary on the back. Gary didn't understand a word but nodded and stuffed a pretzel in his mouth.

"I've never really understood the fuss," Karl Muller/Brand said.

"Fuss?" I asked.

"Kafka," he said. "He was sooo depressing. People read because they want to be uplifted. That's why I wrote "The Remetamorphosis of Gregor Samsa," which was published in the *Prager Tagblatt* in June of 1916. I have several copies if you'd like to read one. My account, I daresay, is much more uplifting and morally sound – in my telling Samsa is rescued from that sickening rubbish heap and the housekeeper who put him there is given the sack. My version tells of the holiday the Samsas take in the country afterward, Father, Mother, Gregor, and his sister, Grete. The countryside does Gregor a world of good and he's transformed in the span of a few days, with some healthy food and good country air, into a productive member of society again. Little by little, he sheds his insect form, first the antennae, then the carapace and last to go are the spindly legs. He even meets a young woman named Marta whom, I intimate in the most nuanced fashion, he will one day wed. Many readers of the *Prager Tagblatt* wrote in to applaud my retelling. Even Kafka, with whom I was already acquainted, paid me a visit in homage to my correction of his dreary tale. But I'm afraid my ears were clogged and I was in the throes of late-stage tuberculosis during his entire visit. I could scarcely hear the muffled sounds he was making as he held up a handkerchief to his mouth but I nodded and thanked him for coming around. I passed on a few months later, a mere twenty-one years of age. Imagine what I might have accomplished had my literary talents been allowed to flower."

"This I've never heard," said Jozef, who had been looking

around distractedly until then, his hand on a mug, his moustache dabbed with foam.

"My friend," Lowy said, putting his hand on the boy's. "You were deathly ill with tuberculosis, is that right? Why would he visit you and put himself in danger? The man I knew was always fastidious about his health."

The boy grew sullen then and a look of fright or sorrow or something like that crossed his face. Jozef put up a warning finger in front of Muller/Brand's eyes to coax him to stay in the here if not the now.

"Don't disappear on us," he said.

"What's going on?" Gary asked. "Someone die?"

"Very well," Muller/Brand said. "I suppose it doesn't matter now."

"What?" Jozef asked, his voice apprehensive.

"I invited him over to see me," he said. "I didn't mention my illness in the letter. By that time, I could not leave my apartment. I lived in the Kleinseite district and my apartment was quite small. I could not even offer him coffee. He could have turned around when he entered the room, but he didn't. He stayed and talked to me as if we'd run into one another at a café."

"When did ... ?" I started to ask Jozef, but as always, he was ahead of me.

"You're asking when Kafka was diagnosed with TB?" Jozef asked.

I nodded as though I had just received a death sentence from my doctor, a second death.

"August, 1917."

The three of us: Jozef, Lowy, and I sat back to ponder this information. We said nothing. Here before us sat Kafka's young murderer, most likely, who had wanted only to tell stories of uplift, and had wound up communicating only disease. What had Kafka hoped to accomplish by visiting the boy? What did he want to tell him? Or maybe he just wanted to listen, patience perhaps his greatest virtue. Patience and that rarest of abilities: to listen. I could have asked Jozef to visit this scene but he wouldn't have taken me out of order, and besides, I too, needed uplifting. There was nothing to be done, of course, nothing to be said, and any anger spent on Mr. Muller/Brand would be wasted. I had been twenty-one and arrogant once, too.

Muller/Brand spoke. "May I go?" he asked. Jozef nodded and the boy left us.

I wasn't sure I ever wanted to return to this Stammtisch now that I knew what went on. Recrimination and earthly sorrows.

Jozef, ever mindful, saw that it was time to change the subject. "You might be interested to know that we were at The Café Savoy on the very night you just read to us from Kafka's diaries."

"You were?" Lowy asked. "Was it when you were alive?"

"Sadly, no," Jozef said. "I was taking _____ on a little tour. He's a Kafka buff and interested in the Yiddish theatre, too."

"Ah," said Lowy. "Well, I can tell you stories, if you have the time." And here, of course he laughed. These tired jokes about time were a habit here and we all humored one another when we indulged in them. "But that was not our finest night. You must have seen how rudely I was treated – first attacked from behind by that madman, Mano Pipes, and then tossed out on my head by Migdal, that brute of a gangster."

"I was curious about that," Jozef said. "What were you fighting about?"

"What else?" he said, shrugging. "A woman."

"Was her name Hanna?" I asked.

"You knew Hanna?" Lowy said. He looked at Katsarida as though Katsarida, who understood nothing, would be as shocked by the news as he was.

"She was my great-grandmother," I said.

He hit himself in the head with such force he would have given himself a concussion had he been alive. "*Mein Gott,*" he said, with that same Yiddish accent I always associated with Isaac Singer. I tried to imagine what Lowy would have looked like in old age, if he had survived to emigrate to New York like Singer had. Would he have met my father? Would he have turned into a great playwright? "Your great grandmother. She was a girl when I knew her. She was the love of my life, I'm not ashamed to tell you."

He leaned forward and gave me the most serious look, his voice almost a whisper. As he had put his hand on Muller/Brand's hand, he now placed a hand on mine. "But you must tell me, my boy, she led a good life? A long life?"

Calling me "boy" gave me pause. He had lived before me, but I had lived longer.

"I didn't know her," I said, "though my older relatives told me stories about her as long as they lived."

Here, he took a sip of his beer and flung it into the ether.

"Dummy," he said to himself. "What a dummy."

"You left her?"

"We were on a bridge near Kafka's apartment. I had a train ticket to Warsaw in my pocket. I kept the ticket and gave her my last two crowns. She took the money I placed in her hand and casually threw it in the river as though it meant nothing. 'You're leaving me as you found me, Yitzhak Lowy,' she said. 'No worse off, no better. Go then, find your future. I hope it brings you peace, if not fame and riches.' I told her she was a beautiful girl and that life would be good to her. I begged her not to do anything rash. Anything else since she'd already thrown all the money we had in the Vltava.

"Over you?" she said. "Just go. You're a coward and I'd rather not look at you again."

"And so I left, and that was the last I saw of her or heard of her in life. But I thought of her often, even in my final hour in the camp, among all the unclean bodies, the shame and degradation. If there was goodness in my thoughts, I found it in her memory." He opened his mouth to say more and tried to speak but nothing. He tried again, and still nothing. And then I understood. He was trying to say the words the living say when they remember someone who has passed – they say, *May her name always be a _____*. But he couldn't complete the wish. The same rules applied. No prayers for the dead. No blessings. Not so much as a _____ when someone sneezed, though no one ever did.

"Look at it this way, Yitzhak," Jozef said in what passed for a consoling tone but just sounded wheedling. "Our friend _____ would not have been born if you had stayed with her."

"Doubly so," Yitzhak agreed. "_____ would have been an impossibility, the great grandson of a ghost. We would have stayed in Poland and Hanna would have perished, too, in a death camp. She survived the War, no?"

"She did. She married a shoemaker and they moved from Holland to New York not long after you parted ways."

This news brightened his mood. "This was a good choice. Better a shoemaker – the world needs shoes, after all. It doesn't need another poor playwright and a terrible actress. You saw her perform as the desert cat in *Shulamith*?"

I nodded.

"The worst. That's what Mano Pipes and I were fighting over that night. After the performance, he insulted her to my face. His opinion that she had the most abysmal lack of talent of anyone in Europe wasn't off the mark, but what choice did I have when he said this loudly as we were taking our bows? He followed that up by saying 'Whoever casts Hanna Reimer as anything but a motionless bush in any performance from this day onwards is a phony and a jackass.' As soon as the curtain went down, I punched him in the eye. But I've never met a worse actor. When she recited a line, my blood curdled. I could never bring myself to tell her until the day I left her. *The Broken Vow* was meant to be her story. I was going to write it for her to star in. I almost convinced myself for a time that she could really be another Millie Tschissik. She definitely believed that it was possible, that her wishing hard enough could make it happen. For a while, I thought she was just trying to please me, but no, she was serious. She saw something in herself that no one to my knowledge ever saw besides her. Finally, I left her to release both of us. I could not marry someone of such ruinous talents. I thought I was destined for greater things. I had my play to write. I never should have left her, and I had to leave her. Both statements are equally true."

"But you never wrote your play," Jozef said.

"It was Ansky's fault," he said. "I met him on a train in 1913. I told him about the play I was writing. He thought it was a very good story and then he simply stole it from me. I was on the verge of writing it. You can't imagine how demoralizing it is to have someone else write your best idea."

"I think I can," I said.

"It wasn't exactly the same story," Jozef said.

"So he made the girl dybbuk a boy dybbuk. He made the vow between two Yeshiva boys, not two pregnant women. So what? You think that's not stealing?"

We didn't answer.

"I always wanted to visit New York," he said. "The Great White Way. A shoemaker?" And he slapped the table. "There's no question in my mind that Ansky stole my great idea. If I ever run across him... "

"You won't," Jozef said. "I'm sure of it."

Jozef, I saw, was not trying to be cruel. He was a pragmatist and I'm sure that while he sympathized with Lowy, he admired Ansky and he had already told me that he had searched the café for Ansky, but he wasn't here.

My teacher in graduate school, Barry Hannah, when I told him

about the loss of my friend Gary Katsarida over the story I'd wri
about his life, said "Anyone with only one idea can't be much
writer." My sympathetic classmates agreed that ideas can't be copyrignt-
ed, and that seemed correct to me, but I had paid for this sentiment
throughout my writing life. Too many times I had suffered the same
disappointment. My third book was to be a novel in which I imagined
the fate of Amelia Earhart and her navigator Fred Noonan. I read every
biography I could get my hands on in preparation and wrote two stiff
chapters, more concerned with getting the setting right rather than possessing the characters. Writing is nothing short of possession and I had
not yet reached the obsessive stage. I was still dabbling, tinkering. That
particular project ended when I walked into a bookstore and saw a display of a new bestseller with the same premise, *I Was Amelia Earhart.*
Was it coincidence? Was it just that some ideas float by for the taking
at the same moment, and a few people grab them simultaneously?
Certainly, that must have happened to the two novelists who both wrote
novels about *Chang and Eng,* the so-called Siamese twins whom P.T.
Barnum made famous. Darrin Straus's novel, Chang and Eng appeared
to great acclaim in 2000, followed by Mark Slouka's *God's Fool. The
New York Times,* in reviewing Slouka's book bemoaned his literary bad
luck, noting in its review the "misfortune of appearing only two years
after another novel about the duo."

I once wrote a story about the Illinois State Fair for *Chicago
Magazine,* the cover story of that issue. A few years later, David Foster
Wallace wrote a piece on the same fair, an essay that helped solidify
his reputation as a great writer. For years, I could not bring myself to
look at it. But this happens all the time –you don't get points for living,
as V.S. Pritchett once wrote. You likewise don't get points for having
a good idea. Or even writing it. The fact that Brazilian writer, Moacyr
Scliar published a novel about a boy trapped on a boat with a tiger
didn't stop Yann Martel from writing his own version, *Life of Pi.* While
Scliar looked into legal remedies, Martel was unruffled. His justification:
"Why put up with a brilliant premise ruined by a lesser writer?" Arrogant and vain of him to put it that way? Perhaps, but the writing gods
are a mean lot, making decisions on who lives and who dies before
they've even had their morning coffee.

What finally distinguishes the Scliars from the Martels? Is it,
as Martel would have it, simply a matter of talent? Scliar perhaps just
lacked Martel's publicity, not his talent, as Martel admitted only having read a review of Scliar's book and not the book itself, and Scliar is

regarded as one of Brazil's major writers.

If you read the story "Der Kondginog," published in 1909 by the Danish writer Johannes Jensen, as I did in the Library of Oblivion, in which a man transforms into a repulsive creature and then read Kafka's Metamorphosis, you'll have to reach the conclusion that Kafka knew of Jensen's story before he wrote his. Many of the details of the creatures are strikingly similar. Jensen went on to win the Nobel Prize for Literature in 1944 while Kafka won almost nothing in his lifetime except for a kind of shadow award in 1915 from the Society for the Protection of German Writers for the "Fontane Prize for Best Modern Writer." The award was given to the wealthy writer Carl Sternheim, but as he didn't need the money, he and other writers decided to pass it on indirectly to Kafka, who everyone agreed was talented but could not at the time be considered "the best modern writer" on the basis of his thin body of published work. As for Jensen's "Der Kondginog," it suffered from the same false uplift of Karl Muller's "Remetamorphosis." In the end, his creature, too, was saved by the love of a good woman. Kafka's salvation, in contrast, was in his realization that there was none.

Still, Lowy somehow moved me even if I kind of hated him for abandoning my great-grandmother on a bridge near Kafka's apartment with no money and no secure future.

All of these grudges, all of these spoiled dreams. Everything and everyone in the Stammtisch moved me, even the solitary figure of Schlaf, plotting still to overthrow the universe and finally make a name for himself. Just like me. Jozef had said it was possible, even in Oblivion. Carl Winterhoven, best-selling author of The Blackhawk Exchange, and Saffron Segovia had done it, but never Schlaf, and obviously not me. Not yet.

I stood to leave and extended my hand to Gary, apologizing for stealing his idea. His story did me no good in the end, after all. Published but forgotten. Moldering perhaps on some distant relative's shelf.

"It would have meant more when you were alive," he said, taking my hand. "But better nowhere than never." He told me to sit down. What was the hurry? We needed to do some serious catching up. He passed me a new beer as though there were such a thing as a round of drinks or anything anymore being *on him,* or *on anyone.* We toasted to new beginnings in Oblivion.

# CHAPTER TEN

## MOVIE NIGHT

# CHAPTER TEN: MOVIE NIGHT

I knew now from whom I had inherited the impulsiveness that dogged me my entire life. And my sense of pride and vanity, which likewise sometimes had self-destructive results. Still, I probably would have kept the two crowns Yitzhak Lowy gave Hanna on the bridge below Kafka's apartment. She was no stranger to deprivation and even starvation, but it's one thing to know such things and another to court them. The gesture of throwing money in the river seemed foolhardy in the extreme, given her circumstances, but I think this is the side of Hanna that made her a legend in my family: the same woman who stuck pins in the hand of her lecherous boss, the woman with a heart condition who nonetheless braved a stormy flight to Cleveland to attend her brother's wedding (not the same one who abandoned his wife and children in Warsaw) at a time when planes crashed almost every day. The defiant idealist who outgrew Brod's Indifferentism, who decided finally that one thing was better than another. But she had also packed away her dreams on that bridge near Kafka's apartment – her time in the Yiddish theatre was a footnote that she barely mentioned to her family, and she had not mentioned once, as far as I knew, that she'd known Yitzhak Lowy, that she'd had dinner at Kafka's apartment. She must have known later who Kafka was, what he became. Why did she keep it from the family?

Hanna was, in a sense, the inspiration for several generations. In her lived a blueprint of all my own victories and defeats, though she, unlike me, had been able to put her defeats behind her. My defeats haunted me and did not make me stronger. I simply buried them until in the afterlife I could ignore them no longer. Hanna had lived for a moment at the apex of Jewish artistic culture in Europe and had wiped it all away like so much stage makeup. How had she done that? How could she have moved so permanently and apparently without regret from one all-encompassing idea of her life to another and have survived it? This was Hanna's great triumph in life – to not care, to move on, to cough out the worlds inside her like so much infection.

When I was twenty-two, on the eve of my brother's wedding in New Jersey, my great-great-grandfather, Hanna's father Abraham, the village mystic from Lithuania who had lived to be in his hundreds, appeared to me in a dream. He stood at the foot of my bed in a black robe, with a large yarmulke atop his head, his beard grey, his eyes as blue and piercing as Kafka's.

"So you want to be a writer," he said, disapproval edging his voice, and in English remarkably.

He sounded like Isaac Singer. It was like something out of *Fiddler on the Roof*, but a lot shorter and without the singing.

"This writing business, is it even a business?" he asked. "Never mind. You have my blessing if at least you don't write about family. Let the dead rest. What's the use of reliving the sorrows of the past? If you want to ignore my advice, then write about my daughter, Hanna. Now that's a story. You should call it, 'My Great Grandmother Hanna as a Metaphor for Transportation.' You don't even have to credit me. But you would be better off studying Torah."

When I awoke, I thought, why not heed my great-great-grandfather's advice on at least one of those points? His words to me were mixed up with my teacher Barry Hannah's advice and Isaac Singer's. Barry was the one who had told me just that week to "write honestly about what you love and put a little music in it" – the best writing advice I ever received. But I had no idea what that title could possibly mean.

Still, I tried that semester and the next to write this story. The problem was that I took his suggestion literally. Like Millie Tchissik's invisible trains, I thought I should write a story in scenes of Hanna on various modes of transportation: the plane trip to Cleveland of course, and the time she said Kaddish for a canoe my great uncle Morty owned, that had been stolen and returned in unusable condition. After that I was at a loss. Should I put her on a zeppelin with the good fortune not to explode like its sister ship the *Hindenburg*? Should I put her on the *Titanic*?

How could I have known that he meant "transport" as in *enchanted, bewitched, spellbound, carried away, possessed?* Hanna had fallen into acting and it had possessed her for a time. It had transported her, though she had been terrible at it, and then her career had just ended. Even so, bewitched and spellbound were appropriate words. Truly the starving artist, she had seemed content on that evening at the theatre when she had watched Else Lasker-Schuler perform. She had certainly dreamed of being on that stage herself. But how did she then forge such a different version of herself, a self that the young Hanna impassioned by Indifferentism would have thought unacceptable? When her daughter, my grandmother, a child prodigy at violin, was given the chance to tour Europe at the age of eight, Hanna forbade it. Even with a chaperone. My grandmother obeyed without complaint, eventually becoming an elementary school teacher and the superintendent of night schools throughout Brooklyn, where others pursued their dreams part-time. As far as I know, my grandmother had no regrets about what might have been. Had Hanna been part of my life, perhaps she would have done the same for me and I would have thanked her. At least, she wasn't languishing in a deli of amateur actors, I felt certain. Still, what would life be like without inspired delusion? What would the world be without bewitched failures?

Jozef suggested we watch the film of *The Dybbuk* in the library. The film, he said, was a faithful adaptation of Ansky's play. "You'll see," he said. "You'll see."

The film was made in 1937 in Warsaw and this fact made it all the more poignant – as I watched this adaptation of my great-grand-mother's story, as reimagined first by Lowy and then by Ansky, I wondered about the fate of the actors in the film. How many of them had perished in the Holocaust? The story, as Jozef explained, was the Yiddish version of Romeo and Juliet, starting at a gathering of rabbinical students listening to the teachings of a famous rebbe. Two Yeshiva students, whose wives are pregnant, make a vow that inevitably will be broken. And in this way the film proceeds, a tragedy from start to finish, the young penniless son of one of the Yeshiva students, making a pact with the devil if he will only allow him to be with his true love. He winds up possessing her and having to be exorcised by the townspeople, but not without the object of his love dying as well.

The film, Jozef explained, was famous for a number of reasons. Widely considered the greatest of the Yiddish classics, it also contained a wild Expressionist scene of the townspeople dancing before the wedding of the young woman to the man she didn't want to marry. The only happy aspect of the film was that both young stars really did fall in love and were able to escape ahead of the Nazi onslaught, to America, where they were fortunate enough to be touring in a cabaret group at the outbreak of World War Two. Lili Liliana, who played the role of Leah, remained in the Yiddish theatre in America, while her husband, Leon Liebgold, who had played Chonen ben Nissn, the young man who became a dybbuk, enlisted in the army and fought the Nazis through Europe, eventually reuniting with one surviving brother in Poland. After the war, he returned to acting in the Yiddish theatre in America. She died in 1989 and he in 1993, and the pair are buried side by side in Mt. Hebron Cemetery in Queens, New York, the same graveyard where successive generations of my family are buried, including Hanna, my grandmother, and my mother.

Watching the film was a distraction, but not enough of one to stop me thinking about my one desire, to keep writing, not uselessly in Oblivion, but in Time, where my words might have consequence. I kept this from Jozef, though it was his fault for planting the idea in my mind. I knew he would find some way to undermine my self-confidence. He'd accuse me of arrogance. But that's what you need to write, a certain amount of arrogance, and even more so when you're dead.

"Why don't we visit Kafka's life again?" I said as casually as possible.

"It's not that I don't trust you _____ ," he said, "but I don't trust you in this instance. Even if you don't think you would do anything ..."

"I'd just like to see his first date with Felice Bauer."

If Jozef knew how to bait me, I also knew how to bait him in return. "You could hardly call it a date," Jozef said, unable to resist. "He simply walked her home although in his mind, he turned it almost immediately into much more than that, and so began one of the most awkward romances in history. Poor Felice."

"Exactly," I said. "Let's go."

"Listen, _____," he said. "You've already put your head through a table. You tried to steal Kafka's typewriter. Let me tell you, Ansky wasn't far from the mark. You think it's bad in Oblivion. It's a hundred times worse if you're a dybbuk. It's a hopeless situation."

"And how is this not hopeless? I'm not planning on possessing anyone."

"No one plans on possessing anyone," he said. "No one plans to become an addict either."

I'd like to write, as the saying goes, *I could have argued for eternity,* but even here, I couldn't have done that, not against Jozef, as resolute as I'd ever seen him. He was determined not to bring me back and I was just as determined to go. There was no room for compromise here. I pretended to be hurt, or more hurt than I actually felt, and told Jozef I'd be in the library. The implication was that I needed a break from him and he didn't say anything to appease me or soften his stance, apparently needing a break from me as well.

# CHAPTER ELEVEN

# A NEARLY ILLUSTRATED
# HISTORY OF THE YIDDISH
# THEATRE IN EUROPE

If you want to avoid someone in Oblivion, it's not difficult.
Solitude is not unavailable – it's just not an option that most people
choose. But I chose it now – preparing myself for the challenge ahead
to return without Jozef's guidance and make my way safely through
Time. I locked myself in a drawing room with a fireplace and maps of
the world and any books I desired. There was a calico cat to pet as
long as I wanted to pet it, and it sat on my leg and purred and dug
its non-existent claws into my non-existent flesh in non-existent delight,
as long as I wanted. When I tired of it, the cat would jump off my lap
into an envelope of air, the same place where Jozef's cigarettes disappeared.

Like inspiration, Fate is not something I ever believed in. Especially after reading, when I was nineteen, Henry James's novella,
*The Beast in the Jungle,* which had a profound effect on my attitude
towards my own life. I didn't want to wind up like John Marcher, the
delusional protagonist of the story, who confides in his youth to a young
woman, May Bartram, that he knows that something catastrophic or im-
mensely grand lies in wait for him like a beast in the jungle, and that
at some point, it will make itself known and pounce on him. He has
no idea what this enormous thing is that lies in wait for him, and it's
not something he will achieve or that will make him renowned. It's some
mysterious change, for better or worse, that will alter his life forever and
that he will be powerless to stop. May asks him early on whether he
thinks it might be love, and while he concedes that yes, it could be
something as mundane as that, he senses it's something much greater.

In the end, Marcher realizes too late that his special fate was to
be "*the* man, to whom nothing on earth was to have happened. That
was the rare stroke—that was his visitation." He had had his chance to
"baffle" his own "doom," when May stood before him, but he missed
it and the beast pounced when, at her graveside, he spied a man at a
nearby grave in true mourning for a woman he had obviously loved.
"No passion had ever touched him," James writes. Abject and devastat-
ed by the realization, the story ends with him throwing himself down on
May's tomb, the one passionate act of his life.

It's hard for me not to see the story as a metaphor for the writers' life, especially this sentence: "He had seen *outside* of his life, not
learned it within... "; the old art versus life battle that Kafka referred

139

n he told a seventeen-year old aspiring writer, Gustav Janouch,
ctual labor tears a man out of human society." Maybe it's worth
it if you're Kafka, but what about the rest of us? Torn between human
society and intellectual labor, we toil compulsively for fruits that mostly
fall to the ground, unnoticed. Most of my life, I rejected the simple di-
chotomy of art versus life all the same. Why couldn't one be a passionate person and a passionate writer at the same time? And if one fails
at life and/or art, does that mean that the failure can be ascribed to
being unable to commit fully to one or the other? Correlation does not
imply causation, right?

I must have been vaguely aware of this dilemma when I was
an aspiring writer of seventeen and dreamed one night of myself many
years in the future working on a story while at the same time living inside a story. In the dream, I was in my thirties, sitting in my study on a
beautiful day. Outside, my two children, a boy and a girl, were playing
tag around a tree. My wife knocked on my door, our maid – I must
have been quite a successful author – right behind her.

"Why don't you go outside?" my wife asked me. "Join us. Don't
you think he needs to go outside, Maria?" she asked the maid.

The maid nodded and gave me a timid look and I realized that
I was having an affair with her and that the story I was writing and the
story I was within were one and the same, both titled, "A Sigh Becomes
a Kiss."

A terrible title but I remembered it and the dream my whole
life, though I never had an affair with "the maid." The dream at least
suggested to me the essential contradiction that formed the life of any
dedicated writer, that of living in a constant dream.

As I was pondering this, the fire crackling in the fireplace, I
considered my own books. Did they deserve rescue? I resolved to read
them and then burn them in the fireplace, or at least try. Self-dramatizing, I know, but that was my mood. My own attempt to control
my own oblivion. Kafka had famously told Max Brod to burn all his
manuscripts after he died, and some people have considered it a betrayal of their friendship that Brod didn't comply. But then we wouldn't
have Kafka to read except in Oblivion, and what would be the good in
that? Brod, in his defense, claimed that when Kafka made this request
Brod told Kafka that he wouldn't comply. Of all the people to instruct
to burn your papers, Kafka should have known better than to ask Brod.
There had been sufficient time for Kafka to find another literary executor if that's what he truly wanted. But strangely, the first thing Brod

published of Kafka's after his death was Kafka's request that his manuscripts be burned. Perhaps he did this as a masochistic act of contrition, but my more cynical side reads it as a stroke of genius on Brod's part – what better way to interest the world than to proclaim the dead writer's wish that you read no further, that everything he wrote be turned to ash? Brod was at least as good a myth maker as he was a writer, even fanning the rumors that the unmarried Kafka fathered a child.

Bukowski might have been right about being honored in Hell, but not in Oblivion. There are no marching bands here, no speeches, only bottomless cappuccinos, though some prefer chamomile. I'd like to believe that the solitary fight itself, regardless of the reception of one's work, is what matters. But for some, the fight is mainly with themselves. Firing squads, not marching bands.

I once knew a writer named Omar, originally from Guatemala. When Omar interviewed me for a position at Fairhaven College, along with several other colleagues, he peppered me with confrontational questions, leaning in as though interrogating me rather than treating me like a potential colleague. Every answer seemed wrong. "Name a Black writer whose work you've taught."

"Toni Morrison. *Beloved.*"

He sat back and snickered. "Really? That's the best you've got?" *"The Bluest Eye?"*

"I mean," he said, "do you know any other Black writers besides Toni Morrison? Or Alice Walker? Anyone less mainstream?" And he started throwing out names of other writers like pins I needed to juggle. "What about Nathaniel Mackey? Ishmael Reed? Audre Lourde?"

After the interview, I did two things. I immediately called my wife and told her there was no way I was going to land this job because one of the interviewers hated me. And then I started smoking cigarettes again, though I'd quit for five years.

Somehow, I got the job and despite misgivings accepted the challenge of being Omar's colleague. He was a few years older than me and from that point on treated me as though the interview wasn't over, that it would never be over. When I told him that I wanted to write a children's book, he rolled his eyes. "Whatever you do, don't make it about talking animals."

"Why not?" I asked.

"Because fucking animals don't talk," he said.

In meetings, he was contrarian. With students he believed, he said, in no barriers and to prove it, he gathered acolytes among the graduate students and rode them like bikes.

A graduate student one day handed in an essay to me in which he wrote of shooting up heroin. In his essay, he had written of doing this with another man. That other man was Omar but I didn't know or suspect it then. I was in my thirties, not trained for this kind of encounter, so I wanted to ask my colleagues what I should do. Omar was the first person I approached. He read the essay and handed it back without a look of surprise or alarm.

"This is not your business," he told me. "You shouldn't do anything. It's a violation of his privacy if you do."

As insecure as I was, this didn't seem the right answer. I approached another colleague who took a blank piece of paper from his drawer, wrote down the name of the school psychologist, and told me to ask the student to seek help. I immediately scheduled an appointment with the student. I told him I was worried about him and he needed to do something about this right away. To my surprise, he did. He went to the school psychologist, entered a rehab clinic, and eventually weaned himself from heroin. He wrote to me two years later from Europe to thank me. I hadn't done much at all, but what little I'd done was apparently the little he needed.

Two weeks after I read the essay, Omar's car was stopped by police in the nearby town of Ferndale, the car completely stationary in the middle of Main Street at 2 a.m. When the cops checked, they found Omar passed out at the wheel, pills and powders strewn across the seats and in the glove compartment.

The college, which had wanted to fire him for sexual misconduct for ages, but lacked the will, now had the excuse it needed and fired him the next day. Faculty and students were split. Some, including me, were happy to see him go. I couched my reasons as concerns for our students. He was sleeping with them. He was shooting up with them. But really, I just didn't like him.

Others thought that he should at least get due process, that he deserved a fair trial, that he should be offered rehab before being summarily fired. The school had acted too abruptly. That was Omar's argument, too, and he sued the university.

A few weeks later, I was invited to a literary event in Seattle. The Martell Cognac company was sponsoring a reading by Yann Martel accompanied by a cognac tasting at the Hugo House. A select group of writers from around the state were invited to attend, including myself. The day before the event, Omar called me.

"So I was wondering if you were planning on attending that Yann Martel reading? My license has been revoked."

I made a clucking noise. Such a shame.

Omar didn't register my fake sympathy and carried on. "It would be really great if I could catch a ride with you. People respect you and it would help me a lot if we could be seen together."

"I'm not going," I said. "I would take you, Omar, but I'm not going."

I had been planning up until that moment to attend. It wasn't moral rectitude that prevented me, but a lack of generosity. And a desire maybe not to be a hypocrite, or at least not an obvious one. I hadn't been shy in public on my views on Omar. My friends, mostly anti-Omar, would be at that party, too. How would I explain him as my plus one?

"Oh, well," he said in a tired voice. "Better things to do, I guess. Who wants to hear Martel read anyway?"

"Too mainstream," I said.

He laughed. "I bet the cognac is good though."

I didn't go, just to avoid being caught out in my lie if he indeed found someone else to drive him. Another month went by and the day before he was to appear in court, he was found dead behind the American Legion Hall in Bellingham. What kills you, apparently, is when you try to wean yourself off heroin on your own and then in a moment of weakness, you give yourself your normal dose again. But your body isn't used to it anymore.

For weeks after that, I could swear that Omar was under my bed, laughing, grabbing at my legs. Perhaps he *was* under there, toying with me from the afterlife. I woke up in a sweat. I felt that I, too, was going through a withdrawal of sorts. I wondered what it would have cost me to just go to the party in Seattle with him? Not so much. And in Oblivion, I blocked him. If he was looking for me, which I doubt, I wouldn't let him find me. I didn't want to know his stories. I didn't want him to tell me things I didn't want to hear. He probably wasn't anywhere near Oblivion anyway. I imagine he would have hated the coffee, the company, and the confines. He wouldn't have wanted to hear our stories. I imagine he might even choose to become a dybbuk, alone in some wintry field, seething among barren stalks, awaiting another maelstrom of his own making, as far away as possible from the mainstream.

Most probably such destruction, (of self, of others) has less to do with choice, and more to do with compulsion, the forces within ourselves beyond our control, providing a blueprint for our obsessions and weaknesses. Brod calling Kafka "chosen," implies either G-d or Fate or even Brod himself, as literary kingmaker. If it's a matter of being chosen, then we should all relax, knowing that only a few can be chosen for greatness, the rest chosen for Oblivion, the whole thing out of our hands.

The cat was staring at me. I made a ticking sound and rubbed its chin, but it pulled away and inclined its head slightly and back again to its original position.

There were stacks of books near the cat, most of which I had read, but the book closest to the cat was oversized with large gold lettering with serifs. The title, which I read upside down, was not a book I had requested: *A Nearly Illustrated History of the Yiddish Theatre in Europe,* by Jozef W.

I bent to pick up the book and the cat rubbed its head against my hand and began to purr but I ignored it and pulled the book beside me. The book was filled with photos and sketches of plump men and women on small stages, their arms outstretched or raised in love, anger, with daggers and guns and scrolls, some dressed like scholars, some like pharaohs or slaves, like Roman soldiers, like demons, others in animal costumes, a pageant of forgotten actors. As I flipped through the pages of the book, I looked into their faces and pondered what I always pondered, who among them had died before the Holocaust, who had perished in it, who had emigrated to Palestine, America, or elsewhere.

Kafka had only escaped the Holocaust through the sheer luck of dying of tuberculosis just shy of his forty-first birthday in 1924, nine years before Hitler came to power, fifteen years before Germany invaded Czechoslovakia and started deporting Jews to the death camps. All of Kafka's sisters were murdered, Elli and Valli at the Chelmno Death camp. Ottla was sent first to Terezin (known by the Nazis as Theresienstadt), the Nazi's model concentration camp for artists that they used as propaganda to fool the world that the Jews under their care were being well-treated. *Brundibar,* an opera by Czech Jewish composer Hans Krasa, debuted at Terezin and was performed by children who had to keep being replaced as the cast members were shipped repeatedly to Auschwitz. Ottla volunteered to be an adult chaperone for one such group, and that is where she vanished from everything but memory.

At least we know what happened to her. Almost every person in this Yiddish theatre book was a mystery, though I recognized a photo of a young woman with long hair cascading down her shoulders wearing a white dress, her hands clasped, biting a thumb as though trying not to speak. Millie Tchissik, her eyes downcast in what seemed like fear and sorrow. Over her shoulder, a large man, well-dressed, had his arm on the shoulder of a man the girl's age, dressed like a Yeshiva student, with sidelocks and a book in his hand. He seemed not to be paying attention to the older man but to the woman in the foreground, upon whom he gazed with longing. Of course, the photo was staged and perhaps a bit stylized in the way of things of the early twentieth century, but it also seemed to capture something genuine. I looked into the young woman's eyes and felt the yearning of the man gazing her way. How sad life was, for a million reasons, many captured in this single photo.

I flipped the page and came to one that was completely blank except for a caption:

*From a production of* The Broken Vow, *Prague, 1919, Yitzhak Lowy's troupe. Herschel Lowenstein as Sender Brynicer ben Henie, Yitzhak Lowy as Chonen ben Nissn and Hanna Reimer as Leah.*

The commemoration of an unwritten play performed by a non-existent cast. Staring at the blankness, I could almost make out the lines of possibility, the straining of potentials striving yet to be realized, portraits of yearnings never born. A once familiar prayer came to my lips, but the words remained unspoken. Still, questions remain, and these can always be asked. Even some of the dead have a curiosity that is insatiable. On Passover, the story is recounted of the four sons: the Wicked Son, the Wise Son, the Simple Son, and the one who does not know how to ask a question. In life, I was at different times three of these sons, but I always knew at least how to ask a question. And the only way for some of us to answer a question is to write it down.

I felt once again...like writing.

# CHAPTER TWELVE

## A REPORT TO KAFKA

## CHAPTER TWELVE: A REPORT TO KAFKA

Marveling at the view from Kafka's window, though I had seen similar vistas on my trips to Prague during my lifetime, I considered how fortunate I was to have found my way here, to enjoy these moments of solitary meditation before I attempted my impossible task. Four stories above the street, there was an unobstructed panorama of the Vltava River and a bridge crossing it. I wondered if I could locate the spot where nearly a hundred years later, Starbucks would stand, or *U Maleho Glena,* the little underground jazz bar I had loved so much on my visits to Prague. No, they were further up the river. Or the Kafka Museum. Who needs the Kafka Museum or his birthplace or the ground on which he once stood, when you're in his bedroom, and know that in a matter of time, Kafka himself will enter? And though living on different planes of existence, somehow you know you will find a way to communicate, to be judged by him (or at least your words) with respect if not exactly on an equal footing.

I didn't know exactly what time it was, but sometime in the afternoon, I guessed by the quietude of the apartment and its rooms. Sometime after lunch perhaps? The elder Kafkas were tending to customers in their nearby shop and Kafka's unmarried sisters were likely assisting at the shop as well. "The girl" was perhaps taking a nap between her chores in her tiny room. Across the river, amid sprinkled churches, stone walls, wooded hills with trees losing their leaves, gardens and squat buildings of varying sizes, Prague Castle dominated with its spires clawing the sky. *Little mother with claws,* he had called the city.

I turned to Kafka's desk and jiggled the drawer until at last I opened it and withdrew a page, which floated to the floor and sailed underneath his bed. Instead of trying to retrieve it, I withdrew another blank paper and this time, I succeeded in feeding it into the platen. Twisting the knob to advance the paper turned out to be the most frustrating part of the process. How much time I spent on this, I'm not sure but it must have been an hour at least and the last thing I wanted was for Kafka to return before I had even succeeded in composing anything. The idea was not for him to witness a poltergeist typing ghostly letters but for him to find what I had written and who knows, be inspired by it? What I hoped to accomplish in this instance is difficult to explain – how to explain compulsions –the logic of the itch that must be scratched.

Perhaps I was confusing Kafka with Eternity itself.

Once I had positioned the paper, I had to consider what to write. My books didn't exist yet, my journals, my phone, myself, only my imagination and future memories. When I was alive, I dreamed prodigiously, nightmares often, but also symphonies, poems, songs, and stories. Whatever I wrote would have to be short as I didn't have much time and I was never good at writing on demand, especially in German. I recalled one dream that had struck me as similar to some of Kafka's parables, but some of the words I would use to describe the dream eluded me. What, for instance was the German word for "report?" I stood there wasting precious time until the right word hit me. Yes, "berecht." I reproduce below all that I was able to transcribe before I was surprised by his arrival.

A Report to the Academy

Dear Members of the Academy:

I am honored by your invitation to submit a report to you about my past life as an ---

I had dreamed of an armadillo, as absurd as that sounds, giving a report to a scientific organization. I didn't know the word for armadillo in German, so I needed to find some easy animal to translate. I thought of a dog, but that reminded me too much of dogs playing poker, and a monkey or ape seemed too obvious and already anthropomorphic, so I chose a tiger. If a tiger was good enough for Yann Martel and Moacyr Scliar (and Blake!), then it was good enough for me. I continued: "Unfortunately, I will not be able to comply with your request. It's been about three years since I was separated from my jungle – maybe a short time on the calendar, but an eternity when you have to race through it like I did. And although I was at least partially accompanied by well-meaning people, sensible advice, and good food, my trip was a frightfully lonely one. My achievements would have been impossible if I wanted to be true to my nature and the memories of childhood. In fact, the first rule I gave myself was to set aside my natural ferocity; I, a free tiger, readily accepted my burden."

I had just finished typing the above when I heard steps in the hallway and I retreated to Kafka's bed and waited. Thinking he was alone, he was talking to himself as he opened the door of his bedroom.

"Now what was that tune," he said. "I can remember the lyrics but not the tune." He paused at the threshold. "Now farewell you little alley," he said in a monotone. "So pure. An exclamation, a lowered head." He hit his brow with his palm and made a sound of disgust. "But I have no ear for music."

I knew the tune *and* the lyrics, but only because of him. I know I fetishized the poor man, in life and death, but I never followed a sports team, never wore a team's hat or a player's jersey, so I indulged in this. It's a little embarrassing to admit but I knew that this was his favorite song, that he had even recorded the lyrics in his journal after he'd heard it at a sanitorium he visited the summer of 1912. He raved about it first to Brod and later to Felice, whom he even sent the page on which he had transcribed the lyrics, ripped from his travel journal. When I read this while I was alive, I sought out the song, memorized it, and sang it to myself in the shower sometimes. It was a sweet tune about a traveler longing for his home and loved ones and his "little alley" as he wandered the world. To many, German is a harsh language, but it somehow conveys sentimentality well, and my voice, a clear tenor, was well-suited to this song, I always thought. Sometimes, I would even stretch the final note to the point of breathlessness and raise my arm to some imaginary audience (Jozef) and take a small and precise bow from the waist as water sluiced off my body. Bodiless now, more or less, I stood and serenaded Kafka so that he might remember the tune.

> *Now, farewell you little alley,*
> *Now adieu you quiet eaves.*
> *Father, mother, watched me sadly*
> *And my dearest watched me leave.*

He stood in the middle of his room, gazing out the window, and I couldn't tell whether he heard me or was simply trying to remember the tune. I was about to begin the second verse when Kafka caught sight of the typewriter and he gasped. He ripped the paper from the machine and stood with his hand over his forehead. He had already taken off his hat at the entranceway of the apartment, as was customary, but otherwise he was still dressed as if at the office. Mumbling the words that I had written as though trying to remember another accompanying tune, he placed the sheet aside but didn't take his eyes off it. He kicked off his shoes, removed his jacket and hung it across the back of the chair, then undid his tie and flung it on his desk next to the marble paperweight from Karlsbad. Undoing the top buttons of his shirt with one hand, he retreated with my words to his bed and lay down on top of me as though falling onto a trampoline. I felt only the slightest pressure, but I did feel something and he must have felt something too as he wriggled a bit as though his back was itchy. I wondered if my frequently itchy back in life had been caused by lying down on Jozef.

For a long while, Kafka lay like that, and I didn't move either. I wondered what he thought, of course, but I couldn't ask him and I dared not possess him, not even for a few moments. I was starting to feel that feeling of being unmoored, a drifting as though holding on to a piece of wood in a flood, in peril of being carried away. I felt a storm-tossed sea in me rise as we waited. He placed his hand over his eyes and the sheet of paper on his chest and seemed to be sleeping but his breath was irregular. With his eyes still closed, he grabbed the sheet roughly and stuffed it under his pillow, then resumed covering his eyes with his hand. Some time later, the sound of the front door closing made its way faintly to his bedroom, and then soft footsteps in the creaky hallway.

"Ottla," he cried, snapping his hand from his eyes but keeping it in a kind of salute as though he didn't want his hand to stray too far from his eyes. He stared up at the ceiling, nowhere else. "Ottla," he yelled again, and once more, "Ottla, come here." He sat upright and retrieved my composition, but did not even glance at it. His eyes were firmly focused on the door.

"I just arrived," she said from the hall. "Let me –"

"Ottla." He sounded like someone on the verge of drowning, his voice weakened by struggle. I suppose if, in life, I had been greeted with something such as phantom words, I would have been baffled, too. But he seemed to be over reacting, a little self-dramatizing. If I had found someone else's words on my laptop I would have merely assumed the culprit was one of my daughters.

Perhaps I should have anticipated a troubled reaction, especially from someone as troubled as Kafka, but to say that I was not thinking straight was a considerable understatement. I had never thought straight the first time I encountered existence. The second time I was making even more of a shambles, but in the moment, I just wanted him to say something, even if he hated it. I could always revise. I was a good reviser. This had been one of my strengths as a writer.

Ottla opened the door. She wore a modest black dress down to her ankles and a white blouse. In her hand, she held her gloves and a wide brimmed felt hat dominated by a faux hibiscus.

"What's this?" he asked, slapping the paper.

She approached him and placed her things on his bed before taking the paper from his hands.

She read it and smiled. "It appears to be the beginning of a story," she said, handing it back to him. "Is it a new story?" He raised his arms as though it might burn him and the sheet sailed to the floor and under his bed, to join its companion blank sheet of paper.

"It is not a new story," he said. "I did not write it."

"You didn't write it?"

He seemed unable to speak. His jaw tightened and he shook his head.

"I certainly didn't write it" she said, sitting beside him, "if that's what you're implying. Maybe you were sleepwalking."

"Do you think?" he asked, turning to her. "It wasn't there this morning. Are you sure you didn't write it? A prank?"

"I would never," she said.

"Then I'm going mad."

"You're not going mad," she said and touched his cheek. "It sounds like you."

"A bit," he said. "But it's not me. I would rather have a tumor."

That seemed uncalled for, definitely the worst endorsement of my career. *I would rather have a tumor* – Franz Kafka.

He asked Ottla to let him rest, but before she did so, ever the solicitous sister, she asked him if he wanted anything, some water, some tea. "Perhaps some water," he said and he fell back on his pillow and closed his eyes. "No, never mind," he said. "I just need some rest." Ottla agreed and so did I and I left with my torments and to him his own.

There are any number of reasons Kafka might have killed himself on any given day. This was an especially stressful period – he was already fretting over his non-relationship with Felice, he was getting pressure from everyone, even Ottla to be a responsible businessman. His writing wasn't living up to his high expectations. He feared going mad. The only thing that saved him, I think, was a breakthrough he had in September of 1912 when he wrote his story, "The Judgement." He had not written any of his other famous stories yet – "The Judgement" was a prelude to them all. But when I returned to Oblivion, I knew that he had written none of them. The library held only his works prior to 1912, the first issue of *Hyperion Magazine,* for instance, which published eight short pieces by him. But there was no *Amerika*, no *Castle,* no "A Hunger Artist." All memories of his works were now my memories, the purest works of fantasy. I remembered now that I had received an "F" in 8th grade for a book report on a book that didn't exist, by an author my eighth-grade teacher had never heard of. I was not even rewarded for my precocious creativity, but that shouldn't come as a surprise to anyone who has passed through the junior high system in America. All I could retrieve besides bits and pieces from the library, was a *Festschrift for Franz Kafka,* edited by Max Brod in 1913, "published on the one-year anniversary of the untimely death of Dr. Kafka by his close friends, associates, and admirers." There were tributes by Werfel, by Brod, of course, and even, though Kafka would have hated this, by Elsa Lasker-Schuler, who wrote a poem in his honor.

A Desert Caravan
(*for Franz K.*)

The Sirocco winds blew us this way and that.
Dunes formed in endless deserts.

The longer we trudged
(Singing to keep our spirits high,

Our mouths rimmed with sand)
The more we were fooled.

By the next summit and the next.
Dumbly we climbed,

Though we had lost sight of the caravan.
Had we known the sandhills formed

A chain of summits,
We might have forsworn our goal.

Turned and run or rolled downhill joyously
Like children in our better skins.

Dear heart, can succor be found at the open flap of a
Bedouin tent or the sight of a dromedary

Drinking at the water's edge?
Do you also kneel and see

The reflection of your broken promise?

The only upside I could see was that most of his ideas were now mine, like a wire transfer, an inheritance from a wealthy uncle I had never known. I had written many of them in my lifetime. I published "The Metamorphosis" in 1997, my graduate thesis. It was good enough to earn me an award for the best thesis that year, but its later publication by a small press in Minnesota brought me nothing but a few good reviews admiring my "quirky talent," and lackluster sales.

Still, present circumstances suggested that he might be here in Oblivion, that I would finally have my chance to meet him and discuss . . . what? I wasn't sure anymore.

He was seated at a table with Jozef, who waved his hands and blew smoke as though he was engaged in the conversation of his afterlife. Kafka's back was to me, but the little doubt I had that it was truly him vanished when he placed a hand on his hair as if to keep it in place. Jozef noticed me and stopped talking – leaning back in his chair and regarding me with his most *look-what-the-cat's dragged-* in look. Condemned men have marched towards their deaths with more enthusiasm than I could muster, and to think this was a meeting I had dreamed of for so long.

"Saffron," someone yelled. "Over here."

Not far from Kafka's table, a man dressed in black leather stood, his hair a shock of white though he presented as someone in his twenties. He looked like he was about to go clubbing in 1983. He was waving at me. "Saffron," he yelled again.

I did one of those things I was always doing when I was alive. I pointed to myself and gave him a questioning look.

Ah, these moments when one's inner fool dances hopefully onstage only to be laughed off, how many had I endured in life? How many had I yet to endure? He shook his head, his look summing up everything: Of course not. Why would I want your attention? Is your name Saffron?

It certainly wasn't, but apparently that was the name of the woman behind me. She towered over me, dressed as if she wanted to be Pippy Longstockings, her hair in pig tails on either side of her face and a kind of childlike frock covered with pins with environmental slogans.

"Your name is Saffron?" I asked.

Jozef had now appeared beside me and in a friendly but somewhat sheepish voice, introduced us. "_____, I'd like you to meet Saffron Segovia."

"You're _____?" she asked me.

Perhaps she had read one of my books or at least my most anthologized short story, "In the Penal Colony."

"Weren't you the Senior Editor of *Hoot and Holler?*" she asked.

"You published some of my early poems. It's such a pleasure to meet you." She stuck out her hand. "Saffron Segovia."

"What are you doing here?" I asked.

"Well," Jozef said.

"That's a deep subject," she said, and burst out laughing. At first, I didn't get the joke, if you could call it that. This was the genius Saffron Segovia who had baffled her own doom? In an instant, I saw what Jozef had done to me. Saffron Segovia was just another writer like me, and that was the extent of it.

"Did you ever collect your poems?" I asked.

"Oh yes," she said and told me she was planning to give a reading from it sometime. She had only published one volume, she said. "*Anatomy of a Mass Extinction*. It includes all of the *Hoot & Holler* poems."

I nodded and told her I had heard of it but I hadn't yet read it. I was looking at Jozef as I said this, but he was focused on the mist swirling near his feet. Saffron was ecstatic that I, a nobody, had heard of her book, though of course I didn't tell her the circumstances under which I had heard of it.

"It's hard for a poet to publish her second collection," she said, as though all poets had this problem. She mentioned a publisher in Minnesota even smaller than mine.

"We'll have to talk," I said. Jozef took a long drag on his cigarette, as Saffron left to join her disdainful friend at his table.

"Does best-selling author of *The Blackhawk Exchange*, Carl Winterhoven, even exist?" I asked him.

"Carl Winterhoven exists," he said. "But I'm afraid The Blackhawk Exchange is a little invention of mine. Would you like to meet Kafka?" He gestured towards the table.

"So no one has escaped Oblivion? This was all a prank to make a fool out of me?"

"Sometimes it's just too tempting where you're concerned," he said in his whiny voice. "But I didn't expect you to become obsessed and ruin Kafka's career, well, more than his career."

We bickered about whose responsibility this was and who should apologize to Kafka, but then something else struck me.

"Who wrote "The Metamorphosis?"

"Not you," he said. "Kafka, of course."

"Does everyone here know this?" I asked.

"Very few," he said. "I imagine we're the repositories of his works because we're responsible for losing them. No one else here will remember a word, except for that man," and he pointed to Kafka who sat quietly eating a bowl of something and reading *The Prager Tagblatt.*

"Wouldn't that be unbearable?" Jozef asked "to know that if you had lived, you would have become the greatest writer of the 20th century? But look at him, eating his French onion soup as though it's the only thing that matters to him now."

I had surely murdered him before Muller had – I had stolen him away from the world. No one cared where he was born. There was no such thing as Kafka-esque.

And all because of my story. Because it was so unworthy that he killed himself.

# CHAPTER THIRTEEN

# DRASTIC TIMES/
# DRASTIC MEASURES

## CHAPTER THIRTEEN: DRASTIC TIMES/DRASTIC MEASURES

Kafka stood in front of his window naked, squatting and then standing up again, arms outstretched.

"He's exercising?" I asked.

"Quite the rage in Kafka's day. This was Jorgen Muller's system – a bestselling fitness guru. Muller advocated exercising naked in front of an open window. Depending on who was doing the exercising, the fad accounted for a lot of neighbor complaints in some cases and a rise in the sale of binoculars in others."

"What's the date?" I asked Jozef.

"It's Sunday, September 22, 1912. Tonight, he will stay up and write his story, 'The Judgment.' It's a monumental night for him, a breakthrough. At least, it should be a breakthrough. It should be his salvation. It was, until you came along."

Generally, Jozef merely implied such put downs, but he had been treating me especially roughly since I'd killed Kafka and appropriated all his ideas. Jozef didn't even wait for me to defend myself, which was fine with me because really, I had no good defense.

"He'll write through the night," Jozef said. "He will be able to see beyond appearances, maybe even the patterns of the fabric of the universe. The most intoxicating of intoxicating moments. In the morning, he will tell the maid that he has stayed up all night and he will wake his sister Ottla and read her the story. But only a couple of weeks later, after this night of elation, he'll contemplate suicide. You understand, he's only supposed to contemplate it."

I nodded.

"Going mad was his greatest fear. That and mice. You understand?"

He looked at me until I said it aloud.

Presently, Kafka stood and closed the window, but he gazed for a while at the river, leaning on the sill as though searching for something in the empty lots beside the water. He didn't bother to dress again before sitting at his desk. Jozef took a cigarette from his endless pack and offered me one, too, then remembered I didn't smoke. But I raised my eyebrows and reached for one before he could put it away. "That's the spirit," he said, giving me the slightest sliver of a forgiving smile, and lit the cigarette.

Instead of placing a sheet of paper in his typewriter, Kafka opened one of the side cubbies and withdrew a silver pocket watch, which he began to wind, staring at the face of it as though into a mirror. After he'd finished winding, he sat back and looked out the window again, then bent his head and shook it faintly. He sprang forward, opened one of the front drawers and withdrew a sheet of letterhead with the words, "Worker's Accident Insurance Institute." Inserting the letterhead in his typewriter, he wound the platen until the sheet was properly aligned in the typewriter.

Both Jozef and I, smoking our cigarettes, leaned over him, on either side of his shoulders. Jozef spoke as though he were dictating the story to Kafka.

> *It was a Sunday morning at the most beautiful time in Spring. George Bendemann, a young merchant, was sitting in his private room on the first floor of one of the low, poorly constructed houses extending in a long row along the river, almost indistinguishable from one another except for their height and color. He had just finished a letter to a friend from his youth who was now abroad, had sealed it in a playful and desultory manner, and then was looking, elbows propped on the writing table, out of the window at the river, the bridge, and the hills on the other shore with their delicate greenery.*

Kafka had not heard the beginning of his story, but Jozef, his cigarette dangling from his lips, made a motion with his hands as though pushing the artist in front of him, urging him to begin.

But Kafka didn't begin. He sat at his desk examining his nails, placing his knuckles against his lips, turning to look again at the window. He took his pulse, breathing slow and steady and afterwards rose from his desk, placed the chair against the front drawer and went to the door where the light switch was located.

"When will he begin?" I asked Jozef, but Jozef said nothing. The answer I received was darkness as Kafka turned the switch. A moment later, the covers of his bed rustled. Neither Jozef or I moved. "Let's wait a bit," Jozef said.

We waited. We must have waited fifteen minutes or more in total darkness and silence. Kafka's breathing evened out – he was asleep.

I wasn't entirely sure of the date I had written the start of my story on his typewriter, perhaps a week earlier, perhaps a month, perhaps that very afternoon. If I glanced under the bed would I find two sheets of paper?

"I'm going to wake him," Jozef said.

Before I could say anything, Jozef was no longer beside me. In life, when you're lost, the wisest thing is to stay in one spot; don't move, until you're found. I wanted to flee, to fly out the window and follow whatever footfalls or wagon wheels I heard, whatever laughter or warm human voice, but I stayed where I was and waited. The door opened and the light turned on again.

Hermann Kafka, in a white nightshirt that hung over his large belly, glared at the bed. His white hair was ruffled, his eyes demonic beneath wild eyebrows. Kafka groaned, then sat up. Still naked, he covered himself with the blanket.

"Father," he said. "What is it? What's wrong?"

Kafka's father tipped as though he were going to topple, but he didn't, and Kafka leaned forward as though he wanted to catch the man but then shrank back, expecting, it seemed, a thrashing. I, too, felt again like running, confused by this man with the blazing eyes. "Stay where you are," Kafka's father yelled. "You think you still have the strength to come here and are holding yourself back only because that's what you want. But what if you're wrong? I am still much stronger than you."

"What?" Kafka said in a soft voice. "I don't understand. What have I done?"

"Up to this point you've known only about yourself," his father said, still yelling. "Essentially, you've been an innocent child, but even more essentially you've been a devilish human being. And therefore understand this: I sentence you now to death by drowning."

Ottla, looking as baffled as her brother, appeared now at the door. She wore a white night gown, her hair disheveled, her lips pursed, her eyebrows furled. She inquired with a glance, but her brother shook his head as if to say, "I have no idea."

She took her father's arm and he bent his head like a child who knows he has done wrong, standing there on the verge of collapse it seemed. His gaze swept across his daughter and then his son. "Something at dinner must have disagreed with me." It wasn't exactly an apology, but in his father, Kafka seemed to see something heartrending.

"It's fine, Father," he said, on the verge of tears.

"You were having a bad dream," Ottla said and started to lead him out of the room, holding him with both hands by one of his arms.

It was easy to see why she was Kafka's favorite. After she was married, and his health grew worse, she provided him with a property she and her husband owned. Later, years after Kafka's death, as life for Jews became increasingly unbearable, she convinced her husband, who wasn't Jewish, to divorce her, in a bid to save their children.

I was a little in love. I considered appearing before her and professing my love, asking her to marry. We could run away to America. We could live with Hanna and the rest of my relatives in Bensonhurst. We could raise children of our own and I could watch my grandmother and mother grow up. I could advise them on investments. Franz would be my brother-in-law.

Jozef appeared before me then, smiling, taking quick drags on his cigarette and pacing. I had no idea what had happened to my cigarette. I must have dropped it when Hermann Kafka appeared. "It had to be done," he said before I could say anything.

"What was that?" I asked Jozef. "Were you ... "

"Drastic times call for drastic measures," Jozef said, though not so proudly, but chastened by the knowledge that he had just crossed a line never to be crossed. "I just let him hear some of the words from his own story. They're from his subconscious, not mine. He merely needed a trigger. You understand, don't you?"

I nodded because if I didn't I thought he might fly apart. The fear on his face, in his voice, made me fearful too. I feared for what was going to happen now. Why had he done that? I loved Kafka, too, but not that much.

Kafka was alone again, but hadn't moved an inch. "Death by drowning," he said. "Extraordinary." He went to the door then and locked it just as Ottla called to him from the other side. "Franz?"

"How is father?" he asked.

"He's resting now," she said. "Fast asleep."

"Good," he said. "You should sleep, too. We'll talk in the morning."

She started to say something and rattled the doorknob, but then she fell silent and the floorboards creaked as she went down the hall to her bed. "Death by drowning," he said again, standing naked in the middle of the room. He looked out the window at the river, pulled his chair from his writing desk and sat down again.

After a moment's hesitation, he began to type.

*It was a Sunday morning at the most beautiful time in Spring.*

# CHAPTER FOURTEEN

## MAELSTROM VERSUS
## MAINSTREAM

## CHAPTER FOURTEEN: MAELSTROM VERSUS MAINSTREAM

Sometimes you're given a Max Brod and you don't even recognize him or her; someone who's able to see the worlds inside another person and forego his own. My friend Kevin was one of those people. When I published my second collection of short stories, my first idea was to title it after one of the stories, "The Holocaust Party." But I chickened out because I thought that was too confronting a title and called it instead after another story with a more innocuous title, "Another Harmless Poison." Kevin, who loved the first title and thought the second too tepid, never let me forget it, especially after the book received some good reviews but few sales and started the process of moldering on the shelves of the few people who purchased it. I saw him last in 2010 at a bookfair in Atlanta, but lost touch, as one does, over the next five years, until, hearing that he and his wife had separated, I decided to give him a call. The voice on the other end, while recognizable, was halting, like someone was twisting his arm behind his back as he spoke, the deep breaths one makes to make pain subside as it washes over you. From the second I heard him speak, I knew this was hardly the same person who had travelled with me down to Prague out of friendship and youthful whimsy, in 1990. In the course of forty-five minutes, he told me that his depression, which I had not even known about, had taken its toll on his marriage and that three years earlier he had moved back home to take care of his 80-year old mother, though it sounded as though perhaps she was the one who needed to take care of him. His psychiatrist had told him he should go on disability, but he didn't want that because he thought there were others who were "more deserving." He said he didn't know how to operate the video link, though he could see me. On his end, he seemed to be in a dark room and I imagined he didn't want to be seen. I asked him what he was reading and he couldn't say. I told him I would send him something to read and that we needed to be in touch more. When the call ended, I went to the bedroom, where my wife was lying down, and I broke down in tears thinking how small my problems were compared to his. She placed our cat, Scamper Jack, on my chest and brought me water and tissues and talked me through my sadness.

Over the next year, we messaged twice more – he seemed at least in his written messages the Kevin I had known when we were young: he was wise-cracking, edgy, and smart. Sometimes his questions took me aback – he asked me if I'd rather have my books pulped or sold in used book stores. He reminded me of book ideas I had had, but never written. He remembered and loved every single one. At a café in the town where we had met, he and I had discussed an idea he'd had for a book in the "dead cat" vein during a fad of such jokey books many years earlier. I had recently read a piece in the newspaper about an author who had spent five years on a novel about nuclear obliteration that sold in the low thousands and a dead cat book he wrote fast that achieved near bestseller status. Not that he was bemoaning the money, just the stark difference between a labor of love and a throwaway. Now people came up to him at parties, he wrote, and only wanted to talk about dead cats. Relating that story to Kevin, I discouraged him from writing anything that was merely "clever". But I was sorry after Kevin reminded me of this in an email that I had ever discouraged him from writing anything he wanted. Nothing in the tone of his emails suggested any rancor, but all the same, he had kept a tally, it seemed, of both our ideas and disappointments, the various ways in which we'd failed to measure up to our early promise.

I told him that maybe in the afterlife we'd get another crack at our abandoned ideas and catch up with our reading, too. I mentioned the fabled ancient library of Alexandria that had been lost forever when it burned to the ground, and he replied that Egyptologists now believed that the famously cat-worshipping Egyptians had filled the library with almost nothing but dead cat scrolls.

That was the last exchange we had, wisecracking to the end.

I thought of him back in Oblivion as I unrolled scroll after scroll from the library of Alexandria, which, like all other libraries, had its resting place in the Library of Oblivion. I wished that I had been able to say something or do something that would have stopped him, a year after we last exchanged messages, from ending his life. I'm not sure what I was looking for in these scrolls as I couldn't read a word of them, but the scrolls were all here, all four hundred thousand, two hundred and fifty-seven, full of illustrations of the cat god Bastet. I wished Kevin were here and that I could show him my new story.

Yes, I had written a new story, upon my return to Oblivion. The only place I had ever channeled my dreams and disappointments was in my writing, and I had been overjoyed that when I searched anew for Kafka's books they were all there, hundreds upon hundreds of editions of them. There was even his story, *A Report to the Academy,* which was really my story, or at least the beginning. I had unequivocally provided the inspiration, though of course I'd never be able to convince anyone of that. Worse yet, he had changed my tiger to an ape. Really? That completely ruined it. I took some satisfaction that apparently it wasn't so much my story that had driven him to suicide, but the manner in which the story had appeared and what he had thought it said about his mental health. When he was able to write "The Judgment," on his own, more or less, a necessary correction had been made. At least, that's what I assumed. But really, an ape? A tiger would have been so much more powerful.

I was free, even inspired to write again, even if only in Oblivion, now I knew that I needed to adjust my expectations. There was no way out of Oblivion for me or anyone else. But that didn't mean I was out of ideas. There was so much I still wanted to write. I located a typewriter, Kafka's brand, an Oliver 5, and a sheaf of papers, and I wrote the following little story:

## THE WINTER SWIMMING CLUB

The air pulses blue outside Kafka's window and across the river the winter swimming club is dark. He opens his window and breathes the night air, humming the first verse of his favorite song, its melancholy tune like a call to battle.

> *Now, farewell you little alley,*
> *Now adieu you quiet eaves.*
> *Father, mother, watched me sadly*
> *And my dearest watched me leave.*

He thinks of Felice, whom he met only five weeks earlier, but this song is hers, this beginning of a story that now twinkles in his imagination like a solitary light in the swimming club. How when they first met at Max's apartment, he alienated himself from her by observing her too closely: the causally thrown on blouse, the coarse blonde hair, the almost broken nose, the bony, empty face, the strong chin, but then he'd walked her to her hotel and they'd chatted and something changed on that walk, something in her was not easily forgotten and he second-guessed his first impressions constantly after that unremarkable walk until he could barely think of anyone else. He had thought of sending flowers to her in Berlin, but had written her instead and she had written back.

Two men cross the bridge over the Vltava, one gesticulating in silence to the other under the evenly spaced lamps towards the Belvedere Heights and its sprinkled churches, stone walls, wooded hills with trees losing their leaves.

That's the last he notices until at 2 am a wagon passes somewhere nearby, and the keys of his typewriter slap the paper in their predatory way, like the wings of some great bird perched on top of a mountain,

Only the maid's rambling in the antechambers alerts him to the new day, which he enters the way a mountain climber returns down a rock face, clutching the rope of his creation as he descends. When the maid comes into his room, she stops at the unmade bed, as though she's never seen it before, and he, at his cluttered writing desk, simply observes her in his shaving mirror beside the typewriter, like some apparition. She gasps when he stretches and reveals himself as though he too is a ghost. As though they have both manifested themselves to the other from some other plane of existence.

"I stayed up writing all night," he tells her, and she seems uncertain how to greet such news, whether it's evidence of insomnia or a greater illness, self-inflicted.

"You must be exhausted," she says. "I'll prepare a coffee for you," and she dashes out of the room. While she makes his coffee, he slips away to his sisters' room.

Entering without knocking, he sits on Ottla's bed, the new pages trembling in his hand. So attuned to her older brother's comings and goings, she has already begun to stir before he even touches her shoulder. She sits up, but doesn't smile. It's an old brass bed she sleeps on with a mattress that only Ottla could love, so saggy you'd have to send a search party after him if he dared lie down, even skinny as he is. He's too jittery to lie down anyway. His sister Valli is also stirring, but only to pull her pillow over her head.

He has that feeling of being emptied, his head buzzing as though he's crossed some great threshold, as though he's either committed some great crime or been released after many years for a crime he didn't commit. In his hands he holds a story, and he's not sure if it's terrible or great, and so he must read it to Ottla.

"What have you written?" she asks. "Can you read it to me?" She tilts her chin to the sheaf of papers, this little ritual of theirs, as though she has any choice. *Of course*, he will read it to her, but she never treats these morning intrusions as intrusions, acting always as though she's invited him in. He begins to read:

165

It was a Sunday morning at the most beautiful time in Spring. George Bendemann, a young merchant, was sitting in his private room on the first floor of one of the low, poorly constructed houses extending in a long row along the river, almost indistinguishable from one another except for their height and color. He had just finished a letter to a friend from his youth who was now abroad, had sealed it in a playful and desultory manner, and then was looking, elbows propped on the writing table, out of the window at the river, the bridge, and the hills on the other shore with their delicate greenery.

It all starts out so innocently but then the father enters the story, and George begins to understand that the world he thought he knew is different from the world as it is. The world he thought he knew contained a frail father, a friend in Moscow down on his luck, an engagement. In the world as it truly is, the frail father isn't so frail, and he condemns George Bendemann for his lies and manipulations of his relations to other people, as though Bendemann and his father have long been spies for opposing sides and now Bendemann has at last been unmasked. The story ends with the father's judgment, sentencing his son to death by drowning.

By the end of his reading, his hand is moving uncontrollably about his face and there are tears in his eyes. When he finishes, Ottla doesn't speak, as though out of respect for someone with a deep grief, and all she can say finally is, "The house in the story is very much like ours," which doesn't insult him in the least because she's his sister, and he knows how she expresses things, that she's still trying to comprehend him, though there is nothing but a tender admiration in her eyes. "If that were so," he tells her, "then Father would be living in the toilet."

She smiles but doesn't laugh – her head bent to the comforter on her bed, she seems to be looking inward. "Otherwise," she says. "It's true."

"Is it?" he asks.

She nods, and he feels a strange joy and conviction that everything can be said, that for everything, even the strangest fancies, there waits a great fire in which they perish and rise up again. That day, he stays back from work and lies on the couch, humming his favorite song, thinking of Felice, of his other sister Valli's engagement. He writes "For

Felice Bauer" under the title, and then he puts down his pen and dozes, dreaming that he's just set a world record in swimming at the Winter Swimming Club, all of them, his mother, his father, his sisters, and Felice, on the banks of the river urging him to step out of the water to accept his medal and his accolades, though he prefers to stay in the water a little longer; it's more comfortable he assures them, though really he fears the land, how brittle it seems, how dry, how the air where they stand burns and fills him with thirst.

There was someone else I thought might appreciate this new story of mine, but I couldn't remember his name. It started with a G or a Y maybe.

I returned to the café, my sheaf of papers in hand. I felt sure I would find the person whose name I couldn't quite remember smoking as always, legs crossed, reading or sketching with that unperturbed look that I envied and that so characterized him. I planned to just drop it on the table in front of him as though he were not only my Brod, but my Ottla, too. "A new story," I would say and walk away. And he would show it to someone else and then someone else would read it and then another until all of Oblivion had read my story and everyone wondered what I was doing here. I should be elsewhere, they would all agree, and Eternity, too, would change its mind – it would have no choice with such a clamor.

Ah, I had thought I was over this, but my ambition was eternal as well, it seemed.

He, the person I wanted to show my story, whoever he was, was nowhere to be found in Oblivion – I asked around but no one recognized my description, though I had seen them chatting with him on many occasions. When I found Maudy, she was writing, and she looked up and gave me a warm smile, my rudeness forgiven, it seemed, but she said she didn't know who I was talking about either. And then I couldn't remember his face anymore. Oblivion is bad enough. To be wiped clean, not even left as the memory of a phantom limb, to be forgotten even by the inhabitants of Oblivion – this seemed the most unmerciful of ends possible. What I was left with was the echo of a voice. *Meet me at the bridge,* it cried. Calling my name, it pleaded with me not to forget.

# CHAPTER FIFTEEN

## THE DYBBUKS

I could have left him there, on his own. As with my former colleague Omar, I could have begged off. The universe wanted Jozef forgotten. To remember him, now a dybbuk, was itself a crime. But he had brought me back so many times, and his crime had not been a selfish one. No crime at all, I thought, though I wondered if he had helped unlock Kafka's genius or if he (and I) had created Kafka. Divine (or almost) inspiration. Had Jozef not intervened, Kafka would have killed himself, his talent merely a fitful dream of frustrated attempts. He would have seen Brod's faith in him as a cosmic insult, the rebuke of the universe for daring to imagine that something great was in store.

I returned.

Too late to promise I wouldn't get into trouble, but I had no plan except to lead Jozef back from the perilous land of the living to the complacent confines of the cappuccino-loving dead. If I could, I would guard myself from the madness Time inflicts on the dead by simply waiting for him in a fixed spot. And then, if I left Oblivion again, it would only be as Winterhoven and Segovia should have, as I had wanted them to leave, in triumph.

I chose a Linden tree beside the bridge beneath Kafka's window. To stay focused, I repeated Jozef's name incessantly but I soon forgot my own. When I remembered it again I forgot I had ever been alive. When I wept for my lost family I soon forgot who was doing the weeping and even weeping's purpose. Time played all of its nasty tricks on me in succession, trying it seemed, to push me back into Oblivion. I waited though I did not know why I was waiting. I knew that what I was doing was wrong, and that what my friend had done was wrong, too, but he had not possessed Kafka's father for selfish reasons. He had panicked perhaps and maybe Kafka would have reawakened anyway without a nudge, and gone on to write the story unaided. Death by drowning. That was the son's punishment in the story, and Jozef's punishment seemed to be a kind of drowning, too. The words of the story came back to me as I sat beside the tree: *"Up to this point you've known only about yourself. Essentially, you've been an innocent child, but even more essentially you've been a devilish human being."* When I remembered the words, it seemed that I was suffering the same fate as George Bendemann, and as Jozef. Perhaps, but existence and remembrance are worth little without the risk of being accused, judged, and even condemned to be forgotten. In defiance of Oblivion, there's a virtue that only selfish people know. My mistake, I saw, was in thinking Jozef was more like the father, that he was judging me, but he had been the most earnest person I'd ever known, though he had disguised himself as an ironist. I would always be like George Bendeman, always the guilty one whose crimes floated above consciousness, just beyond reach because I refused to look up and confront them. Still, I deserved better, I thought beside my linden tree. Jozef deserved better. And so I waited.

I had plenty of time to think and listen to the sounds of footfalls and horses pulling carriages and water flowing and birds calling and dogs barking, rats scurrying, boats whispering beneath the bridge, the sounds of branches occasionally snapping in a windstorm, a muffled blanket of snow falling from the branches, an exquisite sound that I had never heard in life. I thought a lot about this tree. I considered possessing this tree. I thought that maybe when this was over, if the people I was waiting for ever showed up, I might not be punished as harshly as Jozef, that maybe possession of a tree was, in the order of the Universe, nothing as terrible as possessing a human being. What difference would this tree make anyway? What could I make it do?

I possessed the tree to find out, but not for long because I did not want to become trapped in it. But when I entered it, as it turned out, there were some things I could do. I couldn't resist. I shook the branches. I popped out a bud or two before they were ready and mourned them when they froze. I scared a few children and made sure dogs didn't pee on the tree. I wasn't terribly inventive in the things I said to children and dogs. To children, I said, "Boo." To dogs, I said, "Shoo." But the tree did not want me there – it tried and tried to throw me out when I took over, much stronger than the table in the Café Savoy, which was weak and heavy with the accumulated sadness of the Café's patrons.

One day, they walked onto the bridge holding hands, both of them in winter overcoats, Hanna in a tattered fur hat, Lowy's curly light hair dancing over a forehead reddened by the raw cold. They cleared away a spot on the stone wall of the bridge, only a few feet away from me, and leaned over the bridge, looking at the ice below and the uneven frosted ridges on its surface. Neither seemed happy but they seemed still bound together even though they were no longer holding hands. Wrapped in an aura of mutual concern, something that until now had kept them warm.

Yitzhak dug in his pocket and showed her two coins. He said this was all he had left and that he was leaving Prague, probably for good. He said that he didn't want to weigh her down, that she would be better off without him, all the hurtful and transparent things you say to someone to whom you mean just the opposite.

He took her gloved hand and placed the coins in it and she held them but did not close her fist around the coins, gazing at them as though they were two tiny eggs with no hopes of hatching. She looked up again at Yitzhak and seemed about to speak but then she tossed the coins where they rolled on the ice and shone dully against the frost. She sprang on him and beat his chest until he held her by the wrists, and she tried to bite him, but he let go and backed away.

"Coward," she yelled, turning from him and looking at the frozen river, the dropped coins.

A light turned on in one of the windows and she briefly looked up as if someone had called to her, but she turned away and Yitzhak tried to come close to her again, but she put out her hand as though she indeed had eyes in the back of her head, but she had undoubtedly heard his footfalls in the snow. He was biting a knuckle as though he were on stage and he needed to convey that this was killing him, too and that he couldn't properly express what was in his heart. She shook her head and he backed away slowly, his arms hanging as though he'd just let go of something heavy, had let it drop and it was best to just let it lay curled there in the snow by the linden tree that he barely noticed, by the forlorn spirit that he couldn't see. A cart passed and the driver paid them no notice, but he sensed me and spat. For a time, Yitzhak stood there, but then he turned around and walked away, head bent towards future possibilities and triumphs he undoubtedly saw laid out before him if only he just kept moving forward.

Hanna stood immobile, leaning towards the water, one hand brushing in gentle sweeps the dusting of crystallized snow that still covered the ledge. She blew on her gloves, her face red from the cold. With the palm of her hand, she started to knock her forehead, her eyes closed, as though trying to remember something that she shouldn't have forgotten. For her, this was one of the most terrible nights of her life, when two dreams died at once, one of those nights that you think you will never recover from.

She looked up then as though an idea had just occurred to her and she smiled, and I thought yes, this is the moment of her triumph, when she sees what? I didn't know. What's possible to fill you with happiness when you're trying to glimpse past the barrier of your destroyed future? What makes a person smile whose sense of who they were has collapsed entirely? What makes you so shattered that the shattering renews all your strength? What strange fancies was she envisioning? I wanted in on that smile.

Curiously, she kept brushing aside more snow on the ledge of the bridge, though large flakes kept falling, the kind that stick almost immediately. This seemed to occupy her completely as though her entire world had been reduced to keeping a space of about half a meter snow-free. She stared down at the river, a hand shielding her eyes as though searching for something. The coins. She's looking for the coins, I thought, and I went over to see if I could help her locate them, but the snow had already covered them. I stood beside her and pointed to the spot where I thought they lay. "I think they're around there, but the ice might be too thin to support your weight." Of course, she heard none of this. "I think we have a bad connection," I said as though we were speaking on a cell phone. "I'm breaking up." She turned slightly as though she had heard something, and I smiled at her, trying to reassure her. A gust of wind nearly blew her hat off her head and when she brought her hand from her face to adjust the hat, I saw the tears pouring down her face. She hoisted herself on top of the ledge then and stood unsteadily, the ledge barely wide enough to accommodate her boots. In life, I would have suspected something earlier from her history with bridges and her lingering at this bridge. But my mind, which had wandered quite freely when I was alive, had a tendency now that I had spent so much time in Time to skate away completely for long stretches. To stay at all focused took all my energies. This time, Yitzhak Lowy wasn't there to save her and I imagined this was what had made her smile. The second attempt, continuing where she had left off in Warsaw. Still, if she jumped, she might only break some bones and become an invalid. But I saw now that she hadn't been staring at the fallen coins at all but at a blue patch beneath, studying the ice for the thinnest spot where it would be likely that the force of her fall would shatter the ice so that she could drown beneath it.

I had been wrong about her, completely wrong. She, like me, was unable to let the fixed idea of herself go. This was not her moment of triumph. And yet, why not let her? I leapt to the ledge and stood beside her. We both stared down at the river below. "Admire nothing," she said in a low voice as she cupped her own face in her hands, a tender but despairing gesture as she said goodbye to herself. The beauty of those physical commands, the music of the body performing its chorus against the brain's solo, the body and the brain, neither really certain of the true intentions of the other.

Across the road, a door opened, and a butt-naked man walked across the snow as though he were shuffling across the floor of his room after a bath. Chin jutting forward, he seemed drawn by some invisible rope, his arms against his sides. The street was deserted, the snow falling, the lamp light casting its green light on him.

It was Kafka, quiet Kafka, yelling perhaps as loud as he'd ever yelled in his life, "No, Stop. Stop. No."

He started running full speed, an arm outstretched as though hailing a ride. Famous or not, it was a sight. Hanna had turned at the shouts and seemed at that moment on the cusp of two worlds and one decision. She watched him with an expression that was at once curious and horrified but she smiled. My great-grandmother smiling as Kafka ran naked through the snow. I can't explain it, but this filled me with a sudden pride. What, after all, did she have to be afraid of at that moment? *What was it with these meshugga men and bridges?* maybe she was thinking. This writer she was barely acquainted with thought it worth humiliating himself to save her. Perhaps she was touched, or perhaps she thought that the world is too mad a place to give up on at that moment.

Sometimes when we're indecisive, circumstance nudges us in one direction more firmly that the other. In other words, Hanna lost her balance and started to pitch backwards.

It wasn't exactly *It's a Wonderful Life* and I was no Clarence the Angel. There were no bells tinkling in heaven as an angel earned his wings. Just a slight creak as a door to the universe shut forever behind me and I threw myself into her with the force of someone shielding another from a bomb blast. I had thought I wanted her to jump just moments before. I guess that's not what I really wanted at all.

Nothing could have prepared me – as though I had dived through a layer of ice that cracked my soul open into a scalding bath. No one within a block who was still awake could have ignored Hanna's scream. If they had looked out their windows, they would have seen a red-headed woman dancing on a ledge of snow as over coals, swaying to some crazed rhythm and in danger of toppling onto the frozen Vltava. It was a dance worthy of her desert cat. An involuntary encore. Maybe the sight would have frightened them, thinking that she was some kind of demon, an idea much closer to the truth than they might have imagined. As remarkable, they would have seen a naked man, if they could make him out through the darkness and haze of the snowstorm, grab the demon's arm just as she was about to topple backwards and catch her in his arms as she fainted.

I suppose he carried me across the street and the threshold of his building, up the stairs and into the apartment, where nothing stirred. In his room, he must have laid me down and then sat in the desk chair and watched me. When I awoke, I had that by now familiar sense of not being sure of who, where, or when I was. But it was not unpleasant. I don't know how to explain the situation except to say that it was warm, the warmest I could remember feeling, like nestling amongst blankets on a cold day and having nowhere else I needed to be.

Being in a body again was distracting and it was difficult not to simply stare at Hanna's arms and stroke them, which I did by crossing her/my arms and petting them both simultaneously.

"Why did you do it?" Kafka asked presently.

I cleared my throat. "Jump?" I asked. "Why did ..." and here I wasn't sure of the pronoun, "she" or "I?" "Why did I want to jump?"

There was a strange timbre to my voice when I spoke and this, too, was distracting. She spoke and yet I heard an echo of my voice directly after.

Kafka laughed. He looked at his crotch and I looked, too. I wondered if I should act shocked, scandalized, but I felt more curious and confused.

"I suppose I should get some clothes on him," Kafka said. "He was exercising when he saw Hanna. I know why she wanted to jump but you, I was hoping to spare you my fate."

"Jozef," I said, and he sat beside me.

"But look now," he said, "at what you've become."

I had stopped stroking my arms, but I couldn't take my eyes off the dark hairs on his arms, my skin tingling in response.

"I wanted to save her ... " I revised the thought. "I had to save myself, both of us."

"You should have left it to me," he said, smiling that boyish smile of Kafka's. That and his eyes made me smile back and forget for a moment my predicament. But only for a moment. "You're a dybbuk now," he said as though welcoming me to an elite but doomed fighting unit. He scanned the room and took a deep breath. "The worst thing is that Kafka doesn't smoke."

"You asked me to come," I said. "Didn't you?"

He looked perplexed. "I did? It's so hard to remember. I was not in my right mind."

"I was hoping to lead you back," I said. That reverb in my head made it difficult to say more in Hanna's voice.

"Ah," he said. "My Orpheus."

He told me of the ways in which he had kept himself occupied since becoming a dybbuk. He had just come from Berlin where Else Lasker-Schuler had held a séance. She and her friends, six of them, had held hands around a table and had tried to call up the spirit of Napoleon Bonaparte. Jozef had sat under the table and answered their questions with raps, one meaning yes, two meaning no. But he'd soon grown bored with that and went to a movie theatre where Felice Bauer, not yet engaged to Kafka, was watching a melodrama with a co-worker. He'd possessed another audience member, a twelve-year old boy named Wolf, and had kicked their seats and shouted at the screen until he was thrown out. So much fun.

"Why are you doing these things?" I asked. "They're not like you."

He smiled and touched his temple. "It's hard to say. My mind swings now between the devilish and the melancholic."

"That's always been my mind," I said.

He nodded. "That's why I found you sometimes fascinating," he said.

"Sometimes?" I wanted him to tell me more, or expand on the idea, but he was silent and looked down on me as though I were a sick child. Instead of two beds with a fever in each as the Yiddish curse goes, I was in one bed, burning with two fevers, my own and Hanna's.

"What's next?" I asked.

"There is an infinite amount of hope in the universe," he said and made a gesture for me to scoot over in bed, which I did. "But not for us."

"Kafka," I said, finally recognizing one of his quotes. "From *The Trial*."

"Correct," he said with Kafka's voice. "Me."

He lay beside me and we both looked up at the ceiling. "Beyond that? You'll see you have a lot of freedom."

"You've been completely forgotten in Oblivion," I said. "And now, me too, I'm sure. It's as though we've been swept beyond the edges."

"Ah well," he said and propped himself on an elbow. "Chalk it up to experience. It all goes into your biography."

"You're trying to be funny?"

"What do you want me to say?" he asked. He and Hanna were close, and I felt the strangeness of being a body next to another for the first time in a long while. My judgment was already impaired, and I didn't see Jozef in front of me but Kafka, and I didn't feel like myself but like someone else: a woman in her twenties lying on a bed with a naked man. But I thought about his question. Or tried. His breath smelled like cherries and coffee.

"That you thought I might have lived up to my early promise," I said.

He stroked my cheek.

I had always wondered in life if when you landed at an airport in a foreign country but had not cleared customs, could you say you'd been to that country? Undeniably, physically, you had been there. An airport, regardless of what liminal status it might occupy as part of a nation, was still within that country. I was one of those people who said airports counted even if you couldn't claim to have stepped past the borders of that country. That's how I felt now. I felt two connections at once, just as Jozef seemed to feel them, too. One was physical, the attraction between bodies, and the other intellectual, but not between Kafka and me – that second connection was purely between Jozef and myself. We stared at one another for the longest time, neither of us able to commit to a course of action one way or another. I wanted to feel those lost physical sensations, though I didn't know who I was anymore. It's difficult to follow through when you look into someone's eyes and a different soul looks back.

Even if I could never experience Kafka, I was adjacent to him. I could create certain outcomes in his world. He had always been rumored to have had a love child. Why not my grandmother, first daughter of Hanna?

I leaned in towards Kafka. As I did so, he cradled the back of my head, looked into my eyes, and bit my lip.

I shrank back, brought a hand to my mouth. "Why did you do that?" I asked.

"Something for you to remember me by," he said and pushed me away. The chuckle that emanated from Kafka sounded like bad plumbing after a toilet flushes.

The sound even seemed to alarm him and he started to cough. When he had finished, he patted his chest. He stood and pulled on a pair of pants. I stood, too, and ran a hand through Hanna's hair. As he buttoned his shirt, I looked forlornly at the typewriter on Kafka's desk.

Jozef noticed that look. "You might have escaped the café after all that," he said, "in the proper manner. The normal fashion. All those minor writers who should have been seated right beside you, but weren't. You wondered where they were, didn't you? You'll never find them. They put an end to it."

"An end to what?" I asked, imagining multitudes of writers jumping off bridges.

"You mean, after all this, you still can't figure it out? They stopped trying to baffle their doom."

"Henry James," I said. "Beast in the Jungle."

"Correct," he said. "Very good."

"What about you?" I asked. "Why did you stay?"

"This is the first time I think you've ever asked about me. I've always been curious about that. Why did you never want to see my work?"

Ah, so he wanted a Brod, too. He wanted a Jozef, a Cecil Hemley.

"In answer to your question, there was nowhere else I wanted to be," he said. "I was quite fond of the café."

As difficult as it was to admit, I had always needed him to guide me, but had taken too long to recognize this. He had at least tried to correct the mistake he'd made in playing on my vanity and ambition. Or maybe fooling me had been another way, for a time, to guide me by giving me something to hope for. And when that failed, he had saved Kafka, and then the world from me, Kafka's pale imitation. Dooming himself. Finally, he had saved me and my family for a time by saving Hanna's life, a saving that actually had consequence, unlike one spirit pushing another out of the way of a streetcar. Saving had always been his impulse.

When he was finished dressing, he gave me a brotherly hug and I did the old thump on Kafka's back that physically uncomfortable men like myself rely on when forced to hug.

"We've always had a complicated relationship," he said, "since the beginning. But please understand that from this point on, we go our separate ways. There are no dybbuk teams. Dybbuks wander alone."

At that, we both left our respective bodies. Kafka was mostly dressed now but disheveled, as was Hanna, her hair gone wild. Both of them stood blinking at one another, trying to figure out what had just transpired, how to fill in the gaps. For Hanna, she had been about to leap to her death one moment, and now she stood within a hair's breadth of Franz Kafka in his bedroom. For Kafka, he had been exercising in front of his window and now a terrible but beautiful actress stood in front of him.

Neither yelled or fainted but simply stared at their surroundings, though each seemed as though they were pretending to know exactly what had happened between them. Whatever it was, it seemed worth forgetting, a secret gap. I lingered a bit to see what would happen, but Jozef had decided, it seemed, to make a clean break. He was gone.

"Miss Reimer," Kafka said, finally, backing up against his desk, which shuddered and the typewriter bell made a soft ring in response.

"Dr. Kafka," she said.

"Well, goodnight then," he said, staring at his hand as if it held some invisible instructions he could barely make out.

"Good night," she said, rubbing her lip where Kafka had bit her.

She left. Quietly. No slamming of doors. The last thing she would have wanted was a scene. Kafka slowly undressed and climbed back in bed, curled up and put a pillow over his head. He started to shiver, as though just now experiencing the cold he had exposed himself to. But whatever madness he suspected in himself must not have been enough for him to throw himself in the Vltava as Hanna had been about to do. He had already written "The Judgment" and was on to his other great works. He had experienced what he was capable of. Whatever judgment the Universe deemed for him, it was not death by drowning.

I followed Hanna down the stairs and into the street, where she tightened her collar and hurried away through the brisk snowstorm, glancing back, but only for a moment, at the bridge.

# EPILOGUE

## MY GREAT GRANDMOTHER HANNA AS A METAPHOR FOR TRANSPORTATION

## EPILOGUE: MY GREAT GRANDMOTHER HANNA AS A META PHOR FOR TRANSPORTATION

I was lost. For years. I walked through the century as if through a long dark tunnel, though I knew certain outcomes. The opposite of one's life flashing in front of one's eyes – this was a cavalcade of lives parading in front of me, none of them my own, at a snail's pace.

I floated, I drifted. I was unsettled, restless. I sometimes walked without a thought or understanding for a year, or two. I eavesdropped on arbitrary conversations. I invited myself into the bodies of random strangers. I made love with sweethearts who weren't mine. I tasted food that would never be remembered. I was rarely called out as an evil spirt because I was the gentlest of dybbuks. I didn't make anyone do anything he or she wouldn't already have done. I just wanted a sample here, a taste there. I attended my own birth and heard Isaac Singer tell my mother when he visited her in the hospital. "He'll grow up to be half poet and half editor." Just like my father. I regretted not visiting my parents before now, not seeing them in Oblivion where they had undoubtedly forgotten I was once their son. But I spent six months with them in the months before my father died of a heart attack, inhabiting a cat named Ulysses who was especially affectionate to my seven-year old self. My seven-year-old self-petted Ulysses and often talked to him. I fought with other cats and always won. One day, crouched inside the cat, I left it momentarily, drawn to the warmth and innocence of the younger me. My sister somehow saw me and hugged the boy I had once been, yelling "Get out, get out," and I hardly had a moment to inhabit him before the strength of her anger forced me out again. Glad to be a cat for a while, I was glad, too, that Jozef had prevented me from acting out my own worst impulse, that I wasn't my own great grandson even if that meant forfeiting all claims to my beloved Kafka. A tree, a cat, just not my own worst self.

I wandered empty roads and crowded ones, sometimes inhabiting a body, more often not. What prevented me from complete madness, I can't be certain, but perhaps I had built up a resistance to Time, or perhaps I simply could no longer recognize my madness. I mostly stayed away from my own life until the next century when my family was all together and I remembered being happy. My youngest daughter always thought our house was haunted, but I said that was impossible until I climbed the stairs as a spirit and saw her in her room on her bed, drawing portraits of big-eyed girls and clothes for them to wear. As I stood on the top step looking into her room, she called out, "Who's there?" but she didn't see me. Still, she sensed me and instead of spitting like a Czech cart driver from 1911, she went to the room that had been my study, opened the door without knocking, though I had always told her to knock first.

He sat there with an annoyed look. "Remember, you're supposed to knock," he said. "I was in the middle of something."

"I'm sorry, Daddy," she said. "Can you tuck me in?"

"Okay, I'll be there in a minute."

"Can you read to me?"

"Not tonight."

He waited far too long, maybe twenty minutes, writing whatever it was that he thought was so important, until finally he remembered and went to her bedside.

"Thank you," she said in a groggy voice. "Will you stay with me a bit?" she asked.

"Okay, for a little while," and he lay down beside her.

She hugged him and told him he was the best dad in the world and he said he wished that were so, but that he was glad she thought so all the same. He would have stood up again and gone back to his study to keep working on whatever it was he was working on, but instead, I lay down in him and started issuing new commands that overrode the old ones. Instead of leaving my daughter's bed after a few minutes, I stayed put half the night before joining my wife in bed and putting my arms around her as though I had never left. She shifted slightly to accommodate me and said something about oranges.

The next morning, I awoke inside myself as if in a tent at a campground, ready to start a day's hike, breathe fresh air, explore new landscapes. I drank a cup of coffee and returned to my study where I closed the file I had been working on and started a new project. I wanted to write the story I couldn't write in Oblivion. In Oblivion, I was forgotten and even if I could return, my book would be unwritten as I wrote it, an invisible hand erasing the words as soon as I committed them. Here, I could still write. I wanted to write about being transported by the world I lived in and the people I loved and who loved me, by the books I read and dreamed. I wanted to write about the people in my family whom I had never met but whom nonetheless, I carried forward.

Over weeks and months, I relived this portion of my life, attending to all the obligations of a person with mid-life responsibilities. Once again, there was never enough time to spend with my family, but it wasn't as though they wanted to spend all their time with me. They had friends, playdates, sleepovers, school, alone time. Still, I vowed that I would not give up my old body until it died again, and this time I would live better, write better.

Mostly, that did not come to pass. Re-inhabiting myself, my own Remetamorphosis, proved no more successful than the first. I still found myself distracted, pulled in too many directions at once, still spent too much time away from home. At dinner, we still engaged in the same inane arguments, the most heated of these between my wife and eldest daughter, who were so similar, so headstrong, that of course they clashed on an almost nightly basis over the smallest things that were stand-ins for the largest. When I intervened, my wife accused me of spoiling my daughters, which I probably did. In my defense, it's almost impossible not to spoil your children when you've returned from the dead. The only difference between the first time I lived my life and this time was that this time I was writing exactly what I wanted, the book I was meant – though that presupposes Fate, which is problematic – to write.

But isn't the answer to the question, "Why do we write?" really just to still our minds, to come to terms finally with the fact that the whole human experiment is a glorious failure because we cannot blend or mend our many contradictions, though we try? I think that there can't be a cafe for everyone in a profession, only for those who believe that making their mark will dissolve those contradictions and still their minds. Maybe the great writers and the lesser writers who stop measuring themselves against the universe, go to the place of Not Trying, finding contentment finally in a draining of the anxieties that pollute us. If so, then Kafka and many others, now nameless, were simply at peace, at rest, victorious in a way that I could not be.

I still had a writing project. I sorted through various family papers that had been rotting in the basement and enlisted my fifteen-year-old daughter to help me sort – not for free of course, but in exchange for a generous allowance she so desperately needed to buy clothing at vintage stores.

We spent the better part of that summer retrieving from our dank basement boxes and files filled with my mother's stories and letters, my father's papers as well as family photographs and magazines and flyers and ancient calendars left over from my mother's life. The breezeway between our kitchen and garage became cluttered. While my wife was unhappy with the mess, which we promised to clean up, my daughter and I bonded over piles of papers and the photographs of now nameless relatives and family friends, many of them claimed by my daughter to decorate her bedroom wall.

She knew that I was writing about my great-grandmother's time in the Yiddish theatre and her friendship with Kafka. I told my daughter everything, in fact, after drinking too much wine one night: that I had attended a performance with Kafka of a poet Kafka despised, that I had tried to steal Kafka's typewriter, that I had seen Kafka naked, that I had possessed a cat, a tree, and assorted strangers and had wandered aimlessly through the last century, that I had briefly possessed my great-grandmother and had kissed another dybbuk who had possessed Kafka, that I, too, was now a dybbuk, both her father and not her father, transformed into an evil spirit completely and utterly doomed. This didn't mean I loved her any less, I told her. I was that kind of drunk demon, sentimental and nostalgic.

"You're so weird, Dad," was how she responded, still sorting papers and shaking her head, laughing at my utter hopelessness.

Not long afterward, she came across a sheaf of papers, read them through, and handed them to me. "I think this might be important," she said.

The papers, totaling four pages, were typed and single spaced. At the top of the first page was a heading written in a tight script.

*Hanna Reimer Brauer*
*As told to Augusta Brauer Sainburg (daughter)*

"There's nothing about Kafka in here," my daughter said, "or the Yiddish theatre."

As there was nothing about being the inspiration for the most famous of Yiddish plays, though Hanna had related to her daughter the pledge her mother and her mother's friend had made when they were both pregnant, that if one should have a son and the other a daughter, they would be wed. She told of travelling to Warsaw and even of the moment when she almost ended her life.

*In Warsaw, I met my brother. He was not happy with his wife, so he took my money and went back home to join the military and I was left a greenhorn, not knowing the streets, the language, or the people. After several months my shoes were torn, my*

*dresses ragged, and I didn't know what to do. I stood on a
bridge looking below at the water and I thought of jumping in
and drowning and getting carried away with my troubles. As I
stood looking and thinking, I felt a hand on my shoulder. I
looked back in a fright. I saw a young man who knew my
brother and asked me where he was as he owed him some
money. I began to cry and told him my troubles. He said I
should come tomorrow to the place where he worked, and he
would ask his master and maybe he would give me a job.*

That was all that was mentioned of Yitzhak Lowy, not even his
name recorded. She had left out almost everything else from this portion
of her life. The only event she related to her daughter was the episode
at the factory in which she stuck the hand of the boss's son with pins,
but in this version, she was not fired. In this version, the boss's son was
warned not to bother the girls and she kept her job.

I understood why, in this retelling, there was no mention of
Kafka. No mention of the Yiddish theatre, no mention of Brod, of
Indifferentism, of her youthful hopes and dreams and loves. Still, I read
the pages with a profound sense of sadness that she would erase these
events from her life, though realistically I knew that even in the most
recorded of lives, there are encounters that must go unrecorded, little
secrets never meant to be shared, not with one's family, and as time
passes, not with oneself.

She told of how she had decided after a year that it was time
to go home to Lithuania to marry the man to whom she had been
betrothed since before her birth. Her father had softened since she
left home and had overcome her stepmother's objections, sending word
that he would send her money soon for her travel back home and that
preparations for her marriage were already under way.

This was around the time of Purim and she was invited to a
party by her landlady – how she survived the winter I don't know, but I
assume she found work in another factory. At the Purim party she met
a young man who gave her a chair and "was very attentive." Later, he
escorted her back to her lodge. Over the next couple of weeks, they saw
each other frequently, though she wrote that she "didn't like him at first
but he was so good-natured and pleasant that by the end of two weeks,
I found I had fallen in love with him. He had an older brother there
who told my young man not to marry a girl who travelled around the
world all alone. So he heeded his brother and stopped calling on me."

Had she told her suitor that she'd been in the theatre? If so, no wonder he stayed away – her time in the theatre caused her nothing but shame. No wonder she had erased it from her retelling of her life, though she had told my mother of her time in it, perhaps recognizing in my mother a kindred spirit.

Rejected yet again, and by another Yitzhak no less, she didn't know what to do but wait for word and funds from her father to return home. When the day of her departure finally arrived, she made the rounds of her remaining friends and acquaintances to say goodbye. At the home of the host of the Purim party, one of Prague's rabbis, she found the group of men she had met at the party, in the rabbi's parlor, including the young man she loved. After her goodbyes, he said to her, "Wait. Let me escort you."

"No thank you," she said. "I don't like being escorted by strange men."

But he walked beside her to her door and when she turned to say goodbye once and for all, he said, "No, I can't let you go. We'll be married next week. This hand will never belong to a stranger."

> *I wrote a letter to my father telling him not to wait for me as I was married, and he answered me, "You are a child and you did like a child. What is for me left but to send you my blessing so as a father has pity on his children so I have to send you my blessing. I'll send you my blessing if you will keep the peace in your house with your husband, then you will have my blessing."*

I can't say that Hanna always kept peace in her household, but she found in her second Yitzhak a good man who was kind to her even if maybe she didn't love him as much as she loved the first Yitzhak, but she wouldn't think about this because finally she was a pragmatic person. This much I had learned from my family even though she and I had never met, though we had shared, briefly, a body. A strong and practical woman, she had her impulses and she could be cruel later in life to her second Yitzhak as he stood by the radiator and coughed, and she told him to be quiet as though he was doing it to annoy her. She could also be kind to her children, taking their sadnesses and victories, no matter how small, seriously, and they would worship her for that and tell stories about her to the next generation and the next, and within a small but important circle, she would be legendary. As far as I know, she never went to another poetry reading in her life, though she recited poetry of her own making over the battered body of a canoe stolen from one of her children. As far as I know, literature never transported her again in the same way it had in her youth, though she transported others and comforted them: soothing the infant of a terrified mother as she flew in a plane to another brother's wedding in Cleveland, the first and last time in her life she stepped on a plane. I wished she could reach out and talk to me now, her fallen great grandson, to comfort me as only a relative can. I wanted her to acknowledge me. We both had made the other possible.

After that day in the breezeway, I had everything I needed to complete my project and there was little reason and every reason for me to stay put in this aging but comfortable body. I knew my own future. I knew the day I would die, and I knew the jobs I would take. I knew the broad parameters of my children's futures and knew that they would be all right. I made a few lifestyle changes that wouldn't make too much of a difference: ate a little healthier, worked out more, saved a bit more. Never quite satisfied, I stole a couple of ideas for short stories that I had read between my possession of myself and the time I died the first time. I submitted them to the top magazines, but each one was rejected in turn, proving to my satisfaction at last that an infinite number of monkeys cannot produce the world's masterpieces given an infinite amount of time. The same story by a different writer is still a different story.

I understood the same about my life. The same life lived by a person's future self is not the same life. I was in a sense taping over my own life and ruining it for my younger self who had more right to it than I did. And so, on one unremarkable day not much different from the day before, I made ready for my departure as Hanna had once done, though there was no one to escort me, no one to tell me to stay, no one to even know of my true identity, or where I was going. I didn't even know.

To my wife, I recited a translation of Else Lasker-Schuler's poem as we were lying in bed and she was slowly waking.

Can you see me

Between heaven and earth?
No one has ever crossed my path.

But your face warms my world,
All blossoming stems from you.

When you look at me
My heart turns sweetness.

Underneath your smile I learn
To prepare day and night,

To conjure you up and make you fade.
The one game that I always play.

I squeezed her hand, kissed her, then went to say good morning to our daughters. They had always insisted that before I went anywhere I should wake them up and tell them I was going. If I didn't, no matter what time of the night, this felt like a kind of betrayal to them. And so, I woke them and made apologies for waking them, telling them by way of excuse that I had thought it was a school day. "Go back to sleep," I said. "I'll see you in the morning. And if I don't see you, then you at least will still see me." My youngest, who laughed at everything I said, made no exception with this remark. My fifteen-year old simply said, "Noted. Goodnight." And turning her back, she returned to sleep.

I said goodbye, too, to my younger self, the fool. I knew that when I left finally, he would be confused by such a long lapse of memory, but he was often confused in life, and this too would pass. And then when I was almost ready to step outside of myself, I wrote a short note for him on top of my manuscript. *"Admire everything"* it read.

Admire
Everything

## ACKNOWLEDGEMENTS

This dybbuk would like to thank the following people for their generosity in reading and commenting on earlier versions of this manuscript as well as giving me their support, guidance and inspiration: Lee Kofman, Shoshanna Hemley, Olivia Donica, Isabel Hanna, Anne Brewster, Erin Stalcup, Kyle McCord, Malaga Baldi, Dee Dee Debartlo, Josh Mei-Ling Dubrau, Justin Clark, Peter Parsons, Xu Xi, Sharon Solwitz, Eugenia Rico, David Shields, Heidi Stalla, Kaylie Jones, Stephanie Reents, Darryl Whetter, and Suzanne Paola Antonetta.

## NOTES ON DESIGN

The vector images were created from Franz Kafka's original drawings, while the fonts selected sought to mirror the Olive 5 typewriter that he often used (Bohemian Typewriter font). Another font for the bulk of the book was Packard Antique, which is funky and archaic. On the final vector, Franz Kafka's own handwriting font was used to pen "Admire Everything."

## AUTHOR BIOGRAPHY

Robin Hemley has published fifteen books of fiction and nonfiction and has won many awards including fellowships from the Guggenheim and Rockefeller Foundations. He is Parsons Family Chair in Creative Writing and Director of the Polk School of Communications at Long Island University. Hemley lives in Brooklyn.

**Also by this Author:**

*The Mouse Town* (Stories)
*All You Can Eat* (Stories)
*The Last Studebaker*
*Turning Life into Fiction*
*The Big Ear* (Stories)
*Nola*
*Invented Eden*
*Extreme Fiction: Fabulists and Formalists* (With Michael Martone)
*Do-Over*
*I'll Tell You Mine* (With Hope Edelman)
*Twirl and Run* (With Jeff Mermelstein)
*A Field Guide for Immersion Writing*
*Reply All* (Stories)
*Borderline Citizen*
*The Art and Craft of Asian Stories*

CPSIA information can be obtained
at www.ICGtesting.com
Printed in the USA
LVHW021205231121
704191LV00001B/71

9 781637 527818